PRAISE FOR *Smart Girls Like Me*

"Office politics at the scrappy e-mag run true, and . . . The novel's bittersweet tone carries through to a satisfying conclusion."

—*Publishers Weekly* (starred review)

"Anyone who has ever struggled or is currently struggling to grow up will find her character relatable and endearing. Don't be fooled by the simple plot, this isn't 'chick lit.' Vadino's dry sense of humor and quirky writing style keep it miles away from trite or predictable."

—*The Independent Weekly*

"*Smart Girls* can't be masked as anything but a book about a girl, her friend, and a boy, though Vadino is too skilled a storyteller to apologize for that. Dangerous as it may be to forsake literary gimmicks for the confidence to say the things that one wishes to say the most, Vadino risks it all with an ease that's as magnetic as Betsy's good-bye."

—*The Boston Phoenix*

"Diane Vadino is a writer of enormous gifts, all of which are on display here, in her brilliant debut: a keen intelligence and wit, an amazing imagination, and an incisive understanding of human beings and the dilemmas—fantastical and mundane—in which they entangle themselves. She is that rarity: a young artist able to offer wisdom without pretension, inspiration without inhibition. I have no doubt this is the beginning of a long and wonderful career."

—Nicholas Christopher, author of
The Bestiary and *A Trip to the Stars*

"Diane Vadino is a warm, funny, and talented young writer. In her terrific first novel she transports us to the rollercoaster ride that is single life in the city—pleasingly paced, perfectly detailed scenes replete with Diane von Furstenberg dresses, meatloaf sandwiches, a job in media, credit card debt thanks to various bridesmaid honors, and crushing heartbreak at a downtown Radio Shack. Never again will I reflect on those excruciatingly embarrassing moments of obsessive young love and feel alone."

—Jenny Minton, author of *The Early Birds*

"Fabulously entertaining, insightful, and touching in its telling of a young woman finding her own voice, her own path in life. Diane Vadino is an exceptional new discovery in fiction!"

—Kirsten Lobe, author of the bestselling *Paris Hangover* and *French Trysts—Secrets of a Courtesan*

"For many years I have marveled at Diane Vadino's ability to take the plainest little sentence and extend and twist it into something finer, funnier, revealing, and sad. Like this one from the book you are holding right now and ought to buy immediately: 'Or maybe this is all a fabrication, a way to soften the fact that she is sashimi at Nobu and I am Stouffer's macaroni and cheese and that this is less an illuminating metaphor than it is an accurate description of what we both ate for dinner last night.' That's just one of the beguiling double helixes that make up the DNA of this book: a zippy-smart, bitter-funny read with a beautiful, accomplished novel hidden in its genetic code, expressing itself, like a sudden bright blue eye in a family of brown-eyed children, at the most surprising times."

—John Hodgman, author of *The Areas of My Expertise*

Smart Girls Like Me

Diane Vadino

Thomas Dunne Books · St. Martin's Griffin · New York

This is a work of fiction. All of the characters, organizations, and events portrayed in this novel are either products of the author's imagination or are used fictitiously.

THOMAS DUNNE BOOKS.
An imprint of St. Martin's Press.

www.thomasdunnebooks.com
www.stmartins.com

Library of Congress Cataloging-in-Publication Data

Vadino, Diane.
Smart girls like me / Diane Vadino.—1st St. Martin's Griffin ed.
p. cm.
ISBN-13: 978-0-312-38552-1
ISBN-10: 0-312-38552-8
1. Chick lit. I. Title.

PS3622.A3463 2007
813'.6—dc22

2007021036

First St. Martin's Griffin Edition: November 2008

10 9 8 7 6 5 4 3 2 1

For Laura

Acknowledgments

I was the lucky beneficiary of an inordinate amount of support, love, and patience while writing this book—as I am generally, I suppose. My love and thanks go to Jay Adya, Nick Kulish, David Cicconi, Courtney Lilly, John Henrich, and Gautam Chopra; Maureen Callahan, Luke Crisell, and Jamie Pallot; Dave Eggers, John Hodgman, and Jenny Minton; Nicholas Christopher, Jeff Johnson, and Whitney Pastorek; Eli Marias, Case Simmons, and Craig Stokle; Will Richardson; Chris and Peter Athineos; Katie McCaskie, Nicole Ropp, and Lacey Rzeszowski; Robert Hamilton; and MDJ. Finally: Everyone requires a wartime consigliere. Brandon Lilly is mine. A special thanks, of course, to my ridiculously excellent agent, Joanne Brownstein, and my brilliant, generous editor, Katie Gilligan. And: My debt to and affection for DeDe Lahman—a gorgeous writer and an amazing friend—are both just about endless.

One

The beautiful girl takes a step forward, a step back, rocks her hips left and right, acres of white silk billowing beneath her. She is performing an aerobics routine I remember from high school. She is missing the samba shake between the steps, and she is waiting for me to speak, which I do not want to do, because I do not want to make this moment any more real than it already is: It is real enough, Bridget getting married. My approval will just prod this moment along to its conclusion, and Bridget's wedding will arrive even more quickly than it already promises to, and then I do not know who I will be anymore, except myself, without Bridget, which is to say, myself, only less so.

I lean back on my stool, which is so narrow it seems like it was designed punitively, for stepmothers and wicked children. The wall is farther behind me than I have judged, and I nearly tip over. "What?" I say, recovering. "Did you say something?" Soon enough this ruse will not work, and we will be forced to leave the relative comfort of this dressing room: We will open the curtains and invite the opinions of Bridget's bridal party, waiting outside, and it is all I can do not to simply speak more slowly, in an effort to make these moments stretch on as long as possible.

Bridget tilts her head, licks her lips, tosses her hair back, like she is in a chewing gum commercial set in California. A corner of her mouth rises. She is seducing the mirror. "I don't know what to say," she says.

"Just practice saying your vows," says Tracey, Bridget's wedding stylist, whom I have, as a rule, ignored since she popped out of the BMW convertible she drove down the parkway from her Battery Park apartment to this bridal shop in Margate. "It'll make the moment more real."

"I take thee, Bridget Callahan, to be my ever-wedded wife, to have and to hold, from this day forward, forever and ever. Amen," she says. "Like that?" She removes the tiara from her head and hands it to Tracey, who replaces it with another, a double row of golden flowers across the band.

"Is it weird that when you say your vows you use your name instead of your boyfriend's?" I say.

They ignore me. We are settling into comfortable patterns, the three of us, and this is one of them. When Tracey looks at me, her gaze always manages to begin with my feet and work its way up to my ankles, where it stops. I think she interprets my flip-flops as a sign of my casual disregard for this wedding. If she swapped "casual" for "determined, hopeful," she would be closer to the truth.

"That's the Venezia collection," Tracey says. "Baby gold roses with diamond dewdrops, handblown Murano glass beads, pearl sprigs. Thirty-seven hundred dollars, but I think it's totally worth it." Every purchase Bridget makes goes through Tracey and includes, I have learned, an 8.5 percent surcharge that's paid directly to the wedding stylist. Tracey will make more money designing Bridget's wedding than I will in six months. I hate Tracey.

"Glass beads can't be blown," I say. "They're rolled."

"Is that true?" Bridget asks, her eyes meeting mine in the mirror. "You're making that up."

"Maybe," I say. "But thirty-seven hundred dollars is a lot of money."

"I can't believe I'm wearing anything that costs thirty-seven hundred dollars," Bridget says. "You can buy a car for that much money."

"A really good one," I say. "Like a used Saab, I bet, or a—"

Tracey inserts herself into our conversation, something that is proving to be one of Tracey's top skills. "It's your special day," she says. "It's only once. It may seem like a lot of money now, but you'll be thinking back on this day for the rest of your life, and I know you want it to be perfect in every way. And your father gave us carte blanche. What a wonderful father you have."

I don't think Bridget can hear the desperation in her voice, or the greed. And from where she is standing, looking at herself in the mirror, Bridget cannot see me roll my eyes so emphatically that my entire head bobs up and down. Tracey and this "special day" speech have already cost me and the four other bridesmaids $650 each, when she convinced Bridget that only the Vera Wang gowns would do for such a special day.

"Well?" Bridget says to me.

"I think what we need to ask ourselves is, what would Grace Kelly do?"

"That is a really good idea," Bridget says, before she turns around, smirking. "I don't think you meant that sincerely," she says.

"Grace Kelly," I say measuredly, eyes wide, "wouldn't need handblown Murano beads for everyone to know she's a princess."

"Well, she did have the advantage of actually being one," Bridget says. "I always wanted to be a princess." She slips the more expensive tiara off her head and replaces it with the simpler one. "Now?"

"Now," I say. This is true, and this is not what Tracey wants to hear, and I am not too concerned about which motivates me more to say it. I look over to see Tracey frowning, and I hope she is calculating the commission she just lost.

"Are you sure?"

"I am absolutely sure," I say, and she settles, loosening her shoulders, relaxing her gaze. This is and always has been my currency with Bridget: She believes me, because I tell her the truth, and I believe her, because she does it for me.

"I always wanted to be a princess," she says again.

"If you were an Indian princess, you could come in on an elephant," I say. "And wear a veil made of diamonds."

"I saw that on a TV show," Bridget says, considering. "I would like to have an elephant."

We say nothing. I am holding my breath. I can live in this moment. It is all the ones that will follow that terrify me.

Tracey misinterprets our silence and looks up from her clipboard. "Do you want me to see about an elephant?"

Bridget is no longer the girl I grew up with, talking to her bridesmaids, pliant, cheerful, deferential, but neither am I the girl she knows: I am scowling Betsy, the unexpected competition for maid of honor, quiet and grudging. I wish I could pull off a mask—preferably made of human skin—and scare them into silence. They have something on me, and it is that they are all delighted ("Delighted!") for Bridget, that she is joining them on their side of the marital divide: Three are married, and one, Georgina, is engaged. Bridget's vows will only confirm their own, make their choice the popular one.

I am forced outside the dressing room by a fussing, bobby pin–

wielding Tracey, looking like she is struggling to make a visual case for her hourly rate, and we wait for Bridget to make her final appearance. "You're the one Bridget told me about," says Georgina, wearing a miniskirt and a fur vest in the August heat. ("It's a *gilet,*" I heard her correct a sullen-looking brunette named Tamara, who sucks on the ends of her hair when she thinks no one is looking.) "You're the one obsessed with the millennium. With Y2K or whatever."

"I don't know if I'd call it an obsession," I say. Fucking Bridget.

"Weren't you talking about moving to Idaho or something?"

"New Zealand," I say. "New Zealand. Bridget and I were going to go there and kayak and meet surfers."

"It's weird," she says. "You two seem so different."

"I've known her since she was six months old." I shrug, and this shuts her up, partly because I have pulled rank, albeit crudely and simplistically, and partly because Tracey has drawn back the curtain and ushered Bridget into the room, resplendent, commanding.

"Beautiful," Georgina says, and all the girls smile in beatific consent.

Tracey piles the bridesmaids into her BMW, and they set off for New York, five manicured hands waving from four car windows as they pull out of the parking lot. "I really liked Georgina's gilet," I say. "She seems really interesting and worldly."

"She's fine," Bridget says, still wearing the tiara as we cross the highway separating our cars from the Olive Garden. "They're all fine. If you got to know them, you'd like them, but you're too busy sulking in the corner with your Discman."

"I doubt that," I grumble, and neither of us says anything until we are sitting at the restaurant with menus in our hands, at a table immediately adjacent to the janitorial closet. "Enjoy, ladies," the waitress had said. Bridget's beauty is considerably more beneficial, financially and otherwise, when we are dealing with the male half of the service industry.

Bridget is not unaware of any of this, and she sits straight in her chair, back rigid. She knows when she is being insulted. She removes her tiara, the simpler of the two, and drops it on her lap. "That waitress did that to punish us," Bridget says, and I allow her to include me, even though I had nothing to do with it. "I can't believe she put us back here. Can't we get breadsticks and water? They give you breadsticks and water in jail."

"I don't think it's actually bread*sticks,* in jail," I say. "And I think they come with the soup."

"Biscuits, then."

There is a silence. If Bridget recognizes it, she will fill it with seating plans and floral arrangements and more proof that we have boarded the wedding train and there is no getting off it. "Teenagers frighten me," I say.

"That's too bad," Bridget says. "Can you come over today and tie up cheesecloth bags of potpourri for the goodie bags?"

There is a sort of sweet spot where my natural disinclination for chores intersects with my burgeoning apprehension of this wedding, and we are now in the center of it. "Oh, Bridget," I say. "That sounds so boring. It's a national holiday. Can't we go to the beach?"

"How can you say something related to my wedding is boring?" she says, a little screechily.

"Oh," I say. "I didn't know we had to lie to each other now."

This seems to trip her up a bit, as I believed—and am relieved to see—it would, and when she speaks again, it is in a tone I know better. "It's Labor Day. And you should be laboring on my goodie bags."

"You have to make goodie bags four months early?"

"Did you remember that Frank Sinatra CD with the song for the dance I have to do with my dad?"

I have been charged with purchasing incidentals. I have no idea what song she's talking about. "Yes," I say.

"Now you're lying," she says. "I wouldn't mind so much if you'd lied before. Why can't we talk about the wedding?"

"Who said we couldn't talk about the wedding?"

"You haven't even asked me if we've reserved a church yet."

"How am I supposed to know about that?"

"Well, you would if you'd asked."

"I would be extremely delighted to hear that you've reserved a church," I say.

"I didn't say that we had." She is enjoying this, the suspense. A busboy arrives with the breadsticks, and Bridget nibbles from the top of one, like a cartoon rabbit with a carrot. She has forgotten the earlier slight. If it had been me, I would be out in my mother's car, cranking up the *Rocky* soundtrack and plotting my revenge. But that is the point: that it was not me. Bridget's instinct for revenge is minimal, because her beauty is its own kind of preemptive assault. "I said you hadn't asked if I had."

"Bridget," I say, putting my forehead on the edge of the table. "This is only fun for one of us."

"Do you know where it is?"

"How would I know where it is?"

"Guess," she says.

"New York City."

"No."

"Margate," I say.

"No."

"Atlantic City? Are you eloping?"

"No. And I think you can only do that in Las Vegas."

I am out of guesses. "Where's James from? Denver?"

"No," Bridget says.

"No, he's not from Denver? Or no, the wedding is not in Denver?"

"No to both," she says.

"Where's he from?"

"Maine."

"Is it in Maine?"

"No."

"This game isn't as much fun as it looks, Bridget."

"It's perfect."

"That's not really a clue," I say.

"It's just perfect."

"Can you pass me that spoon?" I say, pointing to the silverware on the table next to Bridget.

"Why?" she says. "Are you going to pretend to gag yourself?"

"Shut up," I say, aggravated that she has anticipated this. "Can you please just tell me where we're going for your wedding?"

"A private island."

"Whose island is it?"

"Who cares? It's in the South Pacific!"

"How do you fly to a private island?"

"Via Singapore, I think."

"How much does it cost to fly there?"

I am hoping she will again say, "Who cares?" and then, "My dad's paying," but she does not. "You're missing the point," she says. "We're staying in huts on the Pacific Ocean!"

"Huts," I say. "Huts sound expensive."

"This is not at all what you're supposed to be saying," Bridget says. "And besides, we got a really good rate on everything. The rooms are three hundred and seventy-five dollars a night, but you can share it with the other bridesmaids and I know you'll totally love it."

"Oh my God," I say. "Did you say that as quickly as possible so I wouldn't understand the words 'three hundred and seventy-five dollars a night'?"

"Yes."

"And I have to stay with those girls?"

"The bridesmaids. Yes. Otherwise it's eighteen hundred seventy-five dollars a night."

"Can't I just sleep on the beach, or in a tent or something?"

"See?" Bridget says, kicking me under the table. "I was just about to ask you to be my maid of honor." She kicks me again. "I can't believe you're ruining the moment."

"You can't ruin a moment at the Olive Garden." I point to a painting of a Venetian gondolier stroking the belly of an orange cat. "You can't really *have* a moment at the Olive Garden."

"Aren't you glad you're going to be the maid of honor? Aren't you going to say something?"

"I've been your best friend for twenty years," I say. "I dare you to ask someone else."

"I'm going to ask Georgina," she says.

"No, you aren't," I say.

"So you want to do it?"

"Of course I'll do it," I say. I smile at the idea of myself as the puppet master, pulling strings, rubbing it in Georgina's face whenever possible. "I would be pleased to."

"Do you understand this will be one of the most important things you ever do?"

"Are you serious?"

"I can't wait until you get married, so I can be all grumpy about it. Aren't you excited? We're going to a private island in the middle of the Pacific Ocean!"

"Did you ever think that a wedding invitation is just like a credit card bill, except you haven't bought yourself anything you liked?"

"All I ever wanted was a beautiful wedding," Bridget says.

"That's ridiculous," I say. "You've wanted lots of things, like a Land Rover and knee-high leather boots and Louis Vuitton luggage."

"This is all I've ever wanted," Bridget says firmly, prescriptively.

"I can think of lots of more interesting things to want," I say. I am getting irritated with Bridget's newly tunneled vision. At any other moment of my life I could come up with a thousand things more meaningful than a wedding on a private island, and everything it means—the love, the security, financial and emotional—but at this moment, when I need them, I am struggling. "A dog. A dog would be a wonderful thing to want."

"More than a man who will love you forever, and you're going to love him forever, and everyone is there to celebrate and be happy for you?"

She does not mean to be hurtful. I think she does not remember what it is like not to have made the acquaintance of a man like that. "A dog could love you forever," I say.

"Dogs have limited life spans," Bridget says in the officious, elementary-school-nurse voice she gets when she tires of my blather. "Now do you want to talk about the menu?"

As long as I can remember, it has been Bridget and Betsy, and now it is Bridget and James, and it is good, I guess, and it is right, but that does not mean I have to like it. "The five-cheese lasagna?" I say, eyebrows raised in earnest expectation. I want things to go back to the way they usually are, as quickly as possible, and even this pathetic swipe makes me feel closer to it.

"I meant the wedding menu," she says.

I wrote her college application essays, and she did my phone interviews. I called her immediately prior to taking my SATs, flying across the Atlantic, and losing my virginity. I have called her from the post office, the grocery store, the DMV, the parkway toll plaza, elevators, cabs, the bathroom of the boy with the smallest penis I've ever seen. I do not know how to need her any less than I do.

I look up. "Weddings are so much fun," I say.

"You are so totally right," she says, too obliviously delighted to hear the despair lining my voice like lead.

When I get back to my parents' house, Rebecca, in a bikini, and her boyfriend, Stevie,. are sitting in lawn chairs in front of the garage door. "We can't go inside," my sister says. One of her fingers is in Stevie's mouth. My sister likes to leave it there. "It's warm," she has said. For all I know, this is how, one day, he will slip on the engagement ring.

"Why not?"

"It's a ghost house," she stage-whispers, staring at Stevie as he sucks on her finger. They talk about weddings but only as a sort of theater, and there is something pleasantly calm and ordinary about their plans, like I imagine women in prehistoric times would just wander into a field and pop out a baby, without the thousand-dollar strollers or baby psychics. Rebecca says all she wants is pink-and-white bunting above the snacks-and-soda aisle at QuikChek, where Stevie works, where they will stand in front of the cash register and eat a QuikChek hot dog from either side, until their lips meet in the middle. They are waiting, Rebecca says, for Stevie to finish paying off his guitar. They have also discussed performing the ceremony in the hair salon where my sister is a stylist, somehow simultaneously shaving each other's heads at the conclusion of their vows. Their previous plan was to build a giant terrarium and marry in suits made of moss.

"When you get married, I want you to promise that you won't make me do anything with potpourri or cheesecloth," I say.

"Do they have potpourri at QuikChek?" Rebecca says. Stevie shakes his head, wagging Rebecca's hand back and forth, like a bone. She scratches his chin. They are like two parts of the same dog. "I think not."

My parents leave in the morning for a ten-month tour of the equatorial regions in search of native sunburn remedies. This is true. This is my father's dream, after thirty years of running a chemical lab for a German pharmaceutical conglomerate, to sail from Philadelphia to Puerto Quetzal, Guatemala, to begin his scientific studies. He is working on the formulation of a 100 SPF sun care solution—in pill form. Sun care in pill form. "It'll revolutionize the industry. It'll be like winning the lottery," he explained to us when he announced this plan at his sixtieth birthday party. He was wearing a new brown cowboy hat to dinner, his "traveling hat." "So this is what a midlife crisis looks like," my mother said, cutting his cake in the kitchen. "I had always wondered."

Now she is asleep on the living room couch. We had watched my father's plan build momentum like a runaway cart coming down a hill; once it was truly in motion, it was too late to do anything about it, and so, the house will be shuttered, metaphorically at least, Christmas presents delivered poste restante to francophone islands in the Pacific. All the furniture has been shrouded in bedsheets. If this were a ghost house, if we were a family of aestheticians, they would be white and dusty, but a blue Bambi bedspread is tented over the television and Smurf pillowcases have been pulled over lampshades. It looks less like a ghost story than a tag sale. My father appears from behind the door to the basement, carrying a stack of steaks in one hand and a stuffed Daffy Duck in the other.

"Is that for dinner?" I say.

"The duck?" he says. "Nah, we like the duck." He moves the duck's head up and down. "Quack! Quack! Don't eat me, Betsy!"

I have no idea who this person is. "Who are you?"

"Ah, Betsy, you wound me," he says, clutching the duck to his stomach. "Can't a man change?"

"I didn't think so," I say, keeping an eye on him, slowly walking up the stairs to my room, to take a nap or to avoid another conversation with a person who is becoming someone I do not recognize, to discover that one of the few pieces of furniture in this house lacking a sheet is my bed.

Stevie and Rebecca take my parents to the boardwalk on a last-minute search for three pounds of chocolate fudge, which my mother has decided she will share with the retirees she meets at sea. I am sitting in the back, beside the pool, and even with my eyes closed I can see a figure standing in front of me. "Time for laboring," Bridget says, dropping a mysterious bag on my parents' picnic table.

"I hope there are elves, or kittens, or something really fun in that sack," I say.

"There are one hundred ninety-eight invitations in that sack. And if you look here," she says, digging into a tote bag, "you will see two calligraphy pens, and a calligraphy writing guide."

"Bridget, I don't understand. Shouldn't Tracey be doing this, or one of her minions?"

"Somehow this wasn't included. I don't know why. My father negotiated it. You know my father's a crackhead." I nod. Her father is not a crackhead. He was an investment banker before he was, rightly, convicted of insider trading when we were juniors in high school. He went to a federal prison for three months, came out a self-proclaimed Christian, wrote a book about going to jail, divorced Bridget's mother, started a megachurch in Colorado, and married his secretary. Every once in a while we see his name on a bookstore's bestseller list: *Helping God Help You, The Eleventh Commandment: Thou Shalt Not Be Poor, The Devil in Your Investment Portfolio.* It isn't that he hasn't supported his family; he has, even though Bridget's maternal grandfather built half the condos from here to Asbury Park and the remaining Callahan family would have carried on the same without him—and in fact, did, while he was still in prison, before his conversion from disinterested atheist into redeemer of thousands. "These things happen every day, and they have to happen to someone," was all I ever heard Mrs. Callahan say about it. "You are going to need so much therapy when you're older," I remember informing Bridget one night after the trial while we waited in line to see

Natural Born Killers. I might still be right, but she and her three brothers, the triplets, were all popular and beautiful; they had nine varsity letters among them, and their unified, placid front riveted the school; if anything, their allure only grew. Whether they ever vocalized it between them, or strategized around their dinner table—I doubt it. I might not have known, but I think I would have. Bridget had always been a weirdly steely kid, despite the tights and Peter Pan–collared dresses her mom had sent her off to school in every day: She was the first to dive in the deep end; at our sleepaway camp, she was the one steering the canoe, and not crying for her parents at night. The steeliness, like the allure, was already there; it just became more apparent, more frequently.

"Crackhead" is her shorthand for all of this.

"So here we are," she says.

"Here we are," I say, attempting to delay the inevitable.

"You can do the *A* through *Ls*," she says, "and I'll do the *M* through *Zs*."

"But why should we ruin our day with this?" I say meanly, and too meanly for Bridget, who has put her head down to concentrate on forming the letters.

"Fine, fine, fine," I say. "Give me the pen."

"Thank you," she says. "Jerk."

We sit there silently for fifteen minutes. I have made it to Mr. Edward Brown and Guest when Bridget puts down her letter guide and sighs. "It is a national holiday," she says, "and I know you think the world is ending in four months, so I imagine your time is particularly valuable. Do you want to go to Six Flags?"

We flip coins to determine the order of our ride selections, and Bridget, in a strangely beneficent move, sacrifices a second turn on the log flume to ensure that I get to take my favorite three times. "It's the highest, fastest roller coaster on the East Coast, with speeds of up to 72.5 miles per hour," I babble all the way across the park, reciting facts from our promotional brochure. She wins a stuffed penguin on the basketball toss, which she gives to a small child who'd been trailing her for fifteen feet while his parents searched their pockets for a locker key. We are among the last stragglers to leave the park, and my head is still swimming from the roller coasters and water rides. It is nearly sixty miles home, but the night is warm and starry, and Bridget puts down the top of her brother's convertible. There is an AC/DC CD in the glove compartment, which we immediately insert into the player. "You know, when he told her to come, but she was already there, I always thought that meant they were going to dinner or a movie or something," I shout over the music, before joining the chorus. *"Yeah, you, shook me all night long."* Bridget is singing, too, driving with her knees, arms stretched over her head, and it is just like it always was, and just like I wanted it to always be.

Bridget drives down my parents' driveway to drop me off, but puts the car in park before I get out. "There's someone I want you to date," she says.

"Really?" I say. "That's a strange way to end an afternoon."

"One of James's old fraternity brothers from school," Bridget says. "He works in finance."

"Oh my God," I say. "How many times do I have to say that I don't like investment guys?"

"You always say that," she says, "but you never have a good reason."

"I have a million reasons. They work too hard. They buy sports cars and have affairs with interns."

"Any list of reasons that begins with the fact that you don't like guys who travel to Southeast Asia on business is ridiculous."

"They put prostitutes on company credit cards there, you know," I say, glaring at her. "I saw it on *Dateline.*"

"Would it make a difference if I said he was British?"

Yes. "No."

"Don't you want a date for the wedding?"

"Am I required to have a date for the wedding?"

"Wouldn't you want one?"

I have been thinking of Bridget's wedding in such apocalyptic terms that I hadn't considered the possibility that anything could ameliorate the situation. Anyone. Perhaps a great fraction of my problems would be solved if, as I waved goodbye to Bridget, someone—preferably someone strong and handsome—were holding my other hand, and the more I consider this theory, the more it becomes absolutely indisputable, so that by the time I answer her, I am almost stuttering. "Sure I would," I say. "Sure."

"Well," she says. "Good. I didn't expect you to come around so quickly. I thought there would be more yelling. But he's free tomorrow. I already set it up."

As she is talking, I am nodding my head and formulating a plan. I have always enjoyed plans, gravitated toward them, and the more I think about it, the more I see one emerge: I do not have to be Bridget's sad, lonely, sloppy, barely employed best friend. There is no reason why I could not turn this around. I have four months. Armies have been raised in less time. There is no reason why in that time I should not be able to manage some of what Bridget has, to build my own cocoon, to feather my own nest with love and designer bedding. I have to do it. It is the only way I am going to survive this wedding: if I do not have to do it alone, if I can somehow become someone like Bridget, someone purposeful and focused. I am swimming around who that person would be, and I can define her only by what she is not: She is not me. She is not marginally employed at a failing Internet company. She does not have crumbs on her shirt. She is not alone.

"I will go on this date, and I am going to quit my job, and I am going to be a spectacular maid of honor," I say.

"That would be terrific," she says.

"What's his name?" I say.

"Graham."

We are quiet for a moment. I want what Bridget has, and maybe this is my chance. Maybe he has a castle. Maybe he can hold my hand.

"My little Graham cracker," I say, and she laughs.

Two

In the morning I wake to an empty house: There is a Post-it on the refrigerator door that says "Be good" and "Lock the doors and windows," with "lock" and "and" underlined three times. I take two chocolate Pop-Tarts from the cupboard and then lock the windows. And the doors. I cannot think of what else needs to be done: Rebecca and Stevie began their three-hour return trip to Baltimore before I woke up, taking Boomer, our family dog, with them. I do not miss them as much as I miss the distraction of their noise, their literal liveliness: I have always dreaded the last day of summer—not only because it was that, the last day of summer, but also because it seemed to be an unhappy holding place, between what had happened and what was to come. In college, I would always be the last one to return to school, so I would wander the boardwalk or the mall by myself, mouthing the lyrics to Ace of Base songs so that I would look crazy rather than friendless. But even now what I know is that I have loved this summer: this summer, with half its Friday nights spent on the Garden State Parkway with Bridget, driving to our parents' houses, and long Sunday evenings sitting in traffic above Raritan Bay, the city close enough, almost, to see its skyline in the distance. The three summers since we'd graduated from our different colleges Bridget had always had a boyfriend to occupy her weekends, but this one, even though it had begun with her engagement, was different. James is not just a doctor but the kind of doctor who parachutes into war zones to tend to refugees: He was in Tanzania, or Iran, or Nicaragua, and so we went home, and spent most of our weekends in our car, endlessly merging into lanes for tollbooths. But there was no rush. There was nowhere I would rather have been.

I know what has happened. I am less sure about what is to come, but there is nothing for me here. I cannot think of what else needs to be done: All the plants were thrown away last weekend, in a greenery massacre at the end of the driveway, twenty years of African violets and jade trees tumbling out of crockery and onto the lawn. I look around the kitchen, at the dustless circles where there used to be planters. This is when I see a magnet and forty dollars on the floor, two twenties paper-clipped together, with another Post-it: bus fare. Going back to New York seems like the first in a series of steps leading to the millennium, and Bridget's wedding. It is not as if there is another decision to be made: There is this date with Graham to look forward to, I tell myself, and my friends to see, but I take my time leaving home, checking the rooms one by one before shutting each door tightly behind me.

I live in the closet of a one-bedroom apartment in a neighborhood in Brooklyn that adjoins both a park and the borough's biggest housing project. We are closer to the housing project. The closet belongs to my roommate, Zoe, whose parents bought her this apartment when she turned twenty-one. Zoe is the offspring of some sort of art-dealing German great-grandfather, who, if he were still alive, would be in jail for war profiteering. "So fucking embarrassing," she said when we saw one of her uncles pursued by a reporter on *60 Minutes.*

We met a year ago at a loft party in Greenpoint, when she walked up to my friend Tommy, while he and our other friends huddled, bored, in the kitchen, and asked him for pot.

"Are you asking me because I'm black?" he answered.

"Yes," she said.

"Well, you're shit out of luck," he said, "but let me introduce you to my good friends Billy and John." The former is Swedish, the latter Irish, and together they unwittingly rented an apartment above one of the most successful drug dealers in Park Slope. At first, they were so worried about a drive-by assassination of their landlord that they kept the room above the street empty and put masking tape across the windows; even if a bullet pierced the glass, the tape, they reasoned, would keep it from shattering. This was just one of the plans they hatched while enjoying some of their landlord's housewarming gifts—a residential perk that proved to overwhelm their only moderate interest in marijuana. Now they sell it, or give it away, to people like Zoe. A few weeks after she joined their client list, she complained to Billy that she had so much room in her closet, and so little allowance money left over for drugs. I moved in four days later.

Her family, as vaguely aware of her habit for doing ecstasy with male models as I am acutely aware of it, wisely protected her money in a trust she will not be able to access until she is thirty-four. Every year, she says, that number is increased by one. There is something in this that her relatives enjoy, this effort at middle-class poverty: She is viewed as the family envoy into the world of fleece and polyester, and every month her mother sends her care packages, as if she were a Peace Corps volunteer posted to Mali, filled with poppy-seed lemon muffins and Saks gift certificates worth two weeks of my salary. Forced to account for my existence after her mother opened the door to my room with a clutch of hangers in one hand and designer dresses in the other, Zoe told them I was a homeless student from Dublin she'd taken in and sheltered. "Top of the morning to you," I said in the darkness, a disembodied voice from the back of the closet.

Zoe's closet is bigger than many of my friends' rooms, or their studios, and one of her ex-model ex-boyfriends, also an ex-carpenter, installed a phone line and an electrical outlet. Since I work in an office and she works in a nightclub, we keep different hours, but occasionally there are moments we spend together, usually as one of us is coming home (at nine in the morning) and the other is going out (to work).

"I don't know why I can't get you to do coke," she says to me. This is how Zoe and I communicate: She suggests that I do something I will not do (coke, shoplifting, sex with dolphins), I say I will not do it, and she goes to sleep.

"Because I would die," I say as I search my wastepaper basket for my wallet. I have taken to leaving important things in there, on the grounds that I would never forget leaving them somewhere so ridiculous. "I would just die."

"It would be the most fun you ever had," she says. "Now that is a really fun drug." She leans against the doorframe as she says this, and even in this artificial light I can see the way her mascara has sunk into the lines beneath her eyes. It is easier living with a girl with a trust fund when you pity her. "And I think I saw your wallet in the freezer."

Part of what makes my relationship with Zoe tenable is that despite her obvious advantages, I have not subjected my brain to almost two decades' worth of drug and alcohol abuse, which allows me to feel relatively clever and sharp. When she outthinks me, particularly when she outthinks me while she is drunk, I want to cut all her Missoni dresses into rags, if for no other reason than to lodge my frustration at having to participate in such an unfair fight.

I work, every day, at couture.com, America's leading destination for "the fashionista in all of us" or the more general "sexy best in all of us," depending on which folders the marketing interns feel like sending out. Other Internet properties have puppet dogs or animated babies as their mascots, and so we have Nancy, our editor in chief, who was fired from *Elle* for sleeping with the managing editor's boyfriend. We have no proof that she can access the Internet or, for that matter, read, and she remains blissfully ignorant of the difference in meaning an apostrophe can lend to the word "its."

In some ways, this is a relief: Half the staff lacks an education in the English language sufficient to recognize grammatical mistakes. That group, however, populates the positions of authority, which means that the half who do recognize them don't usually bother. If there is someone who works here who spent the night of their college graduation dreaming of working at a failing fashion Web site, I have yet to meet him: Filling out the ranks, we are uninsured stylists and broke ex-freelancers, MFAs paying off student loans, boys in bands, and vegetarian fashion girls sketching PVC handbags during staff meetings. If anything, I am more to blame than most for my current employment: I actually sent in my résumé, after two months of entreaties to actual magazines had earned me nothing but rejection letters, some handwritten, some not, all on impressively embossed notecards, which I kept alphabetized, in a manila folder, as evidence that I at least warranted their correspondence, however obligatory. Toward the end, my queries had grown transparently, aggressively desperate: "I can only hope this letter adequately conveys my passion for fashion and style, these supreme arts," I'd written to Couture, figuring I had nothing to lose. I did, but at that point I would not have guessed it would be the next two and a half years of my life.

In the end, it was either here or a trade magazine catering to manufacturers of restaurant equipment, and Couture, unbelievably, paid better.

The three couture.com founders, Stanford dropouts a year older than I am, have spent millions of their investors' dollars recruiting a staff of illiterate former models and otherwise unemployable writers editing their novels when no one is looking, and they are the only ones who remain unable to comprehend why their project is failing. Their plan was to be the "first and best" Web site with "original fashion editorial," but what they did not consider was that the fashionistas in all of us might not want to download PDFs of fashion spreads, our "core content offering," when they could just buy an actual magazine. There was, briefly, an organized effort among the staff to call them "the Three Stooges," but like most endeavors here it fell apart due to mismanagement, and they are known simply as the Idiots. Sometimes we work, but mostly we sit at our cubicles and wait for the money to run out, or for the Y2K bug to destroy our site.

I usually show up around 10:50, ten minutes before either of the two women I report to typically appear: Julia, we all know, spends the mornings interviewing at every magazine in the city, and Eva would show up at 2 P.M. if Michael, the executive editor, hadn't threatened to revoke her access to the hall closet where we keep all the clothes that the designers' reps have forgotten they lent us.

I don't know why today I decide to show up two hours early. It is, in some weird way, the wedding: If I am a better, smarter, more successful person, it seems like I will have less to lose with

Bridget's desertion. Marriage. Whatever. And so I spend the morning organizing my files, mysteriously full of interviews with movie stars I think are cute and recipes I will never try, and emptying the bookshelf of review copies that will never be reviewed. I change the desktop image on my computer from the default blue screen to four carefully cropped runway exits, all from the fall Chanel show. I check my in-box, which is empty, and I delete the mail I no longer need, which is nearly all of it. I count the number of orange accessories we're featuring in an upcoming pumpkin-themed story. It is not hard, counting.

Now that I am here, and now that I have given my job my full attention for thirty minutes, possibly longer than I have ever done in the past, it is clear that this job could be done by a well-trained orangutan. I should have known this before, but I didn't, and in some ways, I feel like I have turned a corner: I had always wondered what would happen if I devoted myself fully to my job, and now it is thoroughly, undeniably clear that nothing would happen, because this job does not require anyone's full devotion.

Fuck this. I hate this place. Maybe I will just quit and move to New Zealand. Today.

At ten, after an hour of organizing and an hour of surfing listings for apartments I cannot afford, I decide to go to Rite Aid to buy shampoo. When I return there is an unfamiliar young person sitting at my desk.

"Who are you?"

"Kaylee," she says, holding out her hand, which I shake. She has a firm, adult, sweatless handshake, like a real estate broker. She is wearing silk cargo pants and a half shirt that falls about two inches below where her breasts would be, if she had any. "Who are you?"

"I'm Betsy," I say defensively. I sit in Eva's chair, if only to replicate a seating arrangement hierarchy where I am at the desk of power. "Are you somebody's daughter?"

"Do they let you dress like that all the time?"

"It's office casual," I say, raising my eyebrows, spinning left and right on Eva's chair, not so much looking for her keeper as I am trying to convey my irritation without seeming irritated, in case she is related to someone who can fire me. "Who are you, again?"

"*Kay*-lee," she says. "Do you have the Internet on your computer?"

I nod. She whirls around on my chair and turns on my blueberry iMac.

We are still sitting there an hour later when Michael calls us in for the editorial meting, and Kaylee precedes me into the room.

"People!" Nancy claps. Nancy discovered clapping at a "fundamentalist Shinto" resort she attended after giving up on Buddhism because of "the depressing elements." "I want you to meet Kaylee," Nancy says, pointing to my small friend. "Kaylee is to be the spokeswoman of couture.com, and the star of an upcoming feature on women in the new millennium."

"This will go along with the '*X* of the New Millennium' package, with, like, the moisturizer of the new millennium, the seating unit of the new millennium," Michael seconds, unable, as always, to resist approximating self-parody when he speaks.

"I don't get it," says Julia, who I did not realize was here. "How old are you? Twelve?"

"I'll be thirteen in January," Kaylee says. She is all smiles now, glowing from some sort of inner light source, switched on with a flick of her jewel-encrusted fingernails. "My album drops in February."

"She's twelve," Julia says. "She's officially not a woman."

"Everyone on the publishing side feels very strongly that Kaylee is going to be the voice of the new millennium," Nancy says.

"This doesn't sound like a soda commercial to anyone?" Julia says.

Nancy looks around. No one speaks. "I guess your answer is no."

"How about instead, we have Kaylee the prepubescent pose with an anorexic man, and we'll say something about how they represent the ideal body type for women in the new millennium?"

Nancy twitches when she is getting annoyed, and she is twitching now. We are not sure that she is aware that she does this. Nancy always introduces Julia at industry functions as "our little feminist," which for Nancy rates as an ambitious effort at intellectual marginalization. Really she is just a thirty-three-year-old senior editor who was hired to bulk up the "nonfashion offerings and important women's issues"—this is from her job description, which she framed and hung in her cubicle—and then discovered that these important issues included the incorporation of seven different colors of food into one's breakfast. I had been here for a year when she arrived: I saw she was smart and kind, if a little disorganized; I knew she would be desperately unhappy, and she was. I also knew, from her disorganization, that she owed sixty thousand dollars in student loans, and that she had launched a magazine with a friend that had failed, and that she had been keeping herself afloat through freelancing and waitressing, and that she saw Couture as a chance to stabilize a formerly promising career. For the first year I saw her literally bite her tongue at these meetings and hold her breath before speaking; when she did, it was in increasingly clipped tones. She did not trust herself to speak more than one word at a time. But then Michael, who keeps three bottles of Ketel One behind the Bose stereo speakers on his bookshelf, felt her up at last year's holiday party, and now Julia can say whatever she wants. The only question was why she would stay and argue with them rather than simply sue, and I have come up with only two plausible answers. One, she enjoys it, the fighting, knowing she is on the side of good and knowing as well that she will rarely have to account for her positions, since her positions are seldom adopted as Couture's. And also: She is a true believer, if not specifically in Couture than in the power of mass communication. She believes in her bully pulpit, and for now, at least, and begrudgingly, Couture provides her with one. I do not envy her, any of it.

She has said her piece, in any case, and she withdraws from the discussion to stare at the ceiling.

"In addition to Kaylee, we're including a real-life GI Jane, a United Nations lawyer, and a Uruguayan labor leader fighting rebel forces in the Atacama Desert." This is from Eva, who has appeared from nowhere, possibly straight from her morning blowout. One of the fact-checkers described Eva as Vichy France and Julia as the Free French Forces. "It's either drink wine with the enemy or sleep in the barn," he said, explaining why he was checking Eva's "Tales from Bikini Island" before Julia's: "Seoul Survivor: How I Made It from North to South Korea." "If you can look past the Nazi metaphor problem."

"My one concern with the soldier girl and the lawyer and especially this woman from Mexico," Nancy says. "I expect that they'll all have a certain chic-luxe about them, yes?"

"Oh, definitely." Eva says. "The labor leader was Miss Uruguay 1989."

"What about the Mexican?" Nancy says, looking at Casey,

the copy editor, who is a quarter Cherokee and had once been forced to write about fashion "on the res" ("Make Me Reservations: Call It Cowboys and Indians, in This Season's Gorgeous Prints"). He swivels his head left and right, looking for help from anyone at the table who understands the difference between a Mexican and a Native American, and then, not finding it, offers a minute shrug.

We sit there for several moments, looking at our hands. This happens quite frequently. These meetings, I am realizing, are actually quite enjoyable if you've already decided to quit your job.

I am apparently not the only one here who has recognized this. "Why don't we just put everybody in bathing suits and shoot them sucking popsicles?" Julia asks, eyes wide.

"Great idea, Julia," Michael says, but so quietly that only Casey and I can hear him.

Nancy suddenly claps again, sharply, issuing a clap as piercing as a clap could be. "Does everyone understand that this issue is already resolved? And that we should be spending our time getting to know Kaylee and hearing what she thinks this new millennium will bring?"

"Are you serious?" Julia says, but she's laughing. Sometimes it is clear to all of us that Michael's problem drinking is the best thing that ever happened to her.

Kaylee disappears into Nancy's office after the meeting disperses, or rather, disintegrates, and I return to my desk to discover that she has been surfing disney.com pages. I am snickering about this, a little—some mogul, she's still such a kid—but then I see that Kaylee has been looking at production photos from her upcoming movie.

Until I am sure I am going to make my move, I am going to

sit here at this desk and get paid, which will not be much of a challenge—just having a plan makes the day move more quickly. I am looking up airfares to New Zealand online when Eva sneaks up behind me.

"Going on vacation?"

"I was just taking a little break," I say, hastily closing the Air New Zealand window to reveal a fansite for Jack Cole, my movie boyfriend. Today I learned that he was born in Vancouver and drove to Los Angeles in his mother's Volvo, which he lived in until he landed his star-making role in *The Savior.* I position my chair between Eva and the computer monitor.

"Betsy," she says, slapping my desk, "do you hate Kaylee?"

"Doesn't everybody?"

"Do you think she is a suitable spokeswoman for an online property trying to position itself as a global style bible?"

"You mean, 'spokeschild'?"

"Even if she is soon to have millions of teenage fans?"

"Teenagers also like to have unprotected sex," I say. "I don't think we can trust them."

"Even if she was once a Mouseketeer? With the ears?"

She cups her hands above her head, Mickey-style. Any actual survey Eva has come over to perform is complete. She is now entertaining herself, being clever for her own benefit; this is usually signaled when she exaggerates her gestures into something she believes is a kind of physical comedy, when her voice crescendos into something louder than is required for conversation with one other person. I would like to think that the part of me that does not like her, which is a constantly fluctuating fraction, is the part that recognizes this about her, that sees her through this honest lens. Or maybe this is all a fabrication, a way to soften the fact that she is sashimi at Nobu and I am Stouffer's macaroni and cheese, and that this is less an illuminating metaphor than it is an accurate description of what we both ate for dinner last night.

"And by the way," she says. "Are you stalking Jack Cole? Is he your number-one celebrity crush?"

"Maybe," I say. "But I don't need him anymore. I have a date tonight with a British castle owner."

"Like Jack Cole in *Dragon Keeper*? Are you dating Jack Cole's nonfictional equivalent?"

"Oh my God, it's totally true!" I squeal. She squeals. The problem with Eva, really, is not so much that she is disagreeable but that there is no way around her: To engage her is to surrender to her, a mind-body meld of monogrammed bra tops and relationship quizzes.

Eva takes off the rest of the day "to go to a screening," or, as she whispers to me as she walks past my cubicle, "to go to the Sigerson Morrison sample sale." She may be Vichy France, but she still has a disregard for authority that comes with a father who gave his last name to an energy company in Texas. "If Nancy ever really pissed me off," she says sometimes, "I'll just go live in the East Hampton house and sell vegetables at the farmers' market." This is to distinguish her proposed family home/destination/occupation from the condo/Aspen/ski patrol volunteer, the hacienda/Zihuatanejo/English teacher and the ranch/Hill Country/cowgirl. Like Julia, she can do whatever she wants. Unlike Julia, she didn't have to go through the hassle of being sexually harassed.

Julia only comes into the office for meetings and limits her calls to me to (a) when she needs me to FedEx something for her or (b) if her therapist is unavailable and she has a question about how to handle her boyfriend, who is ten years her junior and one year mine, a blind-leading-the-blind situation if ever there was one. Eva's absence, then, usually means that I get the afternoon off, but I have nowhere in particular to go until I meet Graham, and so I sit and stare out the windows and watch as the room fills up with models.

Our office takes up the entire floor of a Midtown skyscraper, about halfway up, and from my cubicle in the newsroom I can see New Jersey. I do not know if at the time this space was christened the "newsroom" the name-giver was being facetious or not, but it is now where we rewrite press releases provided to us by advertisers so that we can promote their products without the hassle of their buying additional advertising. Today Michael has decided to interview models in his office for God knows what—sometimes they are simply hired to stand outside the venues where our parties are held, so it looks like the parties are so unbelievably glamorous not even these actual models were allowed in—so two dozen fourteen-year-olds are stumbling across the office in stilettos and miniskirts. Casey the copy editor and two fact-checkers, who, with Michael, are the most pronouncedly heterosexual men in the office, sit motionless behind their desks, mouths open.

The three of them are in a speed-rock band together, Heaven Forever. "Look at those two over there," says Tom, the tall fact-checker/bass player, pointing to two brunettes embracing and speaking a language I do not recognize. "They're standing so close together that their nipples are almost touching."

"Do you guys think I'd have to deal with models if I moved to New Zealand?" I say.

"Oh, yeah, they're everywhere," says Tom.

"Do you think if we threw money at them, they'd rub their titties together?" Sooni, the short fact-checker/drummer, says.

"I don't understand," I say. "You all live in Williamsburg. I didn't think you talked like this."

"It's kind of an experiment that went awry," Sooni says. "We were writing a song called 'Show Us Your Tits, Pretty Bitch,' and then we couldn't stop doing it."

"It's true," Casey says.

"You remember Ryan Wells, right?" says Tom (short for Tomomito), who is wearing a Japan-a-Nation T-shirt. He does not seem to notice the way I cock my head at an untenable angle, as if this will allow me to see inside his brain and extract everything he knows about Ryan Wells. "Our old guitarist? The old office manager?"

"Hmm," I say. "Didn't he move to China or something?"

"Tokyo," Casey says. I already know this, and I find it incredible that Casey would not know that I am lying, that I have spent considerable portions of the last three months wondering idly what he is doing there, if he is studying at some bizarre Japanese performance art school, as the rumor goes, if he went there to find a girl he loved, as another, unpleasant rumor goes. "But he's on his way back."

"Back to New York?" I say this in a horrified, tiny, breathless voice.

"He started it," Tom says, because he is somehow still focused on his friends' vulgarities, completely ignoring possibly the most important thing Casey has ever said to me, which is that Ryan Wells is coming back to New York. Which is no great contest, as Casey is the quiet, moody one and rarely says anything to me not related to the proper usage of "lay" and "lie," but still. "He was all 'Suck my titties' or something. He was doing an installation with all these porn movies projected onto a ceiling and picked it up."

I cannot devise a way to pick out the details of Ryan's return without displaying a suspicious, maniacal level of interest, so I say nothing.

"This shit is fucking us up," Casey says. "It's like we're all getting in touch with our inner assholes, and we like it."

"On the other hand," Tom says, "it's very progressive to be retro."

"All I know," Sooni sighs, "is that I have no idea how I'm supposed to have a girlfriend when we have this to look at all day."

Two hours later I am waiting for Graham behind a highly polished bar on the Upper East Side, on Second Avenue, amidst a crowd of women in black suits and pearl necklaces. This bar was Graham's choice, and I am trying to believe that it is an aberration, inconsistent with his cultural views or mores. Or his taste in women. They look as shellacked as Bridget's friend Georgina.

For all my certainty about the New Zealand plan, and the pleasing, quiet tintinnabulation of Ryan's return, I think I would give it up in a second for the surety of Graham. I wait at the bar, hoping the pose I am striking conveys an image of warmth and vulnerability.

"You must be Betsy," someone says without the trace of an accent.

"You're not British," I say, audibly horrified.

"I was born there," he says. "But I grew up in Connecticut."

Graham leads me to a table next to the window, with a half-full tumbler in his hand, and pulls out a chair, which I do not understand he is doing for my benefit until he fails to sit down. He does not look like Jack Cole in *Dragon Keeper.* He looks like he brushes his chest hair. A little sprig of it peeks from beneath his immaculate white shirt, but it looks art directed and fake. I am uneasy, and it shows in the way I gesticulate with a fork in my hand. Graham, with his sprig of chest hair and his talk of mergers and acquisitions, makes me uneasy. "Everyone's doing it," he says, "except for the economically incompetent assholes too slow to figure out how to get a piece of the action."

Regardless of the chest hair, I am looking for a way in, a way to make him into something special, something valuable. "I don't have a 401(k) plan," I say.

"You should," he says, but that is all. We are not going to discuss my financial well-being tonight. That thought occurs to me, and I immediately feel guilty: Why am I being so greedy? Can't I just enjoy his company before getting too wrapped up in how he can help me, whether it is with my retirement planning or the Bridget conundrum? I struggle to think of something brilliant, something witty and generous, but I have nothing, and after a few minutes he cuts in and fixes me with a stare I believe I am supposed to interpret as penetrating.

"Do you have a favorite movie?"

"Babe," I say.

"Is that the one about the pig?"

"Well, yeah, there was the main pig, but there were also many other farm animals, including—"

"What's your favorite rock group?"

"We're done talking about *Babe*?"

"You answered the question, right?"

"I like Stereolab." That is the favorite of all the Heaven Forever boys.

"Anybody else?"

I can't think of any other bands that sound cool and aware. "I like Bruce Springsteen."

"Ah. Right. Jersey."

"It's a great place to be from," I say.

"Every girl in the bar is from New Jersey," he says, rhyming it with "Boise." "You're all about the big hair and the tight jeans and the Bon Jovi concert."

"That's stupid. And besides, you're thinking of Staten Island. We don't pronounce the name of our state that way. People from Staten Island say that."

"And you give lots of blow jobs. I've gotten a lot of blow jobs from Jersey girls."

"Lucky you," I say. "And lucky them." I hate Bridget.

"You having a good time on this date?"

"Are you?"

"What's your favorite book?"

"Where are you getting these questions from?" I drop my head beneath the table. "Where?"

"I like to use them when the date's going a little slow."

"Bridget didn't say you were so honest. I really like honesty in a guy."

"Don't take it personally," he says. "I can just tell we don't have a lot of chemistry."

"How are you friends with James?" I ask, giving up. "Isn't he a noble doctor-without-a-border?"

"We were friends at Penn," he says. "You know what it's like—they change, you change, everybody changes."

"True enough," I say, and for a few moments we are both quiet. I want to hit myself in my stomach, because I feel empty, deprived of a dream, a castle-owning dream, and I do not know how it could have taken shape so quickly, so irresponsibly. I cannot trust my head to act in my own best interests. It will fabricate and embellish when what I need is a gaze that is cold-eyed and true. "It's up to you," I say. "We can either go now or maybe eat our dessert in silence."

"So do you have a favorite book or what?"

"You seemed really normal at the bar, for those five seconds between when you said my name and whatever came next."

"You know," he says. "I like to put it on the table. Get it out there."

"You do make me feel aggressive," I say. "Have you ever been to a prostitute?"

"Now we're talking," he says, setting his elbows on the table, leaning forward. "Saucy. I thought at first you might have a little bit of a nasty side."

"In Bangkok, right? Bridget said you travel to Southeast Asia on business."

"It's not really prostitution there. It's like a massage. It's like having a special maid."

"No kidding," I say. "So what's with all the questions?"

"My godmother's a dating coach," he says. "She says she can tell I don't show enough interest in what girls say."

"Did you like going to a prostitute?"

"What's your favorite book?"

"*The Wind in the Willows.* Did you like going to a prostitute?"

"It's like going to the dentist with a happier ending." He is satisfied with his punning. "Do you think you'd still want to go home with me?"

I laugh. He is serious. I admire his moxie, the way he will not allow any of what has come before to interfere with this moment: In that, he is doing something I have never been able to do, which is to disregard past failures and simply move on from them, to climb the wreckage and hoist myself up from there. I am extracting too much metaphor from this: Really, he is just a guy looking to get laid for $83.36, the sum at the bottom of the check, which he picks up with ease and authority. But still: There is an obliviousness to rejection that seems like it could be valuable, that seems like it is almost worth the ninety minutes of life this wretched dinner has otherwise occupied.

"Wouldn't you rather watch Charlie Rose by yourself, like I would?" I say. "I absolutely know you would."

"You think I don't know who Charlie Rose is?"

"Everyone knows who Charlie Rose is," I say, trying to sound as baffled as I can, even though he is right, and I am just pathetically trying to remind him that I watch PBS and he doesn't. That I am smart and worthwhile and he is not.

"The prime minister of Sweden is on tonight," he says. "Part two of two. Why not watch it at my house?"

He is correct and I am amazed and it occurs to me: Maybe this is the beginning to the fairy tale, these once-crossed signals working themselves out. I shake my head, hard, to force the idea out of it, even if this gesture is more theatrical than effective, but also a little bit to look like a freak, because I want someone so badly to fill this space that if it hadn't been for the fact that he has admitted to sleeping with prostitutes, I would continue to hear this story play out: I would tell myself that he was asking me back to his apartment because he enjoyed and appreciated my company. That our horrible first date would make for chagrined, bashful toasts at our rehearsal dinner. I would hear this play out in my head, most likely in the back of the cab on the way to his apartment. Except for the part about the prostitutes: I do not know why I have moved my line in the sand back so very far, but even so, it does not include prostitutes.

Thank God, it seems, for small mercies.

THREE

The Idiots inform us that Columbus Day is not a holiday recognized by the couture.com "team," but as usual, the senior staff ignore them completely and never show up. Of course, none of the Idiots show up either, so the rest of us wander around the office, complaining loudly about Nancy and Michael. Sybilla, the fashion editor, hands the key to the wardrobe closet to one of the photo assistants on her way to Barneys, and soon the art department is walking around in Helmut Lang samples and Jimmy Choo sandals. Eva, who is wearing a Burberry bikini top and a Dolce & Gabbana shawl, waves me over to her desk. "Why aren't you trying on any of the clothes?"

Because I am discovering all sorts of fascinating things about Jack Cole on various Web sites. I have not been on a date with anyone since Graham, and I have reverted to my default Hollywood crush. "I'm researching that story you told me about," I say, which is pretty much my answer whenever Eva asks me what I am doing because she won't bore herself with the tediousness of asking me to explain.

"Did you see Ryan Wells is back?" she asks.

My mouth almost drops open, like I am hungry, or a cartoon character, and I would let it stay that way if I were talking to anyone but Eva, because I do not trust her. "I didn't."

"Hot hot hot hot *hot,*" she says. "Hotter than before, even."

"Are you going to date him?" I ask, hoping, and convinced, she will interpret my question as naïve and uninterested, the handmaiden asking the princess about her suitors.

"I didn't say I wanted to date him," she says. "I'm saying I want to fuck him and then trade him in for a richer model."

I cannot tell if she is consciously punning the word "model" or not. I am sizing her up, and I think that if nothing else, I can say that any interest she has in him is limited to that: Surely he would see through that, see that I could offer him more than that. Apparently my face is giving me away because she changes the subject, tightening the shawl around her bare shoulders. "You know that religion fashion package we're doing for New Year's?"

"I don't think nuns are allowed to wear couture."

"John Galliano's making these habits with a satin trim and actual gemstones. They're fabulous!" Eva says. She presses her finger to her lips, like she is concentrating very, very hard. "You know, Nancy was thinking you could give those guys in the Nation of Islam a call. They're so fashionable, with the suits and the bow ties. Don't you think they'd look fabulous in Yohji Yamamoto?"

"I have to call them?" I do not want to be berated by militants. "I don't even work in the fashion department."

"We're splitting them up," Eva says. "I have to call Richard Gere and Uma Thurman's people. They're Buddhists. Isn't that fabulous? Marc Jacobs might be doing something for us, something very beautiful and old-school and high-necked."

This is going to be one of those days I do not like Eva very much, not because she is asking me to do something I do not want to do but because she is pretending like I should enjoy it, and like it was not her idea to stick me with the militants while she takes Uma Thurman's publicist to lunch.

I have never seen Eva in the kitchen—I have never seen Eva eat anything—so that is where I go when I am trying to hide from her. It is my sacred space, my nerd laboratory, and it is where I go when I want to eat my leftovers and read things like the catalog from the Millennium Marketplace, with its iodine pills and dehydrated ice cream bars, both of which I recently ordered. I am just flipping to the section on powdered milks and coffees when Ryan Wells, former and now current office manager/Heaven Forever guitarist/installation artist walks into the room.

I did not expect him back so soon. His return has been so theoretical, something I have proposed to myself so many times that it became myth, or fantasy, or like a form of war game: This is what I would do if Ryan Wells came back; this is what I would wear. I would not have worn this T-shirt, without a bra, given that my nipples, as I am horrified to discover at this moment, have a tendency to project themselves in nonparallel alignment when they are unsheathed. Zoe forgot to pay the heating bill so many months in a row that it was finally turned off, and last night I slept in John and Billy's empty front room. I did not go into their bathroom, having observed the state of their kitchen, and I am unshowered and tired, and now Ryan Wells has returned and all I want to do is stick my head beneath the table and not sit up until he is gone.

That is not an option, and so I just sit there and look at him: He is exactly the same, tall and not tanned but . . . that bronzed color that cowboys get, with that same nonhaircut haircut, hair brushed forward, over his blue, blue eyes.

"Ryan Wells," I say, folding the catalog over my chest. "I heard you were coming back."

"Betsy Nilssen," he says. "How are you?"

"I'm good," I say. "Nothing has changed since you left." I am horrified to remember that I also forgot to brush my teeth this morning, and in my bag is a toothbrush and toothpaste I bought at the CVS on the way to the office, but have forgotten, as well, to use. I cover my mouth and hope he does not sit down next to me, which he does.

"Nothing?"

I was speaking loosely, but also accurately. "Nancy went to rehab again."

"You're still eating meat loaf," he says. "Weren't you eating that when I left?"

"It's not the same piece or anything," I say. "I get it all the time."

"You only do that to piss off the girls in the fashion department who don't eat anything but salads."

"It's true," I say, smiling, until I realize that means he can see my teeth.

"You always ordered two sauces," he says. "The red one and the gravy one. Nobody really needs two sauces."

"You're wrong about the sauce thing," I say. "The sauces are delicious, each in their own way."

He reaches toward me, and this is so unexpected, I lean toward him, puffing out my chest, confused. I am thinking: Could this really be it? After four months of waiting for him to return, is it really this easy? But he drops his hand, which had been aimed at my neck, and pulls the catalog out of my arms. One of his fingers touches my skin, above the collar of my T-shirt. I can feel myself flush. Something about him makes me want to remove all my clothing. It is not sexual, exactly. It is beyond that: It is just: *Here I am. Do what you will.*

"What's all this for? Is that a catalog for space food?"

I do not want to move: I do not even want to speak. I want to remain perfectly still, and wait for him to touch my neck again. "It's my other favorite food," I say. "Besides meat loaf. Especially the dehydrated ice cream bars, they're delicious." I don't care how lunatic I sound; I just want to keep him sitting beside me, so there is a chance he will touch me again. It feels like an affliction, something I did not ask for and cannot control. All I wanted was to eat my lunch as far from Eva as possible.

He still thinks we are having a normal conversation. "Is this because of the millennium?"

"I always wanted to be totally prepared," I say. "I thought I'd know how to fish and make jerky from cows and hunt deer, but really I was just too lazy to get it together."

"And now you don't know how to make jerky," he says.

"My mom knows how to butcher a cow, but she's with my dad in the rain forest. Looking for native sunburn remedies."

"Really," he says, looking interested.

Of all the things I had imagined about Ryan Wells, the idea that he would be easy to talk to was not one of them, not least because all our conversations prior to now consisted of the location of, and access to, various pieces of office equipment. "My mom grew up on a farm," I say.

"She didn't teach you how to butcher cows? Raw deal."

"She taught me how to cut the head off a chicken, but we never had any cows in New Jersey."

"So you can cook a chicken?"

"No," I say. "I can only cut its head off. I can't really cook much of anything. I keep restaurant menus in my silverware drawer."

He laughs. He has a nice laugh, warm and low, and I watch, because a past couture.com feature advised me to, to see if the smile reaches his eyes. It does. I am relieved. I realize, for the first time, that Couture pieces like that—*Does he like you? Are you sure?*—are like little missiles sent out into our audience, to terrorize them into reading us again. Talk about war games. "Then how do you eat?" he says. "If you don't have any silverware?"

"Oh, they all know me. They always include plastic forks or whatever."

"I could buy you dinner sometime."

"Oh, that's okay," I say. "I can afford it. I just don't buy a lot of clothes or anything."

"No," he says. "Not because you can't afford it. Because we could go to dinner sometime."

"Oh, okay," I say. I hope my amazement is not playing out on my face.

"Tomorrow? Are you doing anything tomorrow?"

Suddenly Eva appears at the doorway, rapping her knuckles on the refrigerator. "Betsy," she says. "Can we talk about the athletes you're interviewing today?"

"What athletes?"

"The Olympians who took growth hormones and now all their babies have two heads," Eva says. "Julia was going to have some freelancer do it, but they wanted too much money." She looks at Ryan. "Betsy's the best with reproductive disorders. Can we do this now, Betsy? I have to get to a screening."

"Okay," I say. I slowly cut the last bit of meat loaf into small cubes. "I just need to finish up my lunch superquick."

Eva turns on her heel. Her Prada heel. I am going to pay for this. I am going to be sent to Staten Island to pick up props for the Easter Bunny shoot. She is going to send me to get her dry cleaning.

Whatever my punishment, this was worth it. "Sounds good," I say to Ryan.

No one can help me strategize better than Bridget, so I want to bang my head against the floorboards when I get her voice mail six times, at ninety-minute intervals, until I give up at 1:30 A.M. and call Tommy. In a way, this is a good thing: If I did talk to her, my upcoming date will feel small and insignificant, and I do not want it to be one more thing we will silently, rightly, decide is less important than her wedding. Tommy instructs me to wear a garter belt, or, if Ryan is picking me up at my apartment, to answer the door in my bra and panties. "I like to call it the B and P Maneuver," he says. This is useless, but as I fall asleep I feel appeased, and recognized, and that was what I wanted.

I have not had a real boyfriend since my sophomore year in college. This is our sad, collaborative truth, that neither I nor my best friends from college, these three boys of mine, met someone who wanted to go out with us at approximately the same time we wanted to go out with them. They told girls they did not like that they did, and the smart ones would see the outlines of the condoms in their wallets and leave my friends with the check and their hard-ons. I pined after my high-school boyfriend, who, though I did not know this at the time, had already met the woman he would eventually marry. I did not miss him, but I did miss the idea of the life we had planned together, of a house in Margate and Volvos in the driveway and children who would root for the Toronto Blue Jays, whose catcher had once been kind to him. With him, all my choices were made—and then suddenly, they were unmade. If I were a different sort of person I would have reveled in it, these myriad destinies, unknown possibilities, but I was—I am—not: I am conservative and cautious, and I worked too hard at guessing the right answers, so that my path was determined by my own worst instincts, my new and unfamiliar fear of being alone—*alone forever,* that was the only way I ever considered it. I was hesitant and timid when I should have been expansive and brave.

This is how I got here. All that has changed, really, is that this concept of "forever" has become, with Bridget's engagement, not hypothetical but horribly real, horribly actual. Things we do now might, indeed, last *forever.* Here is the glass-half-empty perspective: The mistakes we make now could, indeed, fuck us, permanently. I do not know why I failed to understand this before, but I did, and that realization sort of shocked me not into action but into stasis: It was clear that what I had been doing was wrong. I wanted to stop making mistakes—mostly, flimsy crushes on people like Michael, an old professor, a Couture contributor who uses the money he makes writing about fashion to subsidize a sideline making men's hats, crushes with the substance of gossamer.

I was waiting, and it disturbs me now to think that this waiting has culminated, somehow, in the sudden reappearance of this person. Ryan feels fated, and I like neither the false symmetry of that—that call-and-response of perseverance and reward—nor the fact that I am building a mythology around him, because if I am not careful, however we deviate from the story, I will find a way for this narrative to accommodate his failings. Graham is my proof of that, of my head's capacity for revision, for overlooking, for smoothing down, and it is all I can do not to put my hands together and pray he remains as perfect as he seems.

The next day moves slowly, and I pass it by studying him, observing the way he smiles at the other girls, waiting to see if he leans toward them when he speaks, as he does with me, if he positions his head so that he must look up, through his lashes, to meet their eyes.

He works late, and we go separately to the restaurant he has selected. When I see him walk through the door, I stand up too quickly, rush forward without thinking, too happily, and after those initial false steps I remain unsteady, unsure, alternately tentative and hostile, picking at the lint of the sleeve of my sweater as we study the menu. "I hate where we work," I say. "Don't you hate where we work?" I kick my right calf with my left heel so hard it makes a soft unfocused sound from beneath the table. He looks down, confused. Negativity, Bridget would say, breeds no bedfellows. She would say I must go with my strengths, and apparently the only thing I do well is interview female athletes with reproductive problems. "What is your primary goal this season?" I ask.

"I've been reading *The Iliad,*" he says. "I'd like to finish that."

I look up, smiling quizzically, like I have discovered something fabulous in my lap. "What?"

"The Iliad," he says. "The poem."

"I've read it," I say too quickly, too forcefully, because I am lying. This is why I am at Couture and not in Athens on a Fulbright. I skimmed it. Hector, blah blah. Half of my head feels like I have had this conversation before, freshman year, and the other half is swooning, deliriously. "I loved it. So moving. And

The Aeneid," I go on, because this one I actually have read. "It's like the most terrible, romantic thing in all of literature. With Dido, and the city being built, and then stopping when Aeneas left her. She loved him so much, she killed her city."

"Because that's how it is, right?" he says. "When your heart's broken? Or at least how you want it to feel? Like nothing else can go on, either?"

Sorry, what? is what I am thinking. I am interested not so much in the actuality of what we are saying as I am in his apparently deeply felt understanding of heartbreak, which maybe accounts for his return, for the rumors of the girlfriend in Japan. I am thinking that this could be the best news of the night. I am smiling over my victory and relaxing a little, settling in: I have accomplished as much as I'd hoped to, which was further confirmation on his dating availability, further evidence that this dinner is more than strictly collegial, or even charitable, which has been my tiny unspoken fear since he found out I had no silverware and asked me out.

This is when he picks up the candle that has been burning between us, a thin candle in a tall metal container and tilts it slightly, so that beads of wax drop to his arm. I do not know how we got from *The Aeneid* to here. "It's warm," he says, focusing on the wax. I cannot imagine what I have to do with this. "Give me your arm," he says.

I reach across the table. He takes my right hand with his left and twists my palm to the ceiling, so my inner arm faces up. "Ready?" he says, and I smile, with anxiety, because I am scared that after I tell this story to my friends, which I am going to do as soon as possible, it is going to become myth, and I am going to disbelieve that it ever actually happened. The wax drops on my skin. "Hot," I say. I want him to do it some more.

He pulls me by my wrist so that I am stretched halfway across the table, and he moves the candle away from my hair. He threads his other hand through my hair, so that it rests on the back of my neck, and he kisses me. His lips are soft and warm and right, but it is really what he is doing with the clutch of my hair in his hand that is destroying me, tightening it and loosening it with his fingers, while his palm runs across my cheek.

He lets go of my wrist and leans back, but before he is out of my reach I grab his collar and pull him back toward me. Why would we not kiss, when we could kiss? It is different this time. We take turns pulling on the other's bottom lip, hanging back for a second, hovering, waiting for the other to come forward. Finally we both sit back. The waiter, who has been circling our table, approaches, rolling his eyes, and we give him our order, even though food seems beside the point.

"That's what I wanted to happen tonight," he says. "That's what I wanted to happen when I came back."

I look down at my chest, and I can see my heart beating: Not my heart, exactly, but my entire chest is visibly pulsing beneath my shirt. Again I want this moment to suspend, to hang still, because all I want to do is to feel exactly like this for as long as possible. I stare at my lap, I stare at the ceiling, I stare at anything but him, because as soon as we register each other again, it's done, and I am going to have to wait to be back here again, and I don't know how I will be able to bridge that distance. My chest feels like it is going to explode. I want it to be five minutes ago. I can feel myself trying not to move.

He turns to his right, scanning the wall behind him. "I'm just trying to figure out what it is you're looking for," he says.

I am confused, at first, by his use of "for" rather than "at," wondering if this is intentionally a bigger question than I am crediting him with. *You, you, you,* I think. But mostly I am disappointed that he is the one to end my spell. It seemed like there was an agreement to remain as we were, and I do not like being the one who failed to break it first. Or maybe for him this is something other than what it is for me: standard operating procedure, versus . . . something else. Maybe he pours wax on all the girls' arms. I do not want to think so.

"The bathroom," I say idiotically, realizing that I must make good on this, standing up and walking toward the back of the restaurant, where the eye-rolling waiter turns me around by the shoulder and points me in the right direction, almost kindly, almost like one would a child stepping up to a piñata. I walk into the bathroom, splash water on my face, and leave Bridget another voice mail message.

He pays with a credit card and signs his name with a graceful, looping script that is unavoidably feminine. We go out to the street. It has become one of those fall nights when the air is warm and the breeze is cool and everything smells like it did in my parents' driveway when I was fourteen and walking to the bus stop for my first day of high school. It smells . . . endlessly, academically promising, like there is much learning to be done. It feels like we have reentered the real world, which is both awful and a relief. I have no playbook; I have no idea how to follow what has come before.

"I live that way," I say, leaning left, to the south, "and you live that way," tilting my head back, to the east.

"It's like a fork in the road," he says. It is not, in any way, a fork in the road, it is more like a sideways T-stop, as we were moving in one direction and now he will continue straight on while I turn left. I am noticing this because the great majority of the people I have gone on dates with have also been editors or writers, whose precision with words is their livelihood. His imprecision is exhilarating. He could mistake "their" for "there," and it would be exhilarating.

"I thought about you in Japan," he says.

I cannot believe this, but I do not say so, which is a winning compromise.

"You could come back to my house with me," he says, nodding toward Brooklyn, placing his hand on the back of my upper arm.

I have heard this before, but not from Ryan Wells, and it seems so ridiculous that I have to get away from him as quickly as possible, because I do not know how much longer I can keep myself from saying something stupid. I am almost holding a hand in front of my mouth.

I step back determinedly, looking east for a cab, then west, whistling cinematically when I see one turn right onto Second Avenue. I am almost safely away—he is shutting the taxi door behind me—when I block it with my forearm.

"Do you think the world is going to blow up?"

"On New Year's?"

"Yes," I say.

"No," he says. "I don't."

"I'm glad to hear that," I say, and pull the door closed. He taps twice on the roof, and I am at last on my way home.

I leave Bridget a three-minute voice mail on her office line. I omit the wax thing. It does not feel like it should be the sort of reason why you are besotted with someone, even if it is, at least a new and unexpected part of it. I think she will be able—I don't think there is any way she could possibly avoid the excitement, or the hysteria, in my voice: "You have to understand that this was the most perfect date I have ever had in my entire life, and if I am not totally mistaken, this is a case of the mutual crush, which we both know is the highest and rarest form of all crushes. . . ."

Then I call Tommy, who will still be awake. I can hear the opening chords of the *Law & Order* theme song in the background.

"Dude," I say.

"How'd the date go?"

"I told him that I used to live across the street from a housing project, and that one of my best friends from college was black, and that I am completely down with hip-hop culture."

"You didn't," he says. "But I'm surprised you're two for three there."

"I asked him if he thought the world was about to end." I hear a clunking sound. "Dude, hitting your forehead with the phone is a little melodramatic, I think."

"I made my point. And you are not completely down with hip-hop culture."

"I know that. I still thought that would be less embarrassing than the thing about the world ending."

Tommy sighs. "You white people have such a hard time accepting your whiteness. Otherwise, it went fine?"

"Except for the part about the end of the world," I say, "I think so." I do not mention the wax episode. I don't think Tommy would approve, either.

His attention for legal serials is no longer than it is for this conversation. "Luckily," he says, "that's so stupid, he probably thought you were kidding." I hear him switching to *SportsCenter.*

"Do you know what's going on this weekend?" he asks. "Do you want to go see a movie or something?"

I am not sure what to expect at my office. Ryan has been given a new space, six feet from my desk. I am still possessed by the idea that the more I talk to him, the greater the possibilities are for fucking this up, for allowing him to recognize what a floundering mess of a person I am. I half expect to walk in and see him poking Casey in the ribs, pointing at me and laughing, but he is just typing at his computer, staring at the monitor.

There is, however, a note on my chair, which reads, "Meet me at noon at the NJ Transit waiting room in Penn Station."

I whirl around, like a grade-school spy who has just discovered a clue baked into a pie. He is laughing at me, but it is in a way I do not mind very much at all.

"I'm glad you came," he says. "I wasn't sure you would come."

"That was really fun last night," I say. "Did I tell you that I love New Jersey Transit?"

"I just guessed," he says, and he looks pleased with himself for a moment, but it passes. "After—I shouldn't have asked you to come back with me. I don't think of you like that."

"You mean you wouldn't like me if I had gone back with you?" I *knew* it. "Or do you mean you don't want to make out with me?"

"No—I mean, I don't think of you only like that." He is flustered, and it is adorable. "I mean, I just wanted to spend more time with you."

"Oh," I say. "That's nice. I wish we had gone out sooner." I try to say this innocuously, but I want to be entirely sure of my *Aeneid*-based evaluation of his current romantic situation.

"Yeah. . . ." He looks like he does not think "Yeah" but instead thinks "Not so much," and that is a curious combination.

I am surprised. I felt that the evidence was on my side. And I do not like curiosities. "I mean, if I had known how nice that was, I would've asked you out months ago, but I thought you had a girlfriend."

He blanches. This guy has a face like a weather map.

"Well—"

Now I am waiting for it: the other shoe, dropping. I can feel all the elation from last night leaking out of me. "Well what?"

"You should know that I just got out of a long relationship," he says.

This is exactly what I was waiting for. This is exactly it. The only surprise is that the person ruining this is not me. "How long is long?"

"Pretty long."

"More than ten years?"

"No," he says.

"More than five?"

"Yes."

"Is she the reason you went to Japan?"

"Kind of," he says.

"Huh," I say. Twenty feet in front of us, there is a man kissing a woman, his hands in her pockets. I wonder what I am doing wrong, that I am here, having this conversation, and not that girl, not Bridget, not someone being cared for, not someone being protected.

"It's a little weird," he says.

"Who did the breaking up?" I say. I am not that girl, and so I must be savvy. I must be aware. I must be smart. "You or her?"

"Me," he says.

"Is that why you came back?"

"Kind of," he says.

"Vague," I say. "That is really vague."

"We weren't broken up when I came back from Japan."

"So when were you broken up?" Oh, dear. "I mean, you are broken up now, right?"

"Yeah," he says. "We are." He hesitates, and adds a cough for good measure. "I mean, as of Saturday."

"You broke up with her on *Saturday*?"

"Yeah," he says.

"But this is Wednesday. You asked me out on Thursday," I say. For some reason, now that there is a problem, I feel focused and sure and mathematical in my deductions, safer and sadder than I had in last night's epic poetry-fueled ridiculousness. I need to call it "ridiculousness" now because if I think of it as anything else, as something that I could have rationally expected to experience again, I think I would be sick with envy for whoever I was twelve hours ago. If I had only felt this confident in my evaluations and sensible last night, I probably would have enjoyed it more. I probably would have gone home with him, and who knows: Maybe that would have meant we would not be here today. Maybe we would be at his apartment, skipping work, and I would be blissfully unaware about this. I am all about the hindsight, apparently. "You asked me out while you were still together?"

"I can see how it could look bad."

"Hmm," I say.

"We were together for a really long time, and neither of us had the guts to end it until now. I mean, you're part of that. That whole time we were working together last spring, I thought you were so cute with that meat loaf and everything, but things were all screwed up between me and Stella and she wanted to go to Japan and I wanted to get out of the city anyway. . . ."

Even I—*even I*—know this is a disaster waiting to happen, a wagon perched over a cliff. A wagon filled with puppies and kittens. And if I think about it too much, I am going to get angry and teary because something I thought was so perfect, something I so naïvely thought could rescue me from my small, little world, is as flawed and complicated and real as everything else. Why am I like this, when Bridget is like that?

"I don't think it sounds like a good idea," I say. "I don't think you sound like a good idea."

"I promise," he says. "I'm not like this. I'm a good guy."

"I have," I say, sounding sterner, smarter, than I feel, "little evidence of that."

It occurs to me that Bridget met James while she was dating a photographer, a fashion photographer who'd donated work to her gallery. Maybe this is just how it's done. Maybe the difference is not so much the situations we walk into, but how we handle them. The Betsy thing to do would be to crumble or to cry. If I am learning anything, it is not to do things the Betsy way.

"What does she do in Japan? Your girlfriend?"

"She's a designer," he says, not specifying further, and apparently resisting my pathetic piece of bait to clarify her "ex" status. "We don't need to talk about Stella. What about tonight?"

"I don't know," I say.

"My ex-girlfriend," he says, and I get unconscionably, uncontrollably gooey. I can practically feel the stiffness come out of my spine. "There's somewhere I want to take you."

I know the smart answer. "I have to think about it," I say, aware that this is not it.

He goes back to the office. This is not what I want him to do: I want him to stay here until we have reached a conclusion other than the one we have come to, which is to say, one that denies the reality of this situation. For a few minutes I sit there, waiting for him to come back and tell me to forget everything he just said, that it is a fiction he created because he feared the intensity of his feelings for me. This is ridiculous, and acknowledging this makes me hurry away from where I have been sitting, from the site of my wish-making. I pick up the first pay phone I find, holding the mouthpiece as far as I can from my face, and call Bridget at the nonprofit art gallery where she works, selling donated paintings to rock stars.

"Did you buy the Frank Sinatra CD yet?" she asks as soon as I say her name.

"That is not why I called."

"It's very important!"

"Yes. I bought it."

"You're lying."

"Bridget, that is not why I called!" By the end of the sentence I am yelling.

"Jesus," she says. "What's going on?"

"Nothing," I say, because now I am embarrassed to admit to her that my perfect crush is not perfect.

"What is it?" she says. "Tell me or we're going to talk about the CD some more."

"Do you think it's really bad if someone you like just ended a seven-year relationship?"

"What do you think?"

"I think I'm going to throw up."

"By 'just,' you mean—"

"Five days ago. Or six, six days ago."

"I can see that being something of an obstacle," she says. "Honestly, I would say run. I would say do not look back. Or you will suffer. You will turn into a pillar of salt."

"Well, I think that sounds very melodramatic and Greek."

"Don't mix your allusions," Bridget says. "And don't be naïve."

"I think that's really easy for you to say when you're engaged," I say, trying not to sound accusatory or angry, because then this discussion will be about my bad attitude, and I desperately want to keep her on track.

"Maybe I'm engaged because that's easy for me to say."

Fucking Bridget. "But I really, really, really, really like him. I had a crush on him for ages and he just got back into town and I know you got all my voice mails and it was completely, perfectly perfect."

"Except for the part about him being all fucked up because he's just getting out of a seven-year relationship. Did you ever think that your problem is that you tend to fall for people really quickly, when you don't know them well enough for them to deserve it?"

"He bought me dinner," I say, "and we made out, and there were candles. . . ."

"The problem with you, Betsy, is that you're still the same person you were when you were sixteen."

"Everyone is the same person they were when they were sixteen," I say defensively, feeling young and stupid, because Bridget is right. "Except for war veterans."

"I don't think you should see him for a little while," she says. "At least give him a chance to rebound, or something, with somebody else." Silence. "You're not hanging out with him again, are you?" Bridget says. "Well, you can't hang out with him tonight, since you're going to dinner with me and James. We will discuss this there, and don't be late." And then she hangs up before I can summon the energy to cancel our plans.

Bridget is sitting alone at the bar when I arrive. Or I think she is sitting alone, but before I can process the idea of Bridget sitting alone at a bar, something that has possibly not once happened, ever, a man, who had been crouching on the ground, stands up and slips a bracelet over Bridget's wrist. "She dropped it," he says when he realizes that I am not just a curious bystander eavesdropping on them.

There have been so many of these guys hitting on Bridget, since the time we were thirteen and went to an all-ages party at a dance club in Maine over summer vacation, that they all bleed into a blur of fawning and free drinks. "Did you tell him you're engaged?" I say after the man, who has introduced himself as Sammy, retreats to the kitchen.

"Look at my ring," she says, holding up her hand. "Wouldn't you think I'm engaged?"

"I just don't like to see them wasting their time," I say.

"You're a real humanitarian like that," Bridget says.

Sammy returns from the kitchen with a cake and three candles. "Happy birthday to you . . . ," he sings in a deep, surprisingly velvety baritone, and soon the rest of the bar has joined in. Except me. Because Bridget's birthday is in July.

"What do you think he's getting out of this?" I say, eating my cake. I have been dining on Bridget's beauty for a quarter century now. Sammy has disappeared, off to process some forgotten diner's credit card. Apparently he has been running back and forth between Bridget and his tables for the last thirty minutes.

"He's just being a nice guy," she says. "Some guys are so nice."

"You are from another planet," I say.

"I understand things the way they are," Bridget says. "Like this guy you're talking about. I understand that he is only, only trouble."

This back-and-forth of her willful obliviousness and my grudging replies is as comfortable and worn as the jeans I am wearing, and I am disappointed when she shakes me out of it by bringing up Ryan, so that this way of talking to each other, these intertwined monologues we act out every night with different words but identical rhythms, is interrupted and made sharp, made anxious. "He told me the truth, didn't he?"

"Today he did," Bridget says. "What about last week? And who cares about that? I'm talking about rebound. Rebound. You can't fight it. You can only avoid it."

"What's the longest you've gone without a boyfriend? How many days between that photographer and James?"

"That's not the point," she says.

"Wasn't it less than a week?"

"You know, I was really hoping you wouldn't bring that up, because it clouds the issue. I was only seeing him for like six months, not seven years. There was practically no rebound to worry about. Not even rebound. I'm just talking about the random fucking guys do after they get out of a relationship. Do you want to be randomly fucked?"

"Huh," I say.

"I'm just saying there's no rush," she says. "I mean, you remember that story my dad always tells about my mom, right? She was engaged to someone else when she met my dad, and she broke it off and they got married in like two months. Of course, they did get divorced, so I don't know."

"These are some very mixed messages you're sending, Bridge."

"Oh, crap," she says. "Forget that one."

I roll my eyes dramatically, catching sight of a Macy's bag on the chair to her left.

"Are those goodie sacks?"

"They are," she says. "This is what it means to be a maid of honor. It means being my slave."

"I don't think we're finished talking about Ryan yet."

"What else is there to talk about?"

"What am I supposed to do?"

"Just leave him alone," she says. "I'm telling you. It will hold. Come back to him in six months. He'll still have a crush on you, and he'll be done fucking his way through his favorite bar."

I do not have six months, I want to say. Six months will be two months after Bridget's wedding. But even that is not the point: Now that I know what it's like to be with him, in that space where nothing else matters—not Bridget, not the wedding, not the millennium—I just want more. I did not think it was possible, to be able to shut out those things, but now that I know it is, I want it again. "Okay, whatever," I say. I cannot account, to Bridget, spending our time together on my crush, when we should be talking about her wedding. Maybe she's right. Maybe I could just go to New Zealand and come back, and everything would be exactly like it is now, except he wouldn't be quite so defective. I feel like the kid at the carnival with the smallest teddy bear, saying, "Can't you understand why I love mine so much?"

"Your head is getting ahead of you," she says. "Don't let it do that."

"Goodie bags," I say. "How in the world was this not included in Tracey's tasks?"

"My dad is a millionaire crackhead," she says. "How the fuck do you think?"

"Your dad sucks," I say. She nods. "Why don't you buy me some fried calamari for my work?"

"I can do that," she says. She scans the room for Sammy and waves him over. "My friend Betsy wants some fried calamari," she says. "I bet you can make that happen."

"Sure I can, sweetheart," he says, skipping toward the kitchen so haphazardly that he pushes a woman returning to her seat from the bathroom against an ornamental pillar.

A baseball game finishes while we tie the pieces of cheesecloth into small bags. The whole time Sammy keeps Bridget's wineglass filled and an assortment of snacks on the bar.

"I don't know how you do it," I say, eating nachos and calamari as quickly as I can, before Bridget can get to them. "You have two people here doing your bidding."

"Three," she says, looking at her watch, which reveals that we have been stuffing goodie bags for over two hours. "James is on his way over to pick me up."

"Pick you up? You live like ten blocks from here."

"There's a rapist or something on the loose."

"Seriously?" I say, swiveling around to face the windows. "Why didn't you tell me?"

"I thought you knew," she says. "It was on the front page of the *Post*."

"Who's going to walk me home?" I am saying this mostly to myself.

"Aren't you taking a cab?"

"Not back to Brooklyn," I say. "That'd be like twenty bucks. I'm taking the Four train. To the N."

"So I'll give you cab fare. Or we'll walk you to the Four train," she says. "He's only stalking the Upper East Side. It's not a big deal."

Sometimes Bridget's breeziness, especially when it is this sort of imperial breeziness, is thoroughly irritating. "I don't need to borrow your fiancé," I say, although it is clear that I do.

I follow James and Bridget to the subway, feeling like their sulking dog, and when I see a woman in high heels and jeans walking by herself down First Avenue, unconcerned and idling, I wonder if she is oblivious of this threat, or impervious to it, and whichever it is, I resent the lack of a leash around her neck, like there is around mine.

The next night, Tommy and I buy tickets for *Fight Club,* but we make the mistake of failing to show up at the theater without allowing a thirty-minute seat-gathering window, and we are, apparently, the last to arrive. "Where am I supposed to go?" I ask, exasperated, as Tommy scampers to the front row to take the last remaining seat. "Very freaking gentlemanly."

"Dude, I'm sure there's something better up there," he yells, waving skyward from his seat, which I notice is next to a very attractive young woman in a pink top that reads PRINCESS.

"You're a masturbating jackass," I say, so the girl hears me, but although I have made my point, it is clear I sound like a weird, bitter woman to the two rows of people between us. Tommy's gestures have attracted the attentions of an usher, who surveys the situation and turns to face the audience, which has settled down under dimmed lights.

"Can we get one seat, one seat here, for one person," he bellows to the crowd, shining his flashlight on me, standing alone with my Diet Coke and Jujubes and extra-large bag of popcorn and my anger-management problem, looking like the world's loneliest bulimic. I am twelve, and it is dodgeball all over again. "I hate you," I say to Tommy, talking to his princess, when someone in the back raises his hand and the usher leads me up to my seat.

I am tired of being alone. That is all there is to it. "I changed my mind," I say to Ryan on Monday morning, hand cupped over my mouth, my desk phone mashed against my lips.

"Very good, then," he says. "Tonight."

The day crawls by: There is a fuss when a bouquet of flowers for Sybilla turns out to be from her stalker-y ex-boyfriend, and she makes a show of bringing a traffic cop up from his post on Fifty-ninth Street to observe and witness the floral delivery, but that is the only sliver of entertainment until 6:15, when Ryan and I finally find ourselves alone on the floor except for two of the fashion girls and Michael, who is detailing the size of the Idiots' genitalia for his prey.

"Are you very religious?" Ryan asks as we walk out of the building.

"Not, like, super religious or anything," I say.

"But it's sort of a religious thing, right, to think the world is going to end two thousand years after the birth of Jesus, right?"

"Well, there's the religious thing, where God blows us up, but also the other one, where the white militiamen do it, with their Molotov cocktails."

"Oh," Ryan says.

"I've thought about it," I say, "and I would prefer the one with God, because I don't think it would hurt as much."

"Wouldn't it be reassuring to think of the universe as this gigantic thing that goes on and on without really noticing us at all?"

"Well, yes and no . . . ," I say. The universe's ignorance of the human condition is a conversation for another day. "I guess more yes than no."

"Okay, then," he says, holding the door open for me, waving good night to the security guard. "I know where we're going."

We are surrounded by teenage girls in miniskirts and knee socks, at the center of what appears to be a Catholic school field trip. "I don't remember anyone in my class dressing quite like that," I say, not unlike my grandmother might when we take her to the mall for food and entertainment, as the child in front of us strips down to a tube top. She turns around. "Do you guys know how long this is going to be? This is so boring."

I look to Ryan to field this.

"I think it's half an hour," he says, and I wonder if he wishes he were on a date with a sixteen-year-old Catholic schoolgirl. How am I this person? Who wonders these things?

She frowns, and then purses her lips and blows a bubble of gum toward us before turning around.

"Are they all high, do you think?"

"Do you have a problem with teenage girls?"

"I love teenage girls," I say. No one makes me more insecure than teenage girls, a fact that has been true since I was a teenage girl myself. "They are the future of America." I cannot stop myself from saying, "Especially the ones who wear tube tops and miniskirts to the planetarium."

As if someone, somewhere, was waiting for this thought to be expressed aloud, the lights are dimmed and the opening chords of Beethoven's Fifth Symphony reverberate within the dome as the winter sky appears above us. We lean back in our chairs. Stars begin to streak past us—it is the same effect that accompanies the *Millennium Falcon* into hyperdrive—and it is clear that we are moving back through time, back to the birth of stars, supernovae erupting to the left and right of us, and there is a calming galactic orderliness to it that lasts until we pause to witness the birth of a star, at which point the music morphs into Vangelis's theme from *Chariots of Fire.* That one small star grows into "the stunning eye of the dog, Alpha Canis Majoris, or Sirius," and after another hesitation, the Beethoven resumes and we are thrust several millennia into the future. I sit back in my chair and watch the astronomical fireworks go off, white dwarves blowing up into red giants, planetary nebulae floating here and there, and feel incredibly minuscule and meaningless in the best possible way.

Suddenly I understand what he is trying to do, and though none of this has anything to do with the potential for a militia-instigated apocalypse in a few months, it is undeniably calming, being reminded of the universe's total disregard for humanity and their calendars.

"That was really nice," I say when the lights come back up.

"I'm glad."

"I don't know what to think about the other stuff."

"I'll understand if you don't want to," he says, "but I hope you'll come out with me tonight." He cocks his eyebrow at the girl in front of us, who has decided to do a little lap dance for one of her classmates. And then he smiles, mimicking her for a moment, my own private show, and I am a goner.

Four

Ryan is the guitarist in a band. Ryan is an artist and uses words like "Fluxus" in otherwise regular sentences. Ryan plants roses in the patch of grass behind his apartment. My possibilities are no longer endless and terrifying: They are endless and spectacular, and it is in part because I am so unwilling to remain what I have been—the beautiful girl's best friend, the assistant editor of this terrible Web site—that they are so. I do not know how to be the person I want to be, but Ryan seems already to see me through that lens, even while I am just guessing at the end result: I am the guitarist's girlfriend, bedraggled and messy. I am the artist's muse, cool and bisexual. I am the rose-tender's lover, patient and nurturing. And English. He feels like the ticket to all the possible mes I have ever wanted to be.

Each time we go out, it feels exponentially more exciting: I thought my crush would level now that I seem to have what I wanted from him, but it doesn't. It escalates. Whatever it was I felt two weeks ago, three weeks ago—it is always so much less than I feel now. That is not a wholly positive emotion: Part of it is the fact that he can be so elusive, so enigmatic, in a way that my previous boyfriends, all writers, all so enamored of the quality of their communication skills, have never been. "Maybe he's just not that smart," Tommy suggests when I tell him how Ryan will answer my questions about his band or his artwork with a shrug—a soft, yielding one, but a shrug all the same. I force myself to measure my responses to these small retreats, to recognize that the ground lost is insignificant compared to the advances, the orderly upticks in the crucial statistics: the weekday nights we spend together, the weekend nights we spend together, the simple figure of hours in the week divided by hours together. "I can't believe you're actually doing the math," Bridget says, trying to regulate my mania, but even she knows there is little she can do but stand back and watch. "I hope you know what you're doing," she says, and there is nothing to gain from her words but for us to agree, at some point in the future, that we'll both recognize that she said them.

Sometimes it is easier to make out with him than to talk to him. I do not regard this as a problem, because except for the occasional elusion—I will not call it evasion, just yet—he is full of stories about growing up in army bases around the world and then in Texas, where he graduated from art school after tying two drunk fraternity brothers to opposite walls and egging them on until they wiggled out of their bonds and fought each other in the middle of the room.

"Is that really art?" I say, because it seems more important to understand this than it does to pretend to know the answer.

"Depends on who you ask," he says. "It's not the drawing kind. Do you wish I could draw?"

The idea of this, that there is something deficient about him, that he lacks something desirable, is painfully, regrettably foreign to me, and I try to make a note of it, to remember that my view of him is a singular one, and subjective. I need to construct a back-channel system of alleyways, so that if something does go wrong, I will have this information stored at strategic locations, like a canny squirrel's acorns, and it will sustain me.

"I wish I could draw," I say. "I would draw a picture of my dog. He lives with my sister." I am getting off track. "Do you like being an artist?"

"More like, do I like being an office manager, right?"

"Do you?"

"I get all the Sharpies I want," he says. "Other 'n that, we'll see."

"You're talking like a cowboy," I tease him, but I love it, his disregard for words, his apparent disbelief in their power. He is easy to talk to, but exceptionally easy to make out with, and I feel like I am making up for eight years of neglect, with those wide-eyed, naïve boyfriends of my past, all of us enforcing each other's incorruptibility. But he is different—not bad, but normal, slightly beyond normal: I have never made out in so many public places, and I feel that I am owed it, that I am cashing an overdue check. The waiter at a wine bar just-far-enough from our office knows to seat us in a back corner, where we will not aggravate the other guests. If I saw us, I'd hate us. As it is, one night we are seated behind another couple, who are making out, on display, and we look at each other, aggrieved.

"We can't let this happen," I say.

"Up here," he says, patting his knee, and I jump on top of him, straddling him, mashing his head against the wall. The other couple ignores us, and I wonder if they have won, somehow, by their very obliviousness, but these questions of hierarchy, these questions of winning, matter so much less now than they did before, sitting in the back of a bar with my legs wrapped around the hottest guy I've ever seen.

There are a couple weeks of nights like this, and eventually I start to worry that they will all end, as they have, with one of us getting into a cab. It seems like we are both avoiding asking each other home. I know why I am—how do I explain my closet? How do I explain Zoe? (Of course, what I mean is: How do I compare to my beautiful, rich, blissed-out roommate?) And I blame his reticence on my earlier refusal. I wonder if this is becoming some sort of stalemate as we sit on the deck of the Pizzeria Uno at the South Street Seaport, which I have told him is my favorite restaurant in New York City. "If we were over there at the River Café," I say, waving toward Brooklyn, "this wine would be a lot more expensive." I am trying to say that we are savvy, that the view looking east is just as good as the one looking west, but it sounds more like I am saying that he is cheap. He fidgets with his fork, dragging it across the unfinished slice of pizza on his plate. This is one of those conversational roundabouts I worry over. "Maybe you should come home with me," I say, needing some way of cutting the tension in my head. All the lightbulbs in my closet's ceiling lamp have gone out, and I am scared that if I remove the fixture, I will replace it incorrectly and it will fall on my face while I sleep, so at night I make the way to the bed by turning the TV on from the doorway and navigating by its glow. And when Zoe shaves her legs, she taps the razor against the shower wall, leaving the cut hair there, so it dries stuck to the glass. Plus, she is gorgeous. "Or not," I say. "My kitchen is being painted."

He is paying attention now, to my lies and obfuscations. "I have a roommate," he says. "But I know somewhere else we can go."

Apparently there is a Best Western at the South Street Seaport. I didn't know that. I am not prepared for this, at all: I had assumed that if anyone was staying anywhere tonight, it would be in my apartment, with my razors and my soap and my toothbrush, not here, in the South Street Seaport: I don't know where I need to go to get a razor, and I need one desperately if I am going to be in a position to take off my pants. I tell him I am going to find a delicatessen and some beer, which is a lie, though one I believe to be relatively seductive, but he insists on accompanying me, which in any other situation I would find wholly appealing. I am stymied until I think to disappear to the front desk while he is off looking for ice. The desk clerk gives me a razor and I shave my legs with warm water and hand sanitizer in the reception bathroom. My foot propped nervously on the rim of the sink, it strikes me that Bridget would never find herself in this position, physically or emotionally, so anxious with anticipation that I am nicking my legs with this thirty-cent razor, bleeding into torn pieces of toilet paper.

When I get back, he is sitting on the bed, back against the headboard, a plastic cup of beer in his hand. I smile. He smiles. "Do you want to get in the shower with me?" he says, and I had not expected this, or I would have removed the squares of paper affixed with my blood to my legs, which I had planned to detach on my own solitary trip to our bathroom. It is the only thing in the world I want to do at this moment, get in the shower with him, but I cannot navigate it: I cannot figure out how to clean myself up in time for this to happen. When I begin to think of all the other problems of space and distance—

If I gave him a blow job, how would I breathe with all that water?
What would happen to my hair?
What would my wet hair look like from that perspective?
Can you put on a condom in the shower?
What if the water makes it somehow impossible?

Where would you put your feet?

Wouldn't it be slippery?

—I can almost hear my head break. "I'm already quite clean," I say lamely. I cannot figure out a way to make clear how much I want to do so without explaining my reasons, and as long as I know him, I don't know that I will be able to explain why I have bloody squares of toilet paper attached to my legs. "Super clean."

"Fair enough," he says, not giving me a hard time of it, which I both regret and appreciate: More the latter than the former, because any other time, his giving me a hard time would result in my unequivocal yes to whatever he offered, but this time I do not know how to do it, and I would still say no, and I do not want him to think I am that person, a no-sayer.

But why didn't he give me a hard time? I hear my head say. *Didn't he want me to do it?*

Shut up, shut up, shut up, the other side of my head says. *Sometimes I just don't think you want us to be happy.*

I strip down to my underwear, carefully removing the toilet paper and dropping it, piece by piece, down the space between the wall and the headboard. This is one of those lucky things about living through Zoe's forced winters-in-the-tropics, when we spend New Year's through Easter walking around the eighty-degree heat of our apartment in our bikinis. During one of our rare dinners together we agreed that we would no longer waste money on cotton underwear and even now, it is the one thing that truly binds us together, our bikini wardrobes, and I am comfortable in mine now, which is a brown halter top and boy shorts, my hips comforted by the gentle, insistent encasing of the material. I should have volunteered to wash his hair. I lay on my back and cover my face with my hands until I hear the water taps turned tightly off, and he comes out, hair wet, towel wrapped around his waist.

"You're wearing a bikini," he says.

"I'm always wearing a bikini," I say.

"I always thought it was a special-occasion-type thing," he says.

"It's sort of an everyday-type thing," I say.

He stands up, at the foot of the bed, so that I am looking almost straight up at him. "I think we should get those off," he says, pulling at my shorts. He lifts me from my waist and moves me a few inches down the bed, so that my legs are hanging off it. I am worried he can see the nicks on my knees. Then he pushes my legs apart, kneels between them, and licks the inside of my thigh.

I close my eyes and for once, for a little while, stop worrying.

For the first time ever, Eva is at her desk when I walk in. "Century Twenty-one field trip!" she says, holding up a crumpled dress. "Missoni! Spring collection YSL!" She is not being unfriendly, anyway, so I cautiously approach her desk. "I got these Ferragamo shoes, too," she says, pointing to her feet, "for ninety dollars!"

By the time I am directly in front of her, she is eyeing me closely. I have been reeled in with spring collection YSL. "Hmm," she says, fingering the sleeve of my shirt. "Didn't you wear this yesterday?"

"No," I say weakly, because I am wearing the same orange T-shirt with a hand-drawn picture of a star on it that I wore yesterday, possibly the brightest piece of clothing anyone has ever worn to this office. "I don't think so."

"You totally did," she says, leaning in close. "You didn't go home last night. Somebody got lucky last night! Who was it? Who was it who was it who was it?"

"No one," I say.

At this point, Ryan, who had left the hotel before I did to buy himself a new shirt at one of the wholesale places on Sixth Avenue, appears from nowhere and bumps up against me. "I'm so sorry," he says.

"Hot," Eva says after he is out of earshot. "Who who who? One of those weird guys always hanging around you?"

"No one," I say. "I just forgot that I wore this shirt yesterday."

She deflates, sits back in her chair. If I weren't so deliriously happy to be lying to her, I would be disturbed that she will so easily believe I am a dirty-shirt-wearing slob. As it is, I couldn't give a shit. "Do you have anything else to tell me?" she asks, clearly irritated at the burden of completing our conversation.

"The Nation of Islam passed?" I say, suppressing my grin. This will forever rank as one of my favorite conversations with Eva, I know: I am both disappointing her, for something she could only struggle to blame on me, and deceiving her, keeping from her the only thing that could possibly make her envy me. Maybe I should tell her about this, about Ryan; I could, in front of her, easily give him a too-lingering look, which he would return, even before thinking about it. It could be that subtle, that slight, and it would be enough, more effective than constructing some false opportunity to drop his name, or the way his hair smells. Or the way he kisses, with his left hand always resting, almost carelessly, in the space where my neck meets my shoulder. Even if we hadn't agreed we would keep our relationship, or whatever it is, to ourselves in this office, I would keep it to myself. I would keep it for myself. When we were little, Bridget would run out of her Halloween candy by the teachers' convention holiday two weeks later, while I would still be hoarding and counting and organizing mine at Christmas. "They said it wasn't in sync with their mission statement."

Eva rolls her eyes and shoos me away with a rolled-up copy of *W,* like I am the physical embodiment of the Nation of Islam, but really she just wants me out of her space as quickly as possible. "Militants!"

That night, Ryan comes to my apartment. I play out the scene with Eva and the magazine in pantomime, acting out the parts of both aggressor and victim, a sort of after-dinner play as he washes the plates we used for our Indian delivery. Being with him now, and looking back on how I was even six weeks ago, that old life seems shabby and gray: I would not have eaten on a plate, for example; I would have eaten out of a take-out box. After my performance he takes my hands and washes them for me, in the sink, and then he hands me a piece of paper: It is a pencil drawing of a dog, with big floppy ears and a wagging tail, and beneath it is written, "Everybody deserves a dog who loves them, especially Betsy." The grammar is wrong, but the lines of the sketch are fluid and confident, not what I'd expected after our last conversation.

"You can draw," I say happily, because I had been disappointed in the idea of a nondrawing artist, whether I intended to admit that or not. I am usually horrible at receiving gifts: I inevitably hate them, something Bridget and I have always had in common; every year on Christmas we pick a dollar amount together and then meet at one of the malls in Atlantic City, hand each other the same amount of cash, and reconvene in the food court an hour later with our purchases. But this is perfect, so perfect I want to cry, because at least then I give a shape to everything I am feeling. I don't know what to do with it: It seems so much more significant than its weight would suggest, and it is a relief when I finally just run into my room and pin it above my bed.

It is shaping up to be the night that becomes the First Night We Have Sex. It has that sort of anxious, unsettled sense about it. It is always my least favorite night: This makes clear how tremendously square I am, and I struggle not to admit this in a flurry of apologetic disclaimers, a preemptive effort to lower any expectations he might somehow harbor. It is just this one night, I want to explain, which has the weight of everything else on top of it, that has me so flustered and unsteady and unsure.

There are other girls out there who do not have this problem, I hear my brain say, *who would be fucking him this very moment, who would be turning him into their love slave, who would make him forget all about that ridiculous ex-girlfriend.*

Where are you getting this? the other voice says. *Couture?* Cosmo*? Where? You don't even read that magazine.*

But I do, the first voice says, *when you're not looking.*

This is becoming one of those nights I spend more time inside my head than in the room with him, and this seems like a tremendous waste of what I can only consider a wretchedly wonderful opportunity, just to have him here, in my room, with his shirt off and his jeans kicked under my bed.

My first-night barometer is accurate. It begins, it goes on, and after it is over, I spend a few moments wondering if I should say something out loud like, "I'm sure next time will be better," until I finally do.

"I know," he says. "It's always weird the first time. I thought you were going to make me wait some more."

"—?"

"That kind of makes me sound like an asshole," he says. "That's not what I was going for."

"I'm a puritan," I say, choosing my words carefully, because I want to be clear about what I am, and what I am not. It seems important for him to understand that I have done this with only a handful of people, all of whom I have loved, without suggesting that I necessarily feel all, or any, of that for him. I am having enough trouble tamping down my actual obsession; it seems ridiculous to suggest there could be even more going on than what is there already, and what is, I am sure, ever apparent. "I just like to be sure of who I'm dealing with before . . . you know, before things get . . . fluid-y."

"I can't believe you just said *fluid-y,*" he says, pushing my bangs out of my eyes. "As long as I've heard you talk, you always have the right words, the words you want."

"Fluid-y," I say, laughing, shaking his arm vehemently, "is what I meant, and *fluid-y* is exactly the word I wanted." It occurs to me, for the first time, that there is something inverse going on here: As much as I luxuriate in his disregard for words, maybe he sees something worthy in my dependence on them. I feel newly appreciated, and when I speak next it is without thinking about the possible ramifications of doing so. "I think you should come back again tomorrow," I say, "and come back the next night and the next and not go home until we have had sex at least a dozen times."

It takes a week, but to my surprise I eventually get exactly what I asked for.

"Your boyfriend is hot," Zoe says one morning as she comes out of the shower, towel wrapped around her head, right arm over her breasts and her left hand hovering three inches off her body, below her stomach.

If I needed a reminder as to why I make Ryan leave before she comes home, this is it. "Don't touch him!" I say, pointing my toothbrush at her. I keep it in my bedroom, in case she falls asleep on the bathroom floor, which she sometimes does, so I can brush my teeth in the kitchen sink.

"Okay, okay," she says, sidling past me. "I wasn't going to. I just wanted to give you the Zoe Brundhoffer seal of approval."

I have half-closed the door behind me when I turn back to her. "When did you see him?"

"Sometimes I like to watch you while you sleep," she says, laughing, so that I cannot figure out if she is telling the truth or lying.

I ask him on a date. "Let's go on a date!" I say, trying to evoke a certain 1950s-esque retro Sadie Hawkins–type charm, trying to remind myself that I am a voting member of this relationship, or whatever it is. In the beginning I did not ask myself too many times to name what we were to each other; I was content with quantifying it, making statistical cases, trusting in math to prove the point of his affection. Now, though, I am asking myself that question: *What are you to me?* I thought the only question worth asking was: *Will you be my plus-one at my best friend's wedding?* Now that it is not—it is like that, plus one thousand. Now that this is becoming less and less about Bridget and more and more about feeling the way I do when I am with him as much as possible, it seems exponentially more important to understand it, and I understand things best when they are named, literally spelled out.

I find myself waiting for hints, hoping that he runs into someone he knows when we are walking together so that he will be forced to account for me, in words. What I am hoping for, actually, is "lady friend," which has recently seemed to me to be a pleasant compromise between "friend" and "girlfriend." I have seen my friends do this, having to account for the repeated appearances of a certain woman, and there is a tyranny, or at least a hierarchy to their thinking that words fail to mask. Unless they simply say, as Billy said simply at a party on Saturday night to, or toward, a girl in a yellow tube top, who was holding a beer out to him, "There's Chrissy." I guess that would be even worse than "friend."

We leave for our date, my date, after work, and I take him downtown, making him shut his eyes on the subway even though the conductor announces each of the stops down to Rector Street.

"This is my favorite place in New York City," I say. *Because I am going to get married here someday,* I do not say. What a freak. We are sitting in the front row of a church. "Do you like it? Do you want to go? Do you want to go to McDonald's?" Why did I bring him to a church? Because: "Once I walked in here with my Walkman, and all of a sudden that song from *The Sound of Music* came on, right as I opened the door. The one with all the organs, when the nuns sing."

"How do you solve a problem like Maria?" he asks conversationally.

"How do you catch a cloud and pin it down?" I say, equally conversationally.

"How do you find a word that means Maria?"

"A fibbertigibbet? A will-o'-the-wisp?"

"A clown," he says. He leans back against the wooden bench and stretches out his legs.

"I can't tell you how much I wanted to be an Austrian governess after I saw that movie," I say.

"Yeah," he says. "But the Nazis."

"I wonder if anyone saw it and wanted to be a nun," I say.

"A singing nun," he says.

"Like Sally Field."

"She flew," he says. "She was the flying nun."

"Really?" I say. "Doesn't that sound like witchcraft?"

He laughs and puts his right hand around my neck, pulling me closer, kissing me on the temple.

There is shuffling behind us, the sound of footfalls on stone, and I see a girl, younger than me, walk into the church, stopping at the head of the aisle to do some sort of Catholic-y thing before taking a seat a few rows behind us. Ryan nudges me closer, and while I do not have much of a problem making out in a church, particularly one that is not a Lutheran church like the one my Swedish grandparents attend, I do know something about showing off. I do not know anything about the girl seated behind us, whether she is married or in love or a devoted asexual, but if she is anything like the girl I was before Ryan, I would hate us, and envy us, and feel emptier because of us. Maybe she is smarter than that: We could be anyone, or anything; we could be on the verge of leaving each other; we could be on the verge of boring each other for the next fifty years. I would not have guessed that, if I were her: I would have guessed that they were in love, and they had something I did not, and might never. I would probably have been listening to the Cure, and engineering a way to walk home, by myself, in the rain.

"Time to go," I say to Ryan, pulling him up by his hand. It is not just sympathy for this projected girl, sitting alone in the pew, which is really a sort of sympathy for myself: I feel like we are bragging, in this extravagant happiness, and I absorbed enough of those hard Protestant lessons to remember the relationship between pride and the fall. Pride is not all of what I feel, wrapped up, as it is, in my anxiety and doubt, but it is in there, as unavoidable and gaudy as a vein of gold in rocks, and I am not in the mood to take any chances.

It has begun to snow outside, just enough that footprints are visible on the sidewalk. The McDonald's across Broadway is dark inside. "Where to now, chief?" he says.

"New Jersey," I say. I am disoriented for a second, until I see the World Trade Center over my left shoulder, and I pull him west along Murray Street, toward Battery Park and the Hudson River and Jersey City. "Have you ever been to New Jersey?"

"Everyone's been to New Jersey."

Against the black-orange sky, a jagged line of white lights moves slowly toward Newark Airport, like a mobile constellation. The moon is full, and the clouds are glowing white over the Watchung Mountain range, twenty miles west.

"Everyone's been to the Molly Pitcher Rest Area on the turnpike, not the good parts," I say. "It is a wonderful, magical place." It is. "You should come with me sometime."

He slips his hand under my coat, tucking it into the waistband of my jeans, and turns me around to face him. "You know Casey has a crush on you, right?"

"No freaking way," I say, surprised. "Are you serious?"

"What?" he says, looking a tiny bit taken aback, which I am overjoyed to observe. "You want to go out with Casey?"

"No," I say. "It's just that he's so grumpy and quiet. I didn't think he knew my name. And anyway, Eva totally wants to have sex with you." As soon as I say it, I wish I had not: Maybe he didn't know that before, and now that he does, he will hail a taxi, right now, find her, and fuck her. Goddamn it.

He doesn't. "She's a little intense," he says. "And she smokes. That's gross." He pauses and looks out over Jersey City, and I hope he is thinking how beautiful it looks in this light, how unexpected it is, to be in New York City and see another city's skyline only a half mile away, across a river. "I don't think you should be dating anyone else."

"I don't know," I say. He flattens his palm against the small of my back, so that I am pressed up against him and my lips touch his neck despite the fact I am still trying to speak. "That doesn't seem very fair," I say, muffled.

"Not like that," he says. "Not just you, not dating anyone else."

"Oh!" I say, pulling back from him, so that I can be properly heard. "Oh, now I get it," I say, pinching him on the arm to suggest I understood him all along. "Are you sure? You just got out of a very long relationship; shouldn't you be sleeping around, at this point?" I am trying to exorcise my mention of Eva's interest, to give him the out, even though if he took it, I would . . . I don't know. Blow up. Throw up. Cry and scream.

"I'm sure," he says, and I kiss him, determinedly, while people walk around us, sneering—my eyes are closed but I know they are sneering; I have been sneering at people like this for all of my life—and when someone passing us yells, "Love! It's a beautiful thing!" I am so sure they are right.

FIVE

A few weeks later a cardboard box arrives at my office, full of dehydrated hamburgers and couscous and beef roast with vegetables. "I don't understand why you would get only three different kinds of entrees if this is all you'll be eating until mankind returns to the surface of the Earth," Julia says, but she is smiling as she says it and boils water for us in the kitchen so we can test them. This morning Julia sent around an e-mail with "See Ya, Suckers" in the subject line, announcing that she will be leaving Couture for an art magazine that has, until now, consisted only of photographs and illustrations. She is in charge of the words. She has given her notice and will return for three days after New Year's and then vanish. Waiting for the kettle to whistle, she sings snippets of Britney Spears songs. *"Stronger than yesterday/Now it's nothing but my way/My loneliness ain't killing me no more. . . ."* Before she begins the new job, she and her twenty-three-year-old boyfriend are going surfing for a month in Australia. She's so happy, she seems to be emitting heat. "I'm so glad I'm getting out of this fucking place," she says, leaning against the countertop. "Fuck this fucking fucking place!"

I am not sure what to say. While we wait for the water to boil, the fashion girls, in berets and colored tights, wander in and out of the kitchen, removing free Diet Cokes from the refrigerator two at a time. I want to join Julia in her revolution, but I want more not to be recognized as a traitor-in-waiting. "Totally," I say.

Before I recognize that it is Michael entering the kitchen, probably to retrieve the cranberry juice mixer he keeps in the cabinet under the sink, Julia has turned to focus her entire body, her entire life force, on him, like a death ray in a gray cashmere sweater. "Get out, you fucking asshole sexual harasser," she says tightly but violently, emphasizing the last two words enough for most of the office to hear her.

He turns around so quickly that she is yelling at his back, and for a moment I feel sorrier for her than for him: The tightness in her mouth makes her look older than she deserves, and I am about to ask her if she thinks she has an anger-management problem but the kettle whistles, and she seems to forget what just happened. There's something blissfully on–off about her emotions, as raging as they may be, and even though the rest of the office seems to look down on her for them, for her inability to rein herself in, I wonder now if that was simply part of her plan, if she decided long ago, maybe immediately after Michael removed his hand from her bare left breast, what she no longer needed to bother with. After all, she is the one leaving this shithole, to edit a small but internationally distributed culture magazine and to travel the world with her surfer boyfriend. As smart as she is, and we all know she is the smartest person in the office, she probably wouldn't have gotten all of what she has if it weren't for her glossy black hair and green eyes and the way she manages to turn a pile of rubber bands sitting in a desk drawer into a bracelet we are meant to infer was casually yet artfully constructed. It is not that I want to deny her the credit she is due, but I also want to count the right tally: what she is worth, and what she receives in return, so that I can manage my own expectations.

She would not like my calculus: She regards her own angular, unlikely beauty as irrelevant to her successes, but her insistence on this seems to be one of the few things about her that suffer from self-deception.

Julia pours the steaming liquid into two bowls, both filled with flakes of dried pot roast, green beans, and carrots, and sets them on the table.

"What I really like about this is that according to this invoice you've purchased fifty-two meals. Is that one a week for the year? Or have you calculated that it will take fifty-two meals for society to rebuild itself after the collapse of civilization?"

"They're kind of expensive," I say. "That was all I could afford."

"You don't really think things are going to get fucked up," she says sadly, as if it had not occurred to her that this might be, rather than a pose, the result of actual fear. We will take turns pitying each other today, and there is an equilibrium to it that is pleasing and calm. Instead of answering her I swallow some of my food, which tastes not at all as I imagined it, like sand, which is maybe because on the Millennium Marketplace Web site these meals were always pictured being eating by a solider in a desert, wearing goggles and a gas mask. It is only maybe a half step below a Lean Cuisine dinner.

"This is pretty good," I say.

"Did you ever think about how weird it is that 'roil' and 'boil' are so similar?"

"You mean that they rhyme?"

"Like, a roiling boil. Isn't it weird that they rhyme?"

I think very, very hard, and it is only when I am as sure as I can be that I say, "Do you mean a 'rolling' boil?"

"Ugh, these food words just always fuck me up," she says,

putting down her spoon. "What the fuck does 'roil' mean, then?"

"I think it means to annoy someone, or to agitate, a thing or a person."

"How is anyone supposed to know all these words?"

At this, Ryan appears in the doorway. "Hi, Julia," he says. "Hi, Betsy."

"Hi, Ryan," we say.

"I got you that new chair, Betsy, the one with the roller things."

"Thanks, Ryan," I say, aware that even after he leaves I am grinning so much, I can feel the weight of my own cheeks. "He's a very efficient office manager."

"You think?" Julia says. "He's hot, but looking into those eyes, it's like looking into a well. There's nothing deep going on down there."

This seems a very strange metaphor. "He's nice, I thought."

"He always struck me as kind of flimsy," she says. "He's going here, he's going there. . . ."

I do not know what she means by this, though I assume it has something to do with his going to Japan and coming back. I hope it is not something more than that. I don't think he's ever said her name to me—it is always me saying, "Julia made me buy her boyfriend a suit jacket at the Gap so they could go to some restaurant," "Julia made me FedEx her her passport to El Paso because they won't let her into Mexico." I don't think she could be privy to some information I don't have. That may be my worst nightmare.

"Huh," I say. It is the most neutral word I can think of, and I pray it will not betray me.

"Hmm?" she says, licking her spoon clean.

I wonder if I should say something to Julia. If she does have some horrible piece of information, I wonder if she would share it with me if I told her about Ryan. "What?" I say, at the last minute stripping the theatricality out of my voice. There are just no connections. Julia's avoided the entire staff socially for the last two years, since the Michael incident, which—then I thought bizarrely, but now I think typically—had ended with her looking hysterical and unstable. My calm doesn't last, though: I can't bear the pressure and change my mind. The only thing preventing me from fishing for information is that I am afraid of embarrassing myself, and since Julia doesn't know about us, the embarrassment stakes, anyway, are relatively low. "He seems okay," I say. "He doesn't do that whole gross Tom-sleeping-with-the-whole-Couture-staff thing."

"That guy has fucked half the fashion department," Julia says. "Ugh, I'll be glad to get out of here."

This is all I am going to get without spilling the entire situation all over her lap. It is going to have to be enough. It really is enough. If Julia knew something about Ryan she would have said it then, when I gave her the opening. For all her disdain for the social hierarchy, she is as acute an observer of it as anyone, and she relishes these small moments when she can prove her attention to it. I say nothing, waiting for her to loop back to Ryan if she wants to.

"Roiling," Julia says. "You know, Betsy, you can always come work for me. I'm going to destroy these fuckers."

It is the day before the day before Thanksgiving. Julia is looking at her arm, maybe thinking that she is not sure if I will try to become a Julia or an Eva, if I will try to subvert the system to my advantage, or if I will try to become the system to my advantage. Julia and Eva both want to edit glossy magazines, and their strategies for doing so have varied only because their resources were different: one had smarts and drive, the other had wealth and connections, and I am unspeakably happy that Julia is the one to leap the orbit, to go from her position here as Eva's equal to the editor in chief of this magazine—a promotion in title, function, and medium, all at once. It seems like a victory for all that is good and right in the world.

Probably she is thinking about making it to Penn Station in time for her train to Philadelphia.

"You know," Julia says, "there is going to be a January fifth, and I know that because that is the day I get out of this fucking shithole."

There are forty-seven days left in 1999.

"I know," I say.

Ryan leaves for Austin in the morning. Instead of waiting for the F train to take us to Brooklyn, I pay for a cab from Midtown, because I want to get him into my bedroom as quickly as possible. I sequester him there, whether he knows it or not, shooing him away from the deliveryman waiting at the door, ferrying in plates and snacks and wine and glasses from the kitchen.

"Tell me where you've been," I say. "Japan and Malaysia and Fiji and Kenya and Russia and Texas."

"And Texas," he says. "It's just Texas. It ain't nuthin' special."

I push his knees apart and lie down between them, my head on his stomach, my arm wrapped around his thigh. "All I want to do is see the world," I say. "Bridget and I were going to move to Costa Rica or New Zealand or something, but then she had to ruin everything and get engaged." This is the only way I will talk about the wedding, in this dismissive, aggrieved tone, because

I do not want him to think there is some sort of commitment virus going around that I have contracted from my best friend.

"I thought you were moving to New Zealand. Didn't you say you were moving to New Zealand?"

"I don't know," I say. *Not as long as you're here,* I think, which is immediately followed up by the slightly more hysterical, *Do you want me to go? Don't you care if I go?* I had always conceived of myself as a brilliant adventurer, waylaid only by her fickle companion, but the fact is that since Ryan returned to Couture I have not once considered leaving New York, except for those few panicked moments at Penn Station when I wanted so viciously to be anywhere but there—and even then, that was more a problem of time than geography, how I so desperately wanted to remain in the pre-Stella past. I say "anywhere but there" and even that is a lie: I wanted to be as close to him as possible, because as long as I was, there was a limit to how wrong things could be. "New Zealand seems so far away," I say. "But don't you think there's a big world out there?"

"You mean, outside of couture-dot-com?"

I nod.

"What do you think?"

"I don't know," I say. "I've worked there for ages."

"You do," he says. "Don't tell me you don't."

"I grew up in New Jersey, went to school in New York, live in New York," I say. "My whole life's happened in a hundred-mile radius of Long Beach Island." I flip onto my side and crawl across him to the window, pulling up the heavy metal blinds Zoe installed throughout the apartment after she decided she was being stalked by a mailroom clerk. "I think there might be more," I say, leaning my hands on the windowsill and my head against the glass.

"You think," he says.

"I have a suspicion."

He pulls me, by the waistband, back to the bed. "I could show you some things," he says. "My dad was posted in Indonesia—it sounds like your island's not far from there. I'll ask him about it for you."

Do I ask him to come to the wedding now? Why couldn't Bridget have had this fucking wedding in Margate? Does she not comprehend the difference in asking this person to a wedding in New Jersey and a wedding in the South Pacific? "Have you been to New Zealand?" It can wait. It will have to wait. I can't deal with it right now. "Or Tasmania?" I ask, trying to sound geographically conversational.

"Nope," he says.

This is my favorite thing that we do, lying here and talking, with our heads at the foot of the bed. We are on the top floor, Zoe and I, so I need only to crane my neck a little to see planes from JFK heading north over Brooklyn.

"I want to see the fjords," I say.

"They have fjords in New Zealand?"

"They had glaciers," I say, "so they have fjords."

"They had glaciers," he says, mimicking me, tickling me. Normally it would be difficult to decide which I hate more, but, at this moment, I don't mind so much. *"So they have fjords."*

"It's true," I say, although I am not entirely certain about the glacier–fjord connection. If I stop to think about it, when I am with him, I play loose with my facts, looser than I would with Bridget or my friends or even with absentminded Julia, who, in addition to the roiling/boiling thing, once confused Yogi Bear with Yogi Berra. ("Which one is the cartoon?") Ryan is beginning to cede to me this high ground of facts and figures, and although normally I would like this, normally it would also be more of a challenge. Fuck. Maybe Tommy is right, or maybe—and this is the story I prefer to tell myself—he is simply smart in a way that fails to express itself in standardized testing. I am hoping this is not becoming the push-pull of the Girl Who Is Trapped in Her Head and the Boy Who Loves to Fuck, that we will allow each other to share our natural territory: But there it is, already. When I began this with him, I knew I wanted him to make me into someone other than the nervous, anxious, fact-addled person I have become, but here I am, with my numbers and statistics, and my bikini top. "Actually, I could be completely making up the fjord thing," I say, and although this is true, that is not why I say it. "Why do you have a Texan accent if you lived all over the world?" I say before I can think too long about why I am letting him know about the gap in my fjord–glacier understanding. Maybe it is a good thing: With someone else, I would bluff, successfully. Maybe, with him, I can let myself be wrong.

"Well, you know," he says, because as far as he can tell, this is still a conversation about geography, "Ma and Pa. I sound just like them."

"I love New Jersey," I say. "I wouldn't want to be from anywhere else. But sometimes it can be a little anonymous. Sometimes I wish I were from somewhere like Oklahoma or Wyoming or Hawaii, where if you met someone else from that place, you'd kind of team up and know that you had something in common. Like corn farms or Devil's Tower or lava fields. We don't have that. We have Applebee's and the Gap. It's hard to feel like you're from somewhere when you feel like you're from anywhere."

"They have Applebee's and Gaps in Oklahoma. I think you're giving Oklahoma too much credit."

"You're only saying that because you're from Texas," I say. "Nine million people live in New Jersey, and half of them work in Midtown. We're ubiquitous. We're like Spanish moss."

"There's twelve million people in Texas," he says.

"But you have an identity. You're Texas. You're the Alamo. You're the Lone Star State."

"You're a Jersey girl. Tom Waits wrote a song about you."

"True," I say. I love New Jersey. "Do you want cookies?" I ask, cheered. "I want cookies."

I go into the kitchen without waiting for an answer. Looking in vain for a clean plate, I glance at the clock: It is two in the morning. He is leaving in only three and a half hours, and I will not see him again for five days, which seems like an almost unfathomable period of time. "Why are we talking about New Jersey and not making out?" I say, hurrying back into my room with a glass filled with Oreos.

He is sitting up now, with an extravagantly wrapped box balanced on his knees. "I don't know about that," he says, "but in my family, everybody gives everybody a Christmas present on Thanksgiving."

I hand him the glass and sit down on my bed. I untie the bow and remove the wrapping as carefully as I can, running my finger beneath the inch-long strips of cellophane tape, folding it back into a sheet before shaking the lid loose and poking through the tissue paper.

It is a gas mask.

"It's better than military grade," he says. "And it came with free potassium iodide pills." He reaches inside the box and out comes a small orange bottle with a blue ribbon around it. "They're supposed to keep your thyroid from getting fucked up if there's a nuclear explosion."

I pull the mask on over my head, fiddle with one of the knobs near the mouthpiece, and then push it back, so it sits on my forehead like a visor. The things I want to say most—like *I love you, I love you, I love you*—are exactly the ones I forbid myself to consider expressing aloud. They will have to be content living inside my head. "Thank you very much," I say.

The next day he is gone. He is in Austin by the time I wake up at noon, and then Bridget and I drive south on the parkway toward Margate, blue sky above us and pine forests at our side. Halfway there I convince her to pull over at a rest stop south of the bridge over Raritan Bay.

"Did I mention how tall and strong he is?" I say, apropos of nothing, while we wait in line at Starbucks.

"Oh my God," Bridget says. "You are only getting away with that because you cleverly used the word 'he' instead of his name." Half an hour into our car ride, Bridget accused me of saying Ryan's name twenty-seven times, which I suspect is not so wildly inflated a figure as I'd maintained, and she'd banned me from saying it until we got past Asbury Park. "And in any case, you did. 'Kind of like a cowboy' I think was how you put it."

"And I mentioned he broke up with his girlfriend? And hasn't mentioned her once in the last seven weeks?"

"Can we at least agree that the not-mentioning thing is positive, but not absolute, evidence of his inherent goodness?"

Bridget is only saying aloud what I think to myself, every minute of every day when I am not actually with him, but hearing my own fears enunciated so clearly makes me sick to my stomach, which I can only regard as a traitor, as an unconscionable, uncontrollable barometer of the emotional well-being of my relationship with Ryan. I already feel like Bridget knows too much, is too capable of performing a devastating analysis, but it is the price to pay for the chance that she will say something encouraging. "You must," I say, "you absolutely must have something good to say about this."

"How many nights did you spend with him last week?"

"Six," I say.

"Six out of seven," she says. "I know you know what that percentage is."

"It's hard with sevens," I say. "Er . . . like eighty-something percent."

"You're winning. Stop freaking out."

"You know," I say, because I am sure when I am through saying it I will feel better than I feel right now, "when you said that other thing, I felt all queasy and sick."

"I just don't think there's anything wrong with playing it the tiniest bit cool."

"Oh, seriously," I say. "We are way past that."

"Okay, fine," she says. "Explain your problem, as clearly as possible."

This is better. We are reverting back to how we have been since middle school, which seems to fit the emotional temper of my current situation. "I am obsessed with someone who is only recently out of a long-term relationship," I say, "with a gorgeous, designer-y sex goddess from Japan."

"I bet she's not buying dehydrated food over the Internet, either," Bridget says. It is her way of punishing me for wearing my gas mask for twenty-five minutes while we were stuck in the Holland Tunnel. "If you keep that on," she had said, "I will fucking kill you."

"I can't believe you said that," I say. "It's almost like you want to ensure we talk about nothing but this for the next two hours."

"Okay, fine," she says. "He likes you. He spent six of the last seven nights with you. He would probably be with you right now if it weren't for the fact that he's in another state. So, is there anything else?"

"I don't think so," I say.

"Nothing else? In the world? Bombs going off in Sudan, presidential election coming up, none of that? End of the world, even?"

"I don't see where you're going with this, Bridget," I say testily.

"It's just the way your gaze is so attached to your navel," she says. "I bet your neck hurts."

"I hate you," I say.

"I suppose it's a good thing, the way you've stopped talking about the apocalypse," she says. "I mean, it could be worse."

"Nothing could be worse," I say. "Didn't you ever feel this way about James?"

"No," she says.

Part of me thinks: *There it is again: Bridget's always right, Bridget's always smarter than me.*

And then I think: *Shouldn't she?* "Shouldn't you?"

"I don't know," she says, shrugging her shoulders. When Bridget is being willfully obtuse, she shrugs; she has shrugged like this as long as I've known her, petulantly, dismissively, to the point where I would preface a question by physically, preemptively, holding down her shoulders. Later I will puzzle over this: I will wonder about the substance of this shrug, whether it betrays a lack of interest in answering my question, or an inability to answer it. For now, though, Bridget is rescued by the advance of the line we stand in, and she follows her shrug with an order for two Frappuccinos and a piece of coffee cake designed to shut me up.

Thanksgiving at Bridget's is like the Platonic ideal of the holiday dinner, if you assume the father had been killed in war, or while stopping a crime—violently, maybe, but heroically. There are pies in the oven and candles on the table and an elderly grandfather in a bow tie and sweater vest slicing a turkey his daughter prepared. In the unrealized present that would have come to pass had my parents not jumped down the rabbit hole of their midlife reinvention, someone at my house, just down the road, would be putting on a puppet show with the turkey carcass. Rebecca did that last year, while her boyfriend yelled, "Dance, motherfucker! Dance!" Rebecca discovered a way to make it appear that Boomer was waltzing with the turkey, while Stevie beat the rhythm, one-two-three, one-two-three, on a pie tin with the turkey baster. Then Boomer, presumably enraptured by the scent of all that meat wafting past his nose, attacked Rebecca, grabbed the carcass between his paws, situated it beneath him, and began humping it, grinding turkey skin into my mother's carpet.

"These fuckers," my sister had said when she called me from Stevie's parents' house, in one of those depressed towns on the border of Ohio and West Virginia. "They can't stop talking about the new priest at the church and is he gay or is he not."

"Is he?"

"How the fuck would I know?"

"Where are Mom and Dad?"

"On their way to Tahiti, I think. Remember when Boomer did that thing with the turkey last year?"

"That was the best Thanksgiving ever," I say.

"It was," she says. "That room smelled like turkey all winter.

I wish Mom and Daddy were home. They want to convert me here. Can they do that?"

"You're a Nilssen, and we don't take shit from anybody." Because we are the proud Protestants of the arctic north. "And nobody fucks with the Lutherans." Whatever that means.

This is all she needs. If there were a Danish gang, my sister would lead it, with nunchakus and daggers. "I'm going to go tell them that Mary wasn't a saint, and that that transubstantiation stuff is bullshit."

"I'm very proud of you, Becky," I say, giving her a chance to enjoy our parents' favorite unrealized naming scheme. Years of planning had gone into "Becky and Betsy," only to be lost when we were old enough to understand alliteration, and Becky became Rebecca.

"Next year, let's hide their passports so they can't go anywhere," she says. Day in, day out, we are a little scattered, a little distracted, a little too sure of ourselves. But this is the position in which my family excels: threatened with exile and dispersal, buttressed by nothing but bluster and pride.

It is just four of us at dinner: Bridget and me, her mother and grandfather. The triplets are coming home, en masse, tomorrow night, and I will already be on my way back to New York. James is somewhere sufficiently exotic that he calls Bridget from a hilltop, on a satellite phone. This suits me fine: I have no interest in being their latchkey kid, and I have Bridget to myself for the night. It is snowing too convincingly to attempt the drive to Atlantic City, so we settle on our local T.G.I. Friday's, which, as we had guessed during a moment of hesitation in the parking lot, is filled with other Thanksgiving night refugees. Many of them are drinking blue liquids out of oversized glass mugs. "We're having a special on blue curaçao," the waitress explains, handing us our menus. "The bartender overordered again." Blue margaritas are four dollars, and "blueberry pie shooters" are two.

"I'm not sure blueberry pie shooters are what the Pilgrims had in mind," Bridget says.

"This place is so anonymous, we could be anywhere in America," I say, not so much because this point is particularly apparent at this moment as because it makes me think of Ryan.

"That's ridiculous," Bridget says. "How many T.G.I. Friday's in New Mexico have Ms. O'Connors?"

She is tilting her head at our senior-year biology teacher, who is wearing a black sequined halter top and sitting at the bar. It did not occur to me until now that although we are twenty-four, a teacher of ours might not even be thirty by now. We were Ms. O'Connors's first class of students after Trenton State. "Isn't her name Lisa?"

"Alyssa, I think," she says. "But she should not be wearing that top here. If you were fifteen and you saw her like that, you'd be jerking off to her until you went to college. You could forget about a career in biology."

"Unless you wanted to be an expert in jerking off."

"You're bizarre," Bridget says. "You think she comes here a lot?"

"Where else would you go, if you lived here?"

"Aren't there townie bars or something?"

"Well, we're townies," Bridget says. "I think we would know about them if there were."

"Do you want to talk to her?"

"No," Bridget says. "And if she walks by here to the bathroom, I want you to duck under the table."

"That's a stupid thing to say. We liked her. She was nice."

"If you say a word to her, I will make you drink both of these blueberry pie shooters," Bridget says. We laugh like this is a joke, but when Ms. O'Connors climbs off her bar stool and walks toward us, Bridget stands up to stab me in the arm with her fork. I kick her beneath the table, and in her effort to kick me back, she loses her balance, landing on my arm with her full weight. I shriek just as Ms. O'Connors walks past our booth.

"Girls," she says.

"Hi, Ms. O'Connors," we say. There are four tiny drops of blood on my arm.

"Nice to see you both," she says, her hand briefly covering the *V* of her exposed chest. "Nice to see you." She turns toward the bathroom, and as she walks away we can see a giant diamond on her left middle finger.

"You stabbed me," I say. I press a paper napkin to my arm.

"Why do you think she was wearing a ring on her middle finger?" Bridget says.

"I don't know. Is that bad wedding luck?"

"It's just not done," Bridget says.

"Is there someone we should report her to? A bridal council?"

"It's just not done," Bridget says again. "Why would you do that?"

I hold up my hand so that my palm faces Bridget, and the napkin, still bound to my skin by the drying blood, hangs suspended in the air. "Can we discuss what you did to my arm?"

"I'm sorry," she says.

"You don't sound very sorry. I think you should buy me a piece of cake."

"If I buy you the cake, can we talk about my wedding for the next forty-five minutes?"

"My injury on its own is well worth the cake," I say. "And

did you ever think that maybe I should just be willing to listen to you talk about your wedding out of the goodness of my heart, without you buying me cake, or maybe you shouldn't stab me in the arm with a fork?"

"Not really," she says. "You know, all those bridesmaids girls are married, and the truth is that to the people who aren't getting married, the band-versus-DJ question is a little boring. But to the person who is getting married, a person such as myself, this is an extremely, extremely crucial issue. Isn't it better that I get exactly what I want, and you get exactly what you want, instead of me feeling guilty about talking about this totally boring wedding bullshit and you being resentful about it?"

I like this Bridget. This is my Bridget, the one who admits to the existence of a world outside the one beginning and ending with her wedding ceremony in a few months. And in any case, now that I have Ryan, her wedding feels less a threat, or a terror, than a social obligation. "I'm so happy we agree about this," I say.

"And honestly," she says. "Wouldn't you rather have a piece of cake than a totally meaningless apology about how I didn't mean to stab you in the arm and just lost my balance, which, by the way, is true?"

"You're right," I say. "I'd rather have the cake."

Ryan calls from the airport to say he is taking a cab directly from LaGuardia to my apartment. Ryan says he missed me. Ryan says he went swimming in Lake Austin. Ryan says he is on his way to baggage claim, and there is quite a crowd here, and it could be a while until he is in Brooklyn.

We have had a break, Ryan and I, and I have had a chance to think, which means an opportunity to strategize. There is no, there is just no fucking reason I need to remain what I have been, the Girl Who Is Trapped in Her Head. Unbelievably, I am convinced that Tommy has been right all along, and after I step out of the shower, I call him to tell him so.

"Does this mean," he says, over the din of the Amtrak train returning him to New York from Boston, "you are operating the B and P plan?"

"It does," I say.

"Good luck, and Godspeed," he says. "And call me as soon as possible to tell me how it goes."

The buzzer buzzes, and I make ready. I am prepared to answer the door and discover our landlord, prepared for the psychological spit-take, but it is Ryan, and I know as soon as I see his face that I will be able to report success back to Tommy. "Up here," he says, slapping his side, and I throw my arms around his neck and my legs around his waist. We are kissing and he carries me into my closet, where he sits on my bed.

I am straddling him like a saddle and taking off his shirt. "You don't need this in here, it's so hot," I say. "Did you have a nice time?"

"It was Texas," he says. "We went to the bar."

"Did lots of girls try to talk to you at this bar?"

"A couple," he says. "But I told them I was spoken for."

"You are," I say, undoing his belt buckle. "You are spoken for."

"You look hot," he says, and although I at first want to explain, again, about Zoe's thermostat, he already knows this story, and I keep my mouth shut, as much as it wants to give him the out, to make this a question of climatology versus B&P. Words have always been my friend, my livelihood, and here they are waiting like thieves in the night, threatening to take what by all rights is mine. He is running his finger beneath the bikini strap, and I force, I just force myself to let him speak next. "What's that?" he says, looking closely at the four small dots of dried blood below my elbow.

"Bridget stabbed me in the arm with a fork," I say.

"She shouldn't do that," he says.

"That's just Bridget," I say. "She would stab me in the arm but never in the back." I am so ashamed I just said that. I was so on guard, so attuned to the possibility of my own words doing me in that I did not expect this attack from the flanks. Something about this person makes me say the stupidest things.

"So she stabs you often?"

We are talking about Bridget, and I am thinking about thinking, and his clothes are no longer coming off. This is not what I wanted. "I'm sure you have a friend you punch or something, right?"

"Tastes like blood," he says, licking my skin.

This is better.

"Bridget," he repeats. "She's the one you're maid of honor for."

Is this when I ask him to the wedding? Now he is licking my neck and undoing the knots holding my bikini top together. "I think I'm falling in love with you," I say.

Oh, no. I hold my breath. I knew I was going to say that, and I did not stop myself. I knew what was happening, and I chose not to stop it, and now I wish I had. Depending on what he says next. *Please,* I think. *Say something good next, or I am just going to die.*

"Do you have, like, an office supply drawer?"

I cannot imagine where this is going. Maybe he is going to make me another drawing. Maybe he can only express himself in shapes, like I can only express myself in words. I point to my office supply drawer, which is a Nike box full of packing tape and scissors. I am sitting straight up, cross-legged, holding the ties of the bikini strings at my neck.

"Here it is," he says. "Close your eyes."

Because I am not getting what I want back from him immediately, I focus on what he is doing. He is a physical person. He can only express himself through physicalities. *Like a horse,* I think. I close my eyes.

He pulls back my hair, which is something I like very much. I very much like this idea. After he's twisted my hair into a bun, secured with a rubber band, possibly from the office supply drawer, he pauses, and I hear something ripping. "Are your eyes closed?" he says.

I nod.

It moves left to right across my face. My eyelids are stuck in an uncomfortable position because he has just taped them shut. He twists me around, hard, by the shoulders, and I tip over, hard, so that my face is shoved into my pillow, I am mostly naked from the waist up, and he is pressing against my hips, bringing his hand beneath me to pull down my bikini bottoms. I cannot breathe and I cannot see and so I pull my foot back and kick him as hard as I can in the stomach.

"Oh, shit," I hear him say. "I'm sorry. You were supposed to like it. It was supposed to be a surprise or something."

"I don't understand what's going on," I say, pulling off the tape.

"Did I freak you out?"

"Half of my eyebrows are on this tape."

"I thought—"

"Did you have to use duct tape? Was there no masking tape in my drawer?" I think somehow of a porn movie Billy and John used to watch every night. "Were there no scarves available?"

"I'm sorry, I'm sorry if I was rough," he says. "Stella always liked it like that. She was really crazy in bed."

"Oh my God," I say, so quickly, almost laughing, that I start coughing, and he has to wait for it to subside, while I hide my face behind my hands, to reply. "You did not. You did not just say that."

"I mean—"

"You mean, with Stella. There is no way you just said that. I cannot believe you just said that." I can't. No matter how badly I expected him to answer what I had said, I had never considered this. I had not. I just want it to be twenty minutes ago. It is becoming a pattern here, with this person, that I so often want it to be a time it is not. It is everything I ever wanted, and then it is all that work, all that work to get back to where I was. I feel like a boomerang, always just trying to get back where it started before being tossed away again. "Seriously," I say, because I can think of nothing else. However little I trusted myself to speak before, that reserve is at empty.

"It's not like that. Don't be mad. It's not that. I don't think that. I promise."

I should know, just from the volume and rapidity of his words, that he is trying to express something that is difficult for him, and that he probably trusts his words as little as I do. That is the generous view. The other is that he is lying, that I am just a detour, a sideshow, a freak show, until he goes back to Stella. Who is crazy in bed. I do not know when I am going to be able to stop hearing those words. "Promises, promises," I say, meanly but stickily, because my mouth has gone almost entirely dry. I do not want to leave him here, because right now his hand is on my arm, and if I stop touching him, I do not know how long I will have to wait until I can touch him again. I am not mad; I am not angry. It would probably be better for me if I were feeling something other than lost and injured, if I were not still waiting for him to say he is falling in love with me, too.

More out of disgust for myself than for him, I get up, stomp out, and make my way to the kitchen. I stare into the refrigerator, like I am playing a character, the aggrieved lover, who is looking for strawberry jam, all raised eyebrows and theatrical squats—could it be in the *crisper*?

"Betsy," he says. Zoe's unused kitchen is not big enough for two people to be in it at the same time, so he stands beneath the doorframe. He has put on his T-shirt, which is another terrible development. Maybe he will just leave, and this will all be over. Could it be over, after something like this? Maybe it could. Bridget's wedding looms up like a forgotten disaster, and I see myself standing there alone. Alone, alone, alone. If I say it enough times, maybe it will stop mattering. "Betsy," he says. "I swear, I didn't mean it like that. I don't want to be with her."

Her, her, her. If I say it enough, maybe that, too, will stop mattering. I don't think I will be successful here, either, though. "I don't have any jam," I say. There is nothing left in the freezer to look at but a snowed-over carton of Ben & Jerry's and a frozen Snickers bar I had forgotten. I feel ridiculous; I feel ridiculous that he is standing there while I pretend to be interested in the ice-maker. There is nowhere left to go. "I wish you hadn't done that," I say, my head entirely in the freezer.

"What are you looking for?"

"The strawberry jam," I say.

"It wouldn't be in the freezer," he says.

"I don't care," I say.

"I'll go get you some," he says.

He comes back, holding the jam, my prop, my symbol of thwarted desire. I was not sure he would come back. Is it that I have so little faith in him, or so little faith in myself?

Hours later, his arms wrapped around me, I wake up.

"What is it?" he says.

"Nothing," I say. "Just hot."

I close my eyes and pretend like I am sleeping for a few seconds, and then reopen them. He is staring at me.

"What are you doing?"

"Just looking," he says.

I sit up. Everything feels wrong. "Tonight was horrible," I say. "I hated everything about tonight." I hear the brittleness and certainty in my voice. I am only this certain when things are going poorly. When things are going well, I am clueless, anxious, upended—but now I am on surer ground. I hate that about myself, my perverse confidence, that this place, of dismissal and resignation, should be where I am most at home. I feel like I have been issued the wrong passport: Where is the land of the girls who like to party?

"I am falling in love with you," he says, like he is correcting a mistake.

"Okay," I say.

"Will you please just come here?" He pulls me down to his chest. There is an urgency to his voice that could sustain me for weeks. I do as he asks, because all I want, really, is for him to want things from me.

"Okay," I say again.

"Have you ever seen *Monty Python and the Holy Grail*?"

"No," I say.

"We'll have to make sure you do."

He is almost asleep now, and I tuck my head next to his and behind it, so that I am breathing in his hair. It is calm again. It is like whatever happened in the middle, between when he got here and now, was a misprint, an errant page bound into a book. At least I hope it is.

I like him best when he is silent, immobile, closely guarded. I know he is not asleep. "Say it again," I say.

"Which part?" he says.

"You know," I say, "that one," I say, and he does.

Six

Usually I like calendar-appropriate shifts in the weather: a cold front on Labor Day, snow on Christmas, lilies of the valley blooming on Easter. And sure enough: It is the first of December, and the light in the room is cold and white, a winter light. There are thirty days left until the end of the year, and the muted CNN is reporting that a chain of Midwest banks, in anticipation of a run on their holdings, limited its customers' Thanksgiving weekend cash withdrawals to one thousand dollars. Iowa City customers are picketing in bank parking lots. MY BABY NEEDS ELMO, one of the signs reads. I would have thought milk, perhaps; Elmo, I guess, has his own charms.

I am awake before he is, and I am careful not to disturb him as I get out of bed, dropping a knee to the floor and disentangling myself from the sheets one leg at a time. I do not like the space I am in, the triangle formed between my head and the two edges of the television screen. I wish I could see that there is nothing good for me here, in this space, where my engagement is completely . . . "intellectual" would be too good a word for it, for this mind-jail where I sequester myself, evaluating the ways the world could end, determining preferences in manners (divine, instantaneous) and methods (not an explosion but maybe just a disappearing, a vacuuming—if it's instantaneous it can't hurt too much).

"You know it's arbitrary and ridiculous to think the world is going to end two thousand years after somebody's born?" Ryan says. I had not noticed he was awake. "Why not one thousand years ago?"

"Arbitrary" is the biggest word I have ever heard him use. As soon as I think this, I am disgusted with myself, for judging him on the basis of words, which are currently heckling me with manners less divine (torturous, man-made) and methods more painful (explosions, plagues, bombs, snipers). I take my place beside him and stare at the ceiling.

"No more CNN," Ryan says. He reaches over me to the remote control on the nightstand and turns off the television.

In the quiet that follows I turn on my side to face him. "Did you know that as the year one thousand approached, cathedrals stopped being built? They just stopped and sat down and waited for the end of the world."

"Well," Ryan says. "I bet they felt like real big assholes New Year's Day, 1001."

"Hmm," I say.

Ryan pulls me closer to him and puts a pillow over both of our heads, blocking out the glare of the white morning light. "Quiet now," he says, placing his hand over my mouth.

This is what I want: to be shut down, silenced, distracted from the part of my head that is wondering where the bombs will go off.

Ryan leaves for the office before I do: I walk him to the door in my bikini top and denim shorts and kiss him, barefoot, next to the stairs, feeling both domestic and a little bit like Daisy Duke, which is, I believe, an alluring combination.

I put on a sweater and change into my jeans. On my way through the kitchen I see a note taped to the refrigerator that was not there last night, from Zoe: "I'm going to Mauritius." That is all. I haven't seen her for weeks. I fold the note into quarters and stick it into my back pocket: evidence of someone with the means getting out of here while they can. No. Evidence of Zoe's career as an international partier.

The weather has changed and the wind gusting across this elevated platform has picked up, and I consider, while waiting for the F train, where Ryan waits for it: at the end of the platform? In the middle? Knowing he has come this way before me makes me feel like I am not alone, like I am not about to disappear, like I would be missed if I were.

I spend my trip on the train evaluating the realities of the last dismal eighteen hours: I am who, and what, I have always been, caught up in my head, not a physical being but a mind-jailed one, and unless I can change this, I do not think Ryan will want to be with me: Who would I rather be with? The girl who is crazy in bed? Or the one who counts down the days until the end of the world? Is that even a choice? I have let myself be caught up in my own worst instincts, my most unlikely fears and my laziness, my unwillingness to assume the form and figure of even the most loosely defined adult. I am still the same girl Bridget caught with a forgotten sandwich under her bed. "Pastrami," she'd said, and we'd both laughed and assumed I'd grow out of it. Instead I have just grown into it, my own stunted adulthood, living in this fantasy world of eighty-degree days in December with my brain-addled roommate, tramping to work in five-year-old jeans and a T-shirt with grape juice stains on the hem. Can I not manage something better than this?

Julia is burning off her vacation time painting her apartment, and Eva has left for a Missoni-sponsored trip to Milan, so I have a week to myself until the office party, which I spend at the

World Trade Center mall. First, Victoria's Secret. It is overwhelming, the sheer amount of silk products. The sheer amount of sheer products. If it is like the Gap, where I worked in high school, the employees have a discount, and they all wear these red outfits to bed. I have not ever bought a bra. They are so expensive, and other things are so much more interesting. Ryan had said once that he liked it, my "free-spirit[edness]," and I did not have a problem with that. But now I feel like a hippie, an unattractive hippie, with increasingly saggy breasts tumbling out of faded tank tops. I am the avatar of patchouli.

A woman my grandmother's age, a yellow measuring tape wrapped around her wrist, approaches me. "Can I help you?"

"I have come to buy a bra." I say it too loudly, and grin widely so she knows I am being ironic.

She nods. She is a model of efficiency. "Do you know your size?"

"Somewhere between a two and an eight, depending on where I am."

She narrows her eyes at me, looks through raised eyebrows at my chest. "Are you European?"

"I'm from New Jersey," I say.

"Your accent," she murmurs, "is peculiar."

I do not know what this means. She leads me into a changing room, grabs my hands and raises them above my head. I like this position. My breasts are perkier than ever before. I am going to have to remember this position.

"Take off your top," she says.

I hesitate. "I'm not wearing anything else at the moment."

"I've seen it before," she says.

I slowly take off my top. This woman has a tremendous chest. I wonder if this woman is wearing the padded push-up bra featured on the mannequins in the store windows and if she purchased them with her employee discount. I wonder if Ryan has ever done something like this, something so remedial, to ensure that I care for him.

"Thirty-four B," she says.

"That's a good one, yeah?"

"It'll do," she says, like I am a loony European with unspectacular, 34B-sized breasts.

I meet Ryan at a bar near the Williamsburg Bridge, and when he puts his hand up my shirt, which I have encouraged him to do, he jerks it back. "What's *that*?" he says, looking quizzically at my chest. "That's not a bikini top."

"It's new," I say.

"Hmm," he says, and I am uneasy. I said I would never change myself for a man, but now that I have begun to do so, I will be extremely disappointed if it does not work.

He does not look uneasy. He looks like he is paying attention. "Can I see it?" he says, and I let him follow me into the women's bathroom.

The bra is a success. We leave the bar and return to my house and we are making out in the hallway before making out in the living room. "Did I tell you I'm going away tomorrow, through the weekend?" he says during a break, as I scour the kitchen cabinets for something to open a wine bottle with other than the plastic knife in my left hand.

"No," I say, hoping the distance between the kitchen and the living room will soften the disappointment in my voice. My first thought is he is making this up, inventing a five-day break from me and un-wild ways. But he wouldn't have to work that hard; he could have just told me that he had band practice or was working on some made-up art project; he'd know I wouldn't investigate too thoroughly, that I would at least pretend to trust him.

He is still talking. That is the most amazing thing to me: What percentage of what I think about this person do I actually speak aloud? Five? "A bunch of my friends from art school are here," he says. "We're going camping on the beach in Long Island."

Friends who are girls? Friends who are more fun than me? Friends who are friends with Stella? And in December? "That sounds cold," I say. I am one for four.

"It's kind of a send-off for my friend Russ, who's getting married," he says while I wait for him to continue, for him to answer the questions I haven't been able to ask. *Precisely what portion of your time will be spent (a) fucked up, (b) flirting, (c) in the company of girls with breasts larger than mine?*

"So it's sort of like a bachelor party?"

"Sort of," he says. "But with shrooms and without strippers."

I feel my way through my stack of delivery menus to Zoe's half of the kitchen drawer for a corkscrew, which, delightfully, appears. I pass it to Ryan and sit down next to him. "But then who do the single guys make out with?" *And you would consider yourself single, or not?*

"Each other?" he says. He is smiling, but it is not in a way that tells me whether or not he is joking. "You know, artists."

"You better not make out with anyone, stripper, artist, or otherwise," I say, trying to sound breezy and unconcerned. "You're spoken for." I am hoping he remembers this from last night—can that only be last night?—when he, himself, had said he was. I am not suggesting anything he did not suggest to me first, and surely I cannot go far wrong there.

"Deal," he says, extending the hand that is not holding the wine bottle. We shake. "Why do you call it making out?"

"Isn't that what it is?" I say, trying to at least provide an impression of someone who is barely even aware that her quasi-boyfriend is disappearing for the next five days to get stoned with his morally derelict friends.

"But you sound like you're in middle school when you say it that way," he says.

"I thought that's what all the guys wanted," I say. "To have sex with middle-schoolers." I am barely even paying attention to what I am saying: I am thinking only of how this situation would be improved if he actually were my boyfriend, if I could stake that claim to him, pin him, pin him down. Once again my metaphors are betraying my intentions.

"That's a little young," he says. "I think it's sixteen-year-old cheerleaders guys want to have sex with."

"Do you want to have sex with a sixteen-year-old?"

"When?"

"At this moment," I say, walking over to the open window and sticking my head out, peering down to the street. "I'm sure we could find you one."

"I've already had sex with a sixteen-year-old girl," he says. "I don't think I need to do it again."

With Stella? But the math doesn't work. It must have been someone else. Sometimes it is so clear how little I know about this person. But I am scared to ask because there are answers I do not want to hear, answers about other girls, girls who would not seem like an accident, an oversight that will be corrected.

"Let's make out," I say.

"Sure thing," he says.

By the time I wake up at eleven thirty, Ryan has left for his bisexual artist bachelor party. I wish we were establishing a pattern other than this: He leaves; I feel empty and lost. This cannot be the right idea.

It would be easy for me to just stay in bed, staring at the ceiling; with Julia and Eva out I have no obligation to go to the office, and with Ryan gone I have little interest in it. Again, I think: This cannot be right; this was not what I planned when I came back to the Couture office after Labor Day weekend. And even if I allow that I have a meaningless, worthless job, which I do, and which I do allow, maybe the kind of self-improvement I knew was so necessary then was simply mischanneled into my job; maybe the point was not to submit to those circumstances but to change everything but them. I already have this new bra, which Ryan seemed to appreciate. I sit up, alone in my bedroom, and hop up and down, amazed at the new level of support I have purchased for only thirty-two dollars. I have six days on my own, to do with as I please: Surely there are other paths I could follow, to similar ends. Worlds are created in less time.

"Bras are a really fantastic invention," I say to Bridget, phone cradled under my ear, as I dump raspberries and a cut-up banana into a plastic cup. It is not quite a precise operation, but it is still an improvement on Pop-Tarts, and small improvements are undoubtedly my only key to success.

"Are you at your office?" she says. "Isn't it almost noon?"

"Nobody's really working this week."

"Is it Christmas already?" I can see her confronting her calendar. "Is it *New Year's*?" She sighs dramatically into the phone. "I wish I worked in publishing."

"No, you don't," I say. "Because then you wouldn't get to say, 'La la la la, I'm saving the world.' "

She is all mock outrage. "Well at least I'm not giving teenagers in Fiji eating disorders," she says. She had e-mailed me a news story about how the debut of fashion magazines in some island nations was nearly simultaneous with the rising incidence of anorexia.

"You can't make me hate my job any more than I do already," I say. "It's impossible. But you know what? Instead of a Pop-Tart for breakfast today, I went to the store, bought fruit, then brought it home and cut it up."

"Anything else?"

"If this trend continues, I will be sitting with my boyfriend, wearing a bra, and not eating Pop-Tarts at your wedding."

She pauses, and I am sure it is an appreciative pause. "Do you think you can put all of this in motion in time for my engagement brunch?"

"You're having an engagement brunch? Is that new?" These things just never end. "Hold on," I say. "Do I have to buy you *another* present? Do you know that your wedding already accounts for five percent of my annual salary?"

"Maybe you'd have a bigger salary if you went into your office occasionally," she says. "And did I tell you that all the girls are spending a few days there before the wedding? It's kind of an extended bachelorette party."

"Oh my God," I say. "That has to be at least eight percent."

"I have really enjoyed this conversation," Bridget says, "but I'm not allowed to have personal calls at my desk."

"When is this brunch?"

"The Saturday after New Year's, in the city. You'll be there, yeah? You have to be there."

"The Saturday after New Year's Day?"

"Did you have other plans?"

"Okay," I say. "Fine, sure, whatever."

"Are you saying it like that because you think the world is going to end, in advance of the New Year and my engagement party?"

"No," I say. "I sure hope not, anyway. It would be such a shame to miss out on all that cash."

There is a moment of silence before I hear the dead air. Bridget has hung up on me. If anyone else had done that, I would have been annoyed, put out, but with Bridget it is just part of what we do: There is an indescribable grace in being allowed to be your own worst self with someone, completely unedited, and it is something I would not trade for the world, for Ryan even, for anything.

Rite Aid has lipstick, wall displays exhibiting tube after tube, and I study my options with the put-upon precision of a witness at a police-station lineup: I want to make the right decision but have zero faith in my ability to do so. A Color Me Beautiful expert had once, mysteriously, donated her services to my junior high Girl Scout troop, a gaggle of eleven-year-olds whose concept of sexuality was, until her appearance, derived entirely from Duran Duran videos. This vast land of desire and seduction and cosmetics had not appeared on any of our maps before she showed up at our Monday night meeting in the Margate Public Library, where she warned the large contingent of Autumns against makeup involving pinks or reds. I have forgotten calculus formulae, the order of presidents, and who, exactly, was involved in the Teapot Dome scandal, but I have remembered this warning for nearly fifteen years, and I dutifully gravitate toward an area filled with plums and peaches. I apply half a dozen to the back of my hand.

They all have names like Berry Berry Dramatic and A Rose By Any Other Name, which is written in tiny type down the side of the tube in my hand. A rose it is.

The girl at the cash register is six, maybe eight years younger than I am, and carelessly gorgeous: She is wearing only a white button-down shirt, hanging out over cheap jeans, and a tie loosely knotted around her neck, no makeup, no jewelry, but there is no arguing the fact that she is the most beautiful woman in this room. I am not the only person who sees this: The woman in front of me, carrying a Fendi bag and wearing equally expensive shoes, pretends to examine a rack of Haribo candy, which I am sure she has never even considered eating. The girl's beauty is undeniable, and unavoidable, like Bridget's, and all the rest of us can do is stand back and appreciate it.

The lipstick in my palm feels thoroughly inadequate.

"Seven forty-three," she says to me.

I give her a ten and wait for my change.

At home, in the bathroom, my hand is shaking as I apply it, and I wipe it off with toilet paper and reapply it three times, until I have managed to stay within the desired area. Lip liner. I have written stories about how women should never apply lipstick without liner, and here I am, spitting in the face of accepted beauty practices.

I walk into Zoe's bedroom, where the light is better, and close my eyes before looking into the mirror above her bed.

I look exactly the same. I would rather have gone on believing that I had untapped lipstick potential, that I could be as beautiful as that girl at Rite Aid, if only I would conform to overly rigid standards of beauty, and now that I have at least attempted to conform, I want the benefit, the payoff, and yet I look exactly the same. In a fit, feeling like a furious five-year-old, I stomp back into my room and pitch the lipstick out the window and down the airshaft.

"Are you wearing makeup?" Bridget says, standing in my doorway, lifting her blond hair into the kind of loose ponytail we would describe as "effortless chic" at Couture, with a dozen directions for how to attain it. The thing about Bridget is that it really is effortless. "You have something on your mouth."

"I bought lipstick."

"You did?" She sails into the living room, dropping her Kate Spade messenger bag on the floor on the way into the kitchen. She returns with a can of Zoe's Zima in her hand.

"And then I threw it out the window."

"You are so weird," she says. "That window?" She pulls back the curtain and looks into the courtyard. "How much did it cost?"

"Seven dollars or something."

"You bought a tube of lipstick, paid seven dollars for it, applied it, and then threw it out the window?"

"I thought I would like it more than I did," I say hesitantly. You cannot describe feeling irredeemably unattractive to someone like Bridget: It is like describing sugar to salt. Some loose string will always hang from my hem, some forgotten sandwich will be stowed beneath my bed. "I'm an idiot."

"You are," Bridget says. "I don't think it was the right color, though."

"You think?" I'm torn between the self-preservation tack of pretending like everything I've done has gone exactly to plan, and the self-improvement tack of asking Bridget for help, something I am always loath to do, not because she is unkind about it—she isn't—but because I feel that my only weapon against her effortless chic is my effortless lassitude. But why do I need a weapon to use against my best friend? "I couldn't really tell."

"We have sort of the same coloring," Bridget says, reaching into her messenger bag. She turns me, by the shoulders, to face her. "Open your mouth. Look up. I said *up*." She wields the lipstick as I would a pencil, with authority, grace, dismissiveness. She runs her finger along my lips, evening out the color. "Okay. Look."

"I look like a clown," I say, taking in the dark violet color.

"Don't be contrary," Bridget says. "You look hot. You're just not used to it. Let's just watch TV and you can get all cranky about it later." She flops down on Zoe's couch and turns the television on.

"What *is* a tangelo?" I read from the screen, attempting to sound sincerely curious, looking into the mirror when I think she will not notice.

"It's a cross between a tangerine, a grapefruit, and an orange," Bridget says before the selection of possible answers appears.

"Everybody knows that," I say.

"No, they don't," Bridget says. "You thought it was a special form of the tango."

This is the problem with best friends: They know everything. "I did not."

"Liar," she says. "Raise your hand if you think Betsy's lying." She lifts her arm, like she is answering a question, to reveal a clear sticker below her armpit.

"What's that?" I say. "Is that the smokers' patch?"

"When have I ever smoked?" she says. "It's like birth control in patch form."

"So you two don't just use condoms or whatever?" I do not tell her that I hide under my comforter when Ryan puts it on. I have, in fact, never seen him put it on. I cannot explain it, but it is the same reaction I had to deodorant when I was eleven. I went to school smelling like burnt chocolate for two months before my mother yanked my hands above my head and applied it for me.

"Condoms? Are you serious? Condoms are for sex acts performed in Volvos owned by parents. Do you really think that's adequate?"

"I am quite sure that that is adequate!"

"Are you really quite sure?"

"No," I say, burrowing my head beneath the pillow between us, a tactic of avoidance I am realizing is my key tactic for not losing an argument. "I am not sure."

"You need a backup."

"Like . . ." All I can think of is the day in kindergarten when I cried for four hours because my mother was at the hospital having her tubes tied. Whatever that meant. "Like an intrauterine device?"

"Are you being serious? I can't believe someone as paranoid as you is like this. You never had a condom break?"

"I don't think so."

"You don't *think* so?"

"Wouldn't he have said something?"

"What are you, fifteen?"

"I don't want to be," I say helplessly.

"Seriously: Where were you in high school?"

"Standing outside in the rain listening to the Cure?"

"When I was fifteen, I was wearing makeup and buying bras, and exploring various methods of contraception, and you were my best friend when we were fifteen, so I'm not sure how you missed all this."

The *Who Wants to Be a Millionaire* contestant walks away

with $125,000, unwilling to wager $90,000 on the identity of the Zeus conquest he "seduced" while disguised as a swan.

"Why is this show requiring us to imagine how a swan would sexually assault someone?" says Bridget.

"It's Leda," I say. "And I would like to be a swan."

Two days later I am in a "family planning" clinic on Elizabeth Street. A girl wearing a pink tube top and capri jeans from the Gap is setting next to me, and I am fairly sure she is getting an abortion. Not that I am judging. But when I was her age . . . I was not getting an abortion. I was boycotting the Sadie Hawkins dance in favor of a "political protest" that consisted of me watching reruns of *Gimme a Break!* on NBC until I fell asleep on my parents' living room couch. The girl next to me is patting the head of a stuffed bear she is strangling between her knees, and a woman I believe is her mother is staring at her from across the room, New Jersey neat in a maroon polo top and khaki pants and Keds and a diamond, or diamanté, tennis bracelet, and I think she is wondering where it was she went so wrong.

I am here, at this clinic, rather than in the plush office of my beautiful, angelic gynecologist because the couture.com staff health insurance does not provide for birth control. Or dental care, for that matter, but that is a separate issue.

So this is twice, in one week, I have been in a position of naked supplication with a wise, learned woman. There must be a better system of doing this. I don't like this: I just want to be where I normally am at ten in the morning, which is asleep in my bed. I would even rather be in the Couture office. I want to be anywhere but here. I want better health insurance. I miss my doctor. I want to get back to my little nerd-land of facts and figures and comforting statistics, not here, where everything seems so blurred and assaulting and viscous. This seems to me the opposite of a medical office: It seems like a place you leave in more distress than you came. It is only the thought that if I stay, I will never have to return that keeps me here. If I stay, maybe I will become more of a woman, more of a buxom, desirable adult, and less of a slurring, thumb-sucking toddler.

It is this, I think, this childlike terror of what secrets my body might hold—and I think here only of the ways it might betray me—that's behind my unwillingness to shower beside him, that curdles into something that Ryan can sense. I am not completely wrong about that.

"Do you agree that this is the best choice of preventive birth control for someone like me?" I sound like a robot. I sound like a writer, in search of a story, one she could sell, one that means nothing. I am wondering if perhaps I should have asked this question before I took my clothes off, and I am wondering again what Ryan ever did, like this, so removed from anything he would actually want to do, to make me like him, the way I intend for this, somehow, to make him like me. At this moment, he is not laid out on a doctor's table. He is having fun with his friends, and I, most assuredly, am not.

"Oh, sure it is," the nurse says in my aunt's Midwestern accent, which, in this context, is both comforting and icky. "No pills or hormones to worry about. The only problem is, someone as young as yourself—"

"Well, I'm not *that* young."

"You don't look like you're a day over sixteen," she says.

What? What? Goddamn fucking bullshit American health

care system. It is good, though, because all my anxiety and worry and angst are being catalyzed, by her question, into anger, and it comes as a welcome, pulsing relief. "Didn't I write that on the form they made me fill out downstairs?"

"Okay," she says, picking up my folder and observing, for what I imagine is the first time, the fact that I am considerably older than she thought, which would be pleasing if it were not in the context of a medical history disclosure. And still I think, despite all this, I think: *Maybe I could use this to my advantage with Ryan.* "Twenty-four," she says. "This'll be great for you, then."

Raising my hands in exasperation and anxiety, in this position, looks like I am only stretching. I must look as powerless as I feel, and this is only the most physically expressive manifestation of that: I must look like I always feel now, stretched out and waiting and vulnerable to any parry, friendly or otherwise. "Better than if you thought I was sixteen?"

"Sixteen-year-olds, they forget everything that's not stapled on their hands," she says. "We tell them and tell them, and they think it won't happen, but it does."

"I feel like there are girls here who are maybe using abortion as a form of birth control. I bet you see a few of those every week." It is better, now, this abstract discussion, these facts and figures. It is better than thinking about how naked I am.

"Oh, I think that's true, terrible thing," she says. "I believe in choice. Abortion's not the problem. The problem is girls who believe that oral sex isn't sex. It's a slippery slope from there."

"Do you think this is a national epidemic?" This is not even the first interview I have conducted with my jeans off, just the first one I've conducted in person with my jeans off.

"Sure I do," she says. "I lived in Topeka, Kansas, for fifteen years and the situation there is much worse. New York girls are smarter. All the girls we get here are from New Jersey, Connecticut, Long Island, trying to get away from their parents."

"Would you be willing to talk to a journalist about this?" I say, feeling better, feeling safer. As much as I have come to distrust my head and the way it operates, so frequently, to my own disadvantage, I am so grateful for it now, for this miraculous alchemy, this turn we have taken into manicured grounds. "I think this is an important issue the women of America should know about."

"Oh, sure," she says. "In Topeka, our clinic was real small, and I also handled the public relations."

"I would have to think you are the only nurse here with public relations experience," I say.

"True," she says.

"Well, I write for couture-dot-com," I say. "It's the world's most popular fashion and lifestyle online destination."

"Oh, I've seen your posters," she says. "I'd be happy to talk to you. It's so sad when parents don't care until they have to come in here and sign insurance forms."

Julia is going to love this. This is going to be an actual story, of actual substance. "I think that would be great," I say. *Thank you,* I say to my head, my nattering, chattering head, which this once has done me a recognizable service.

"Great, great." She passes me the diaphragm. "But at the moment, we have something else to discuss."

I leave the clinic with the nurse's cell phone number. As soon as I walk through the doors, into the sunshine, it is as if the life I temporarily abandoned picks up from precisely where I left off, and as I turn up Eighth Avenue toward the Couture office, I am walking so quickly, I might as well be running.

I leave Julia a message on her home voice mail about Marthe, my diaphragm fitter/story source and her experiences attempting to provide birth control to the teenagers of Topeka, and to my surprise, she calls me back before I've made it to the office.

"Marthe, huh?

"She's great," I say. "Very helpful."

"And she's definitely a registered nurse, at a family-planning clinic?"

"It was some kind of clinic," I say. "The kind they make you go to when you don't have any health insurance. But she worked at the other kind in Kansas."

"And what is your relationship with her?"

"I was her patient."

Silence.

"Not for that," I say. "Not for that. For a diaphragm." I feel like I just sneezed health ed all over Julia's face, but she is talking too fast for me to come up with suitable lies.

"Oh, good, okay," she says. "It could get complicated otherwise."

"No," I say. "No, no. Not that. I understand that."

"Not that I'm saying it's wrong," she says quickly. "Just complicated."

"Got it."

"This may be my last official assignment, Betsy, but you've got it. You're sure she can give us a first-person, front-row look at the tragedy of today's teenagers, trading oral sex for rides to football games, yeah?"

Football games? Who ever said anything about that? "Well, she didn't specifically say anything about sports events. . . ."

"You're going to need to elicit that kind of specificity and details and personal tragedy from her, Betsy. I'm sure you can do it. You think you can do it?"

"I can try. . . ."

"There is no try," Julia says sternly. "There is only do, or do not."

I pause in front of a Gap storefront. "Is that from *Star Wars*?"

"*Empire Strikes Back,* actually. But you know what I mean."

"I do."

"Your first feature, Betsy," she says. "This is very exciting. It's a whole new thing now."

"Okay," I say. I have heard this dialogue one hundred times before: It is the speech Julia gives to the young writers she uses, the only ones who will accept Couture's subterranean rates, and at this point she can hardly hear the words as she says them. But what she does not know is that looking at my reflection in the storefront windows, with a diaphragm in my pocket, that the new thing we are discussing is not a feature for a women's lifestyle and fashion Web site but something like an adult female, the way I am beginning to believe that change can be willed if directions are followed; the only secret has been decoding the formula, and following it to the letter. I have a job, newly meaningful, and an almost-boyfriend I obsess over; I have an apartment and thanks to Couture, an idea of what length the skirts will be this spring. Isn't this what I have always wanted, dreamed of, and waited for, desperately?

The afternoon of the office party I buy a halibut and then forget it, sitting in the bottom of a plastic D'Agostino bag, in the hallway of my building, where I'd left it after I dropped it before dashing into the bathroom. Eight hours later, after looking for it in the bathroom, in the kitchen, behind the sofa, I find it hanging from the doorknob, which means that one of the four other tenants who live above me in this building has gone to the effort of picking it off the floor but stopped short of actually ringing my bell and alerting me to the fish's location. I am wearing lip gloss and a bra, and despite the problem with the halibut, which I drop into a garbage can on the way to the F train, I feel strong and present and fully protected against accidental conception, a reasonable facsimile of a global consumer, and just a little bit like a made-up fraud.

I meet Bridget at a Mexican-themed bar across the street from the office party. I have not seen Ryan for almost a week, the longest since what is between us began, and I need her to act, as I always have, as my lodestone, to remind me that I have existed before him. I do not want to finish that thought to its foregone conclusion.

"You look very dressed up," she says.

"I do?" I say it loudly, sharply enough that three girls doing happy-hour tequila shots look over at us.

"Not in a bad way," she says. "Jesus. I just mean compared to normal."

"Shut up!"

"I knew you were going to take it that way," she says. "What's your problem?"

"I haven't seen Ryan in a week," I say. "Anything could have happened."

"How long have you been seeing him?"

"I don't know," I say. "A month and a half? Two?"

"At a certain point," she says, "you are going to have to stop worrying about things that aren't going to happen."

"Don't jinx me," I say meanly, and meaning it.

It takes my eyes a few moments to adjust to the darkness: I hate this bar, and whoever picked it, who I believe to be Michael: I hate him for valuing the ponyskin walls and the faux-ironic disco balls and the line for the hot tub, which stretches from the entrance off to the back, culminating in a point I can see from here only if I squint. I hate him most of all for the après-ski-themed cocktail girls, in furry white miniskirts and knee-high white boots, identical, blond braids hanging beneath their identical furry hats. I hate him for hiring this magazine's staff, which seems to be represented solely in a mass of girls with straight hair sipping pink drinks from martini glasses. "Who are all these people?" I say to Casey, the only recognizable face, as he stands in another line, ending in what skiing-themed fantasy I do not know.

"Sales, I think."

"That's why they're dressed so much more expensively than us," I say, and he nods. This is the first time I've talked to him since Ryan told me about his supposed interest in me, and I don't see it in him. "Have you seen anyone we know?"

"Julia was here for like five minutes and took off with that surfer guy," he says. "Nancy and Sybilla and all them have been in the bathroom for like three hours. Eva and Ryan were on the dance floor."

It is absurd, so absurd, how he is just going along and then pommels me with these words. I realize Ryan has not told him about us, because if he had, Casey probably wouldn't have volunteered that information. Unless he knew it was harmless. I can't decide which is worse, which is better. "There's a dance floor?"

He nods. "Back behind where all the sales girls are standing."

I pause: I do not want to go there. I do not know what I will see. I do not know how it will affect this crystalline bridge I have built in my head. "Why are Nancy and Sybilla in the bathroom?" I ask dumbly.

Casey puts a finger against his nostril and breathes deeply. "I mean, like, if there were coke in front of my nose," he says. "That breathing thing is from yoga."

"Oh," I say. I still want to die, but a tiny part of my head is holding out hope that Ryan will emerge and see Casey talking me up, if that is what he is doing, if that is what I could suggest he is doing. "I thought Nancy was all nature foods and grated beet root."

"I think Nancy's coke is probably organic."

"Can you have organic coke?"

"I don't know," he says. "It's 1999. I thought people stopped doing coke ten years ago."

"Are you in line for something?"

"Hell, I think," he says.

I love Casey for a moment: for his surliness, for that tiny joke, for standing here, where if I were lucky, Ryan would see him talking to me. For being so different from Ryan, who can make me laugh, but not from the acuity of his observations. For reminding me, in a quickly extinguished flash, that Ryan lacks certain things. I want to give him a hug. Sometimes, and now is one of those times, it feels like I just want, so badly, for anyone to love me, that the fact that this puts me at a disadvantage, with everyone, is nowhere near reason enough to stop it. "Me, too." I say, and head off for the dance floor.

And then there they are, like Casey had said: not touching, but there is no mistaking that they are there for each other. Mostly I focus on Eva and her tan skin, and the rainbow camisole from Missoni, and the shoes I know are from Balenciaga, because she had me pick them up for her. I can see her expression, not his, and it is something I could never manage: reserve and desire at once, get-me-if-you-can. I should not have extended myself like this, once I knew it was for him: I am who I was, a week ago, a year ago, at twenty-one and sixteen, and none of this has changed me in any meaningful way. It has best served as a way for me to understand, and calculate, my own deficiencies. I am continually deficient, and acting like I am not is precisely that, only acting, a pose, empty theater, and when I at last catch his eye and then turn to walk out, I feel less like myself than like an actress in a high school play, calibrating her prayers to her circumstances, holding her breath and hoping for nothing but an elegant exit.

I push out the way I came in, past Casey, out to the street. My only ambition is to make it into a cab before I can tell if Ryan has followed me, and in this one, wonderful way, I am a marvelous success.

When I get home, I swallow two allergy pills and fall asleep, still wearing my new white shirt and expensive jeans, but not before realizing I am wearing the uniform like everyone else, that I can make fun of those girls, those Evas, for their shopping addictions and their denim fetishes, but in my week of rediscovery I have just turned myself into a poor replica of something I have always purported to hate, a sales girl automaton on an editorial assistant's salary.

My phone finally rings, as I have been praying it would, as I have, nearly immobile, waited for it. "Betsy?" he says. It sounds like he is on the street, not at home. Why has he been out all this time? Why didn't he call me before?

"Yes," I say. "Yeah?"

"Where did you go?"

"I think you wanted to be with Eva," I say. "If you want to date Eva, date Eva." Or Stella, I am thinking. Even as I say it, I wonder if he can hear the bluff, and how he will call it.

"I don't want to date Eva," he says. "Or Stella. I don't want to be with Stella. I want to be with you."

No, no, no, no, no, I am thinking. *Do not, do not, do not do this.*

"I don't want to be with Stella," he says again. "I want to be with you. I love you, Betsy."

Oh, this is not how I pictured it. I close my eyes, like I am making a wish, which I am, and it is that this moment is not happening the way it is. "I love you, too," I say.

"I do, I do, I do," he is saying, mumbling. I hear him say something away from the phone: "Tom, hold on, I'm coming." So maybe he is out with the Heaven Forever boys. He is not with Eva. Maybe all is not lost. "I do, I do," he says to me again. "Don't worry, Betsy, I love you," he says.

"I love you, too," I repeat, and before anything else can happen, I hang up the phone.

In the morning, I discover a Post-it on my computer keyboard. It reads: *Your hot.*

It seems very important now to remember that his grammar is imperfect.

Later that night, we are eating black bean quesadillas and chicken fajitas on the floor of my bedroom. We are watching the *South Park* movie, which is the only one I can watch without constantly thinking about the end of the world. Our shoulders are touching, both of our backs resting against my mattress; he is sober and here, physically, and, as far as I can determine, mentally, and I am willing,

I am aching to blame his behavior at the party on the three gin and tonics he said he drank before I arrived. "I was bored," he said. "You weren't there." This way that he holds me accountable for his entertainment eases my mind. We move from DEFCON 1 to 3.

I am unused, though, to this sort of advance, this two-steps-forward, one-step-back. I cannot meter the movements at all, and I find myself wanting more than ever to have units of measurement. "Do you think," I say, excessively casually, "someday you'll be my boyfriend?"

"Do you want me to be your boyfriend?"

I had not expected him to turn this around so quickly, and I stare at the television screen, trying to swallow the lump of avocado in my mouth. "Do you want to be my boyfriend?"

"Do you?"

Do I what? Want to be my boyfriend? How long can this go on, this talking, talking, and communicating nothing? "I'm not pathetic," I say. Ha! "Don't you think it's good to talk about things like this?"

"It's a big thing," he says. "Boyfriends, girlfriends."

"I know," I say. "I agree entirely."

"I think it's just a question of time."

"That's what I would have said, too."

One step forward, two steps back. No steps forward, two steps back. I have watched this movie a dozen times in the last two weeks, and this is the part where Satan sings. This is my favorite part. This must be a sign.

"I love you," I say, staring at the television.

There is a silence so pronounced that I almost start laughing, even though my stomach feels like it is being wrung out like a wet towel.

"Thank you," he says.

Seven

It's not really your fault," Bridget says, "if he said it first." She puts down the croissant she has been eating for extra seriousness, to focus my attention on what she is saying. "But you must never, ever say it again."

I have begged Bridget to extend her lunch hour, so that we can review and evaluate my situation in the depth I am sure it requires, so we have been sitting here, in a corner table at Au Bon Pain, for the last two hours. I am struggling to bring new evidence into my argument, to make it less damning than it deserves, but I have nothing, just repeated snippets of my conversations with Ryan over the last difficult two weeks. I think "difficult" but I want instead to think "challenging": I knew, even at the beginning, that he could inspire this determined revision, that I would find a way to shape facts into something loving and warm. Everything, I am learning, is context. "Don't worry," I say. "I won't."

"I mean, I would avoid following the word 'I' with verbs beginning with the letter *L*. You cannot say 'I leave' or 'I lost' or 'I love' anything—no 'I love Pop-Tarts' or 'I love it when I leave sandwiches underneath my bed.' "

"What am I supposed to do with this person?"

"He did tell you he loves you, even if he was drunk when he

said it," Bridget says. "That does count for something. How many nights a week does he sleep over?"

"Three or four."

"And how many times do you stay at his house?"

"I don't," I say.

"Not ever?"

"No."

"Not *once*?"

"No," I say. "Why would I? I live closer to Midtown. Why would we go all the way out there?"

Bridget says nothing, and I am glad for this small reprieve, because even I can hear how ridiculous this sounds. Every stray thought I have expelled from my head over the past eight weeks has returned: *Why don't you stay at his house? What's at his house?* Almost silently, in the back, the reassuring, familiar one: *If there was anything bad to this, why did he invite you to his house on your very first date? You're just being ridiculous.* I calm down, and then, in that quiet, which I am realizing is only the eye of the storm: *Maybe he has another family there. Maybe that's where Stella lives.*

"I'm fucked," I say. "I hate him." I put my forehead on the table, feeling overdramatic but also thoroughly, legitimately, completely defeated. "I love him," I say from beneath the arms covering my head.

"Do you really? Love him?" she says. "Are you sure?"

"I want to be with him all the time, I think about him all the time, and I feel sick when he's not around," I say. "Is that love?" I do not mean this rhetorically. I really want to know. "Is that how you feel about James?"

"I don't think so," she says thinly. "Not exactly. And I don't know."

She stops there, and I decide I have had enough: Even talking about this feels like I am courting a mental breakdown, so before she can continue I ask her what she thinks about Mulder kissing Scully because in her secret nerd heart she is an even bigger *X Files* fan than I am. I judge correctly; she is distracted by this and rambles on while I puzzle over why Bridget might not have been able to answer my question. Since they met three years ago, Bridget and James have become such a simple, solid unit that their entwined fates seemed sealed ages ago. I was never jealous of James, only jealous of their preoccupation with each other. James always seemed more willing to bend to Bridget's will, and at times she seemed to rule with a royal indifference. But this was how Bridget always operated: She had recommended it to me, in fact, as the only way to have a relationship; one person would always need the other more. It was better, she said, to be loved too much, than to be the one left holding the bag, writing the poems.

And here I am, with my lyre and my strained metaphors. I do not have the kind of love that Bridget has. I have something that borders on obsession, something that demands a second-by-second account of another person's actions and thoughts. I will not need to tell him that I love him because what I really mean is that I need him, desperately. Until I heard the tin in Bridget's voice, I would not have thought it an enviable position.

The next night is Ryan's last in New York before he leaves. He will not be back until the day after New Year's. I have wondered if I should ask him to stay in New York with me, but it seems too much, too soon—or at least that it could be construed as too much, too soon. I have had such a hard time locating any dignity with him in the last few weeks: By not asking I am clutching at what little I've found. In so many ways I am thinking: If I can just get through these next two weeks, through Christmas, through New

Year's. Only the tiniest sliver of me is convinced that I will be able to do so without losing something precious to me. But I can see it: a new day, a clear dawn, all of that. I will be a grown up with him, I will learn to dance like Eva, I will be confident and cool, like I'm sure Stella is. I will invite him to the wedding, and I can see it: This is what I dream of, not the beach, not the ceremony, not the drinks and the dancing, but the airport, the security line, the flight to Tokyo and then Singapore and then finally to this island. Almost imperceptibly, over these last two months, my focus has shifted: It is as if the pressure of losing Bridget has completely lifted, only to be replaced by something else. In some ways it is a relief, and there is a lesson in it, as well: I thought nothing could be worse than facing this wedding alone. Now, of course, there is something worse, and it is facing it *without Ryan.* The lesson is that there are so many, so many more things worse than that I have not yet taken the time to invent. But at least now I know they are out there.

That is why I am so desperate to make this, our last dinner, special. I take him to my favorite Italian restaurant in Cobble Hill. This is as close as we will get to a holiday meal. I do not know what I could do to ensure that this means to him what it means to me, so I sit there dumbly, anxiously, smiling too hard and too often. If he notices this, he doesn't say anything, which maybe is as much of a problem as the painful smiling itself. Or maybe, again, my head is to blame: Behold the power of negative thinking. Maybe I am creating problems where none, as yet, exist.

I push my food around my plate and wait for him to say he loves me.

In the morning, while he takes a shower, I feel a loneliness distinctly different from the . . . usual one. It is the loneliness I remember from college, once my friends had left with their families, while I waited on the curb for my tardy parents to show up.

Then he walks into my bedroom, in a towel, and everything brightens. It is like adjusting the brightness on a television screen.

"Do you realize we may have only eight days left to live?"

He shakes water out of his hair and slaps me on the side of my thigh, hard, like a butcher would a side of beef.

"I always thought I would be home, on the beach or something," I say. "Not here."

"Like Téa Leoni in *Deep Impact*?"

I do not like the fact that he has, correctly, recognized my end-of-the-world fantasy as having already happened, in an expensive movie about a comet. "I forgot I saw that," I say.

"I'm sure it'll be fine," he says. "I'm sure. I have no doubt. I am doubtless. You should have come to Austin with me."

What does that mean? What does that mean? What does that mean? A week ago his asking that would have made me sick with glee and despair, but now it just seems like one more thing I cannot respond to in any meaningful way. "Yeah, well, how could I miss New York at the millennium?" How can he believe what I am saying, if he has paid any attention to anything I've said for the past two months? "So I'll see you later today?" I am trying not to say it like I am pleading. He is going home to pick up his bags and then stopping by the office to say a proper goodbye.

"You will," he says. "I promise."

"Okay, then."

"It would be nice to be at the beach at New Year's, end of the world or no end of the world," I say.

"I'll be thinking of you," he says.

Will you? Whatever. I look past him, outside, to the courtyard. "I should put sandbags around the windows," I say.

Eva had told us to plan on a full day of work, but since all the top editors, Nancy and Michael and Eva herself, have fled the city for St. Barts, Long Island, and Goa respectively, we all sort of sit at our desks and wait to go home. Around eleven there is a groundswell of sentiment for walking out, but Cynthia, the production manager, who leaves her cubbyhole only on the rare occasion when she is in charge, sort of the way the chief justice of the Supreme Court becomes president if the rest of Congress is dead, announces that in their absences, the Idiots have arranged for a personal security expert to give a lecture titled "What to Do If the Lights Stay Out," or, as someone has written across the wipe board before the security expert arrives, "Apocalypse Soon!"

We are advised to stock up on a week's worth of fruit and vegetables and milk, and up to ninety days' worth of nonperishables, and to withdraw a paycheck's worth of cash from the bank. If I had that much cash in the bank, I would have quit this stupid job.

"Do any of you have supplies?" asks Kylo, the security expert. It is rumored that Kylo is both a millennial safety expert and a yoga teacher who makes house calls when Nancy is in Long Island.

Casey kicks the back of my chair. "Betsy does," he says.

"Really?" Kylo says in a surprisingly gentle way. Clearly he takes issues of millennial precautions seriously.

I cannot hit Casey in front of all these people, and it would be pointless to lie; too many people saw the packages from Millennial Marketplace. "I have fifty-two boxes of dehydrated meals." I choose to regard the silence that greets me from my coworkers as a measure of respect. I would not have thought this before, but I am convinced that at least one of them is coveting my store of freeze-dried meals. This, maybe, is what I was waiting for, this fractional, survivalist's leg up on my coworkers. Sometimes I am proud of absolutely nothing I think, and nothing I do.

"Good for you," he says. "And you have what you need to heat them up if there's no electricity?"

His seemingly serious regard of my planning measures is more disturbing than reassuring: I like it better when I am being treated like a crank. "I do," I say. "They're the self-heating kind."

"Good investment," he says. "You wouldn't want to wake up with all this delicious food to eat and no way to heat them. I've seen that before, and I can tell you it made for some uncomfortable nights. Do you have a panic room?"

Sure I do. I have rooms where I panic. I do not, however, have a steel cell hidden in my town house where I can wait out the marauding villagers. I look at Casey, again a familiar, if annoyingly amused, face, and the photo assistants, who are giggling. Kylo does not pick up on any hesitation, and this is just as well, because part of me really does want to have this conversation with him. "I have a bathroom without any windows," I say.

"That's practically as good!"

This is a disappointment. I do not know what to say. Kylo the millennial expert is bullshitting me, because he knows that my security precautions are inadequate. "Oh, dear," I say.

"Would you like me to show you a little martial arts defense move?" He says this to the room, but he is waving at me to come up and join him.

What is this for? Is this for the zombies? I smile to the two dozen people watching me from behind the conference table. Kylo takes my hand, presses his thumb into my palm, twists my arm up and behind my back, and brings me to my knees.

"Did everyone see how I did that?" he says, still exerting

pressure on my arm, which remains raised toward the ceiling like some sort of dictatorial salute.

The lecture concludes with pizza, grape soda, and cake. "To shit blowing up," the photo assistants say, tapping plastic cups.

I take my pizza back to my desk to await Ryan's call, which is fifteen minutes overdue, unless he phoned while I was being physically subdued and held prostrate on the floor of the conference room, in which case I will be extremely angry. While I am replacing my handset, having ascertained for the third time in five minutes that I have no new voice mail messages, I am tapped on the shoulder. It is my compatriot from the panic room. "What was your name again?" Kylo asks.

"Betsy," I say in a voice that does not hide the disappointment involved with his forgetting it.

"Thanks for doing that Krav Maga move with me," he says. "It'll be cool." He says this with such breezy confidence that I wonder if his whole millennial shtick is just that, a ruse deployed against idiot Web site editors by touchy-feely yoga instructors looking for extra cash.

"I hope so," I say.

"Just keep your head down," he says, and all the anxiety I had dismissed for one gloriously cynical second swims right back into my chest. "And stay out of Manhattan."

At last Ryan calls. "Meet me at the Radio Shack on Seventh Avenue," he says.

I wait for fifteen minutes in Radio Shack, patrolling the space from the windows to the cash register, standing guard outside the door, quizzing salespeople on possible sightings of 6' 2" men from Texas. I am the only person in the store. I run out of things to discuss with them; first Ryan, then various technical issues that they are surprisingly well equipped to answer. We are discussing the merits of a USB hub when my cell phone rings.

"Where are you?" I say. The salesman I had been talking to nods: He is relieved for me.

"Radio Shack," he says.

"I'm at Radio Shack," I say. "There's no one here but me and two sales guys."

The line is scratchy, amplifying our unsteady silence. We are not phone people. This might already be the longest phone conversation we have ever had. "Which Radio Shack?"

"Seventh Avenue and Twenty-sixth Street," I say.

"I'm at Sixth Avenue and Twelfth Street."

What? "You told me Seventh Avenue," I say. The Radio Shack salesmen hear the anxiety in my voice and try to look busy unpacking television cables.

"I'm sure I said Sixth," he says.

"Well, what do we do now?" I am desperate. There are tears in my eyes. I knew it. I knew this would happen.

"Betsy, I have to get to the airport. I'm supposed to be at LaGuardia in twelve minutes."

"Oh," I say. "Okay."

"I'll see you as soon as I get back. I promise. I'll come straight from the airport to your apartment."

"Do you think," I say, wanting to cauterize at least one wound today, "we could go to your apartment?"

"Of course," he says. "We have the whole next millennium. I love you."

My heart floats, swells. I swoon. He has just promised what

I want more than anything else, which is (a) a future and (b) a future with this person. "I love you, too," I say. I end the call and look at my phone, like it is my best connection to him.

"It's okay now," I say, grinning wildly, to my friends with the television cables.

I spend the rest of the day at my desk weighing the possibilities: that I misheard him, that he lied. That he was mistaken. There is room to move in this third one, space to breathe, a way out. And besides, he said: *We have the whole next millennium. I love you.* He said those words. He did not have to. He would not have said those words, in that way. He could have placated me without them; he knows, I think, that I accept what he gives me, without complaint.

When I think clearly about the person I am with him, I know that she is neither the person I was, nor the person I believed he would make me.

Every Christmas I can remember before this one, the Nilssen family has celebrated the birth of Christ with fried dumplings and General Tso's chicken at the Hunan Garden, in the company of the considerable population of Margate's Jewish and Asian communities. This year, though, we are dispersed to three continents—two continents and an ocean, anyway. My parents are en route from somewhere to somewhere else. My sister calls me from a parking lot outside a warehouse in Glasgow.

"The Y2K Santa's-a-Tattooer Convention and Holiday Ball," she says. "is the stupidest thing I have ever heard of."

"Uh-huh," I say, flipping between the pope's midnight Mass and a cable channel that is for some reason screening *Deep Impact*. I am trying to forget about the fact that *Deep Impact* is on and to switch, with absolute, unswerving resolve to *It's a Wonderful Life,* but I cannot make myself turn away. This is the part where Téa Leoni decides not to get on the helicopter that would take her out of the reach of the upcoming tidal wave. If I were within range of a tidal wave and no helicopters were available, I believe I would just start walking in the opposite direction. But then I think about how I live off of Ocean Avenue, how I am only one hundred blocks from Coney Island and the Atlantic and even fewer from Times Square, and how I believe shit is going to begin falling from the sky in eight days and I am still sitting here, watching cable.

Rebecca is coughing and sniffling into the phone. "My boyfriend is walking around in a Santa costume, with like three thousand other people in Santa costumes, and because he is an idiot, he thought he was being original, the only one, in a Santa costume, at a tattooers' convention on Christmas Eve. 'No,' he says. 'It's a secular country. They barely even believe in God.' So when it's clear that he is not particularly smart, he makes us drive thirty miles until we find a department store open at five P.M. on Christmas Eve, and he bought this stupid pig mask, and then when we got back to Glasgow he has to pay the thirty-dollar entry—excuse me, thirty-*pound* entry, which is like nine thousand dollars—all over again, and he spent all his money on the pig mask, so I had to pay for both of us. And now there's a little pig nose around his neck," she says. I can hear the thump of what I believe is the earpiece of the phone being hit against her thigh. "Why do I have a boyfriend? Why am I in this country?"

"Because we don't have a home anymore?"

"Where are they?"

"On their way to Kiribati," I say. "They said they'll call on New Year's. Does this mean your boyfriend thinks Santa is a pig?"

"That would be a horrible thing to think," she says, sounding wounded, and this Santa affront seems to make her nostalgic. "I wish we were getting Chinese food like usual. What are you having tonight?"

"Pop-Tarts," I say. I feel like my body has rejected the transplant, this failed makeover of mine. "Maybe some fruit."

"I think we're having 'bangers and mash,'" she says, punctuating her sentence with an extended retching sound. "Which we had last night, and the night before. Bangers and mash, and my boyfriend is wearing a pig nose." She makes the vomiting sound again.

The tidal wave engulfs Téa and Maximilian Schell, and the spell breaks; I change to *It's a Wonderful Life,* and suddenly the room is filled with "Hark! The Herald Angels Sing." I am sweating, but I am not sure if this is because of movie-related stress or the fact that the thermostat is still clinging to the low eighties: I thought Zoe's extended absence would give me an opportunity to adjust some of her settings, but it turns out that most of the dials have been glued in place.

I feel like I have just woken up from the sort of nap one takes in the backseat of one's car, in the driveway, after the house keys have been lost at the movie theater and before the assault on the garage windows has begun. "And how are you dressed?"

She pauses, and in the quiet I can hear what sounds like a punk reinterpretation of "Good King Wenceslas." "Like Mrs. Claus," she says.

I say nothing, shaking my head awake.

"Shut up," my sister says.

Bridget asked me to come home to Margate with her and James. What she had said, specifically, was, "Do you want the backseat?" which she had thoughtfully saved for me, like I was their friendly

Labrador puppy, happy in their hatchback, my little puppy tongue planted against the window. I passed on the offer, not so much because of the backseat, which I would have been perfectly happy with even though every time I have ever sat in Bridget's Volvo I have sat in the front passenger's seat, but because I want to keep my movements as small and inconspicuous as possible. If I leave New York now, I am not sure I would come back, and I want to stay. I want to see what will happen. Curiosity killed the millennialist.

I tell Bridget that I am staying in town to see *Any Given Sunday* in one of those theaters with stadium seating, and that is exactly what I do.

I make my last pre-event trip to the supermarket and the video store the day before New Year's. I have eaten eight more of my dehydrated meals in the interim, which indicates (a) I need to find a job that pays a living wage so I can buy some groceries and (b) I am an extremely shortsighted survivalist. I shuffle around the apartment like a retiring general examining his mutinous troops: On top of the refrigerator is a half-filled jug of water, and boxes and boxes of the couscous/hamburger mix I am rapidly tiring of line the countertop from the oven to the sink. For all my weeks of preparation, I have nothing I would want to eat or drink in a postapocalyptic society except for the items I've just bought, and if the lights do stay out, I will be living on Gatorade, granola bars, Hot Pockets, chocolate chip cookies, and rapidly defrosting chicken potpies.

Tommy calls later that night to ask if I know when, Eastern time, the millennium officially begins on Earth.

"Did you know," I say, "that in 1995, the international date line was moved so that the island of Kiribati, which at one point was split in two by it, would no longer be divided, and now Kiribati and Hawaii, which are on the same line of longitude, are sometimes a day apart?"

"You mean," he says. "like sometimes it's Monday night in Chicago and Tuesday morning in New York?"

This piece of information was the only thing my parents left on my voice mail, and now it turns out to be completely worthless. "I think it'll be four in the morning here when the New Year starts in Kiribati."

"So they're twenty hours ahead of us?"

I am counting on my fingers. "No, hold on, that can't be right. We're five hours ahead of Hawaii, so that would mean there's twenty-eight hours in a day."

"So do you think they're sixteen hours ahead of us?"

"Maybe," I say. "This is confusing."

"Forget it, forget it," he says, but now I am realizing the significance of his questions and am surprised I had neglected to figure it out earlier.

"I think it's . . . eight in the morning, New York time."

"Eight in the morning. Excellent. Thank you."

"You don't think there's some weird daylight time adjustment or something?"

"No, no, I'm sure that's fine," he says.

"Are you sure? Are you *sure* sure?"

"Why are you so concerned about it now?"

"No reason."

"Is this about God or something?"

"No," I say.

"Is this because you want to be awake for the end of the world?"

"No," I say. "Shut up."

"Sheesh," he says.

There is a lengthy pause, and I know he is hoping I will just drop this and get off the phone.

"Do you think the world's going to end?"

"Dude, give me a break."

"Okay," I say.

"Okay, then," he says.

"So why did you need to know when it would be?"

"I'm going to John and Billy's to smoke. You want to come over?"

"Do I want to get up at eight in the morning, walk over to their house, and smoke pot so I can spend the millennium stoned?"

"When you put it that way, it sounds so . . . disrespectable."

"Well—"

"The way we're thinking is that if the shit does go down, we'll be too stoned to notice."

"What?" My voice goes up three octaves. "What shit? What do you know?"

"You didn't get the memo about the shit going down?" he asks. "Because I thought everybody got that memo."

"I have to go," I say. "I have important things to do."

"Memo!" he says. "Ha!" And I hang up the phone.

He calls back fifteen minutes later, as I am removing a pepperoni Hot Pocket from the microwave. "Dude, Hawaii is east of the international date line—so it should be an hour *ahead* of Kiribati, like we're east of Chicago and all that. But oh, no, no. The deal is that when it's, like, two in the afternoon on Wednesday in Hawaii, it's two in the afternoon on *Thursday* in Kiribati. The international date line is where yesterday goes to *die.*"

"That," I say, frozen, Hot Pocket in hand, "is just unbelievable."

I wake up when my alarm goes off at 7:55. I pull the curtains apart and see that the sun is shining. I pick up a sweater under my desk, fold it, and put it on my bed. Maybe I will need the sweater, if the world starts breaking apart. It is 7:56. I need to brush my teeth. None of this can happen before that.

When I come back, it's 7:59. I put on the television. I close my eyes, hold my breath, and wish Ryan were here. I take another breath. I count to sixty, and then to seventy-five, just to make sure. I open my eyes. The sun has gone behind a cloud, but it is still quite bright outside. Champagne is flowing on the *Today* show. And then I pull on my running shoes and head out to Billy and John's apartment.

My parents call at nine o'clock from Tarawa, to report that the millennial midnight is clear and starry. Drums beat in the background, and I picture my mother sharing her candy from Margate with indigenous tribeswomen until my father explains that they are staying at the Otintaal Hotel and my mother is playing a Putumayo CD. As he describes the exotically Polynesian room service (pigs' heads! pineapple chicken!), it occurs to me that once again my parents have led my way into the new world, and the force of missing them hits me so hard, so quickly, that I keep from crying only by pinching my nose between the pads of two fingers and breathing slowly through my mouth.

All afternoon I watch coverage of New Year's celebrations around the world: Maori dances in New Zealand, fireworks in Sydney, fireworks in Beijing. Fireworks everywhere. I watch their faces, and it is fair to say that revelers in at least fifteen countries look unconcerned. In fact, they look happy. Happy and drunk, except for the monks. Billions of people are dancing around, singing traditional songs, and I am beginning to think that I am one of the few who were not looking forward to this. *This is what you get for being a loser,* I think, but of course, CNN isn't showing footage of the militiamen holed up in their Idaho shacks. My philosophical comrades. I order a salmon dinner from the fancy restaurant on the corner to celebrate the non-smiting of the world's population.

I have stopped thinking about Ryan. He is going to call tonight.

He loves me. I am sure he is not with Stella. Why would she be in Texas? Unless she went home for the holidays? She lives in Japan. Japan! Where millions are gathering at Shinto temples!

No fire and brimstone. The worst-case scenario is only occasionally also the most likely.

It's not even like I really wanted to go to Texas. And I could have. He asked.

I am spending New Year's Eve lying to myself.

This is the biggest New Year's I could ever live to see, and I am doing it all wrong: I should be drunk on a yacht on the Aegean Sea or just, really, doing something other than what I am doing, which is running to the bodega below my apartment to buy two six-packs of Coors Light, a bottle of crème de menthe, and some Snickers in case the party my friends have chosen to go to has no snacks.

I stand on the corner of Ninth Street and Seventh Avenue, waiting for my friends to pick me up. I left my mittens at Tommy's this morning, and my bare fingers, clutching the plastic bags, have frozen into beer-carrying claws. I wait, looking down the avenue, holding my breath, scanning the street for anyone looking unhinged, or drunk. The person I want to be with is far away, and I wish I were with him. I wish and I wish and I wish. I never wanted it to be like this, so dependent. I just wanted someone to keep me company while Bridget said her vows and danced with her relatives.

I am still lying to myself.

I open the bottle of crème de menthe and pour myself shots in one of the plastic cups.

When Billy and Tommy and John finally show up, I open the car door and sit down into a little sauna of pot smoke and the body heat they have generated wrestling God knows who into submission. I'll die tonight, not as part of a global apocalyptic event but a one-car crash into a bridge pillar with a stoned asshole behind the wheel. I would have preferred the former.

Three hours later, Billy is drunk, making out in the kitchen with the girl John had the crush on. I leave Tommy passed out on the floor of the coatroom/bedroom, nestled in the remains of a toppled acacia tree, and sit on the sofa in front of a barren cheese plate, eating my way through my bag of Snickers, trying to look like I am waiting for a friend to come out of the bathroom.

I would just be happy if I could find some Brie, and some crackers, and maybe some wine, but the crème de menthe is beginning to give me a headache, so I get up from the warm, safe seat on the couch and make my way over to the end of the line for the bathroom, which stretches across the living room into the foyer.

A man in a rugby shirt and pressed khakis, crease down the middle of each leg, is in front of me.

"So," he says. "How do you know Emily?"

"Who's Emily?"

"It's her apartment," he says.

He is not unattractive, but he is also not Ryan, and talking to this guy just reminds me that I am not with him. His awkward slacks and his forced conversation just say: *This is what you should have. I am as good as it's going to get.*

Ugh. He is just being nice. "She's my friend's cousin's boss," I say, suddenly feeling sick. There is no psychological component to this: My stomach feels like it is undergoing its own sort of perfect storm.

"What do you do?"

"For a living?" I say, but this cannot be it, this just cannot be how I begin this century, in line for the bathroom talking to this person about this job that I hate, so I turn and push through a crowd of girls in shiny black tops and black pants to the coatroom, to wake up Tommy. When I get there, though, he has a girl on his lap, and they are stretched across the coats, watching Dick Clark in Times Square count down the final seconds of the year—from 3:00—2:59—and then another wave of nausea courses through my body, and I turn, again, to leave—

"But, dude, the ball's about to drop," Tommy says, grabbing for my arm, curiously unmindful of the way my head keeps lolling to one side, and I close the bedroom door tight behind me, pushing again through the crowd back to the line for the bathroom, which by now is mercifully short, as everyone has given up, in deference to the time remaining in 1999. I am busy concentrating on standing upright when a woman I will later recognize as the former, despised president of my former, despised sorority says, "Oh my God! How are you!" to which I say, "I really need to sit down," which I do, on the floor, while she stares and I stare until, thank Jesus, the door opens and I stand and stumble and puke nineteen dollars' worth of salmon all over myself and the floor and a bit in the toilet, not once but three times. It is done and I wipe off my shoes and my face and the floor and I think, *I am going to be fine, I am nearly shipshape here,* when I sneeze and a piece of salmon flies out of my nose. Salmon, pink salmon with traces of green asparagus sauce has just come out of my nose, but I am less horrified than amazed, so I blow my nose to check, and again, salmon, and I laugh, and then cry, because I desperately want someone, someone who is Ryan, to come in and pull back my hair and tell me that salmon will never again come out of my nose. There's a knock, my heart stops, and I think, *Please, Jesus, let that be Ryan,* but it is just Tommy, and Billy, and John behind him, who says, taking in the fact that I am no longer retching, "I think we're done here."

"I have a bad feeling," I say, although the millennium has come and gone. It is 2000. "I have a very bad feeling right now."

"It's called puked-up fish," Billy says.

"Is it over?" I say.

"It's over," John says, offering me someone's scarf to wipe my face with.

"I think so, too."

They take me outside, around the corner, toward the lights and confetti, still in the air. We are on the northern edge of Times Square, and if there had been one place, in the world, that I did not want to be tonight, it is exactly here. It is light and open and beautiful and completely devoid of the killers I had imagined, and I am embarrassed for ever thinking we should not be here tonight, for ever being such a fucking pussy, for always denying what was staring me in the face.

I think to myself: *Sometimes the worst we can imagine is not the worst thing out there.*

And: *I don't think I have to worry about Stella anymore.*

Back in my apartment I watch the end of the millennial celebrations, in Hawaii, where laser shows mesmerize thousands in Honolulu. I peel off my clothes and sprawl across my comforter, pleased at the idea of sleeping off nine shots of crème de menthe in my underwear. Propped up by some pillows, I turn on the Weather Channel, comforted by a storm moving across the Rockies, lulled by the meteorological certainties of jet streams and high-pressure systems and frontal boundaries impervious to computer bugs and germ warfare.

Before the local forecast finishes, the phone rings.

"I missed you a lot tonight," he says.

"I missed you," I say. "I wish you were here."

"We have the whole next century," he says, and falls quiet. I wait, wondering what he will say next. I wait and wait and wait.

This is becoming a familiar posture. It has been so long, five years, since I was in love with someone that I had forgotten everything about it. I had not remembered it feeling so precarious.

I lay my head on the pillow and place the phone against my ear, listening to his breathing.

Eight

Something is not right with Ryan. I knew it when I puked that fish out of my nose, and I knew it when he called me that night, and I knew it when he told me to go to the wrong Radio Shack two days before Christmas.

He is on his way back from Austin, and if I am to believe him, he will come to the office, and then we are going to go back to my apartment, together. I only have about an hour before he returns.

I tell Julia I want to take her out for a goodbye ice cream trip.

"Are you excited?" I say. I buy her a banana split, and we sit in the booth like twelve-year-olds, like friends, taking spoonfuls from each other's sundaes. "About your new job?"

"Oh my God, totally," she says. "And you know, if you ever decide that Couture's not going to work out for you, you have my e-mail address. I really think you are going to do a lot of great things, Betsy."

"That is so great," I say.

"I mean, why would you stay there?" she's saying. "There's nothing good there. Nothing."

This may be the only entry point I get, and I have no choice but to take it. "There are a couple cute guys there," I say.

"Who?" she says. "Name one."

"Ryan's kind of cute," I say, and I am trying hard to remain still, to channel Perry Mason, the investigating lawyer, but I am literally, physically squirming, twisting my body so that I am looking ninety degrees to Julia's right.

"Ryan?" She is not squirming. She is staring directly at me.

"He's cute," I say, offering a tiny Bridget-shrug, going for an approximation of innocence and light.

There will be neither innocence nor light at this table. "Betsy?"

"Yeah?"

"You're not doing anything with him, are you?"

"Is that against company policy?"

"He's bad news, Betsy."

She says this, and my stomach seizes up, and I hear in my head, over and over and over: *I told you, I told you, I told you, dummy.* "What do you mean?"

"Are you hooking up with him?"

Perry Mason! She's Perry Mason, and I'm her crumbling, twitching witness. "I'm not hooking up with him," I say, making a decision. She just doesn't like him.

"Good."

Oh, I give up, I just give up. "We're kind of dating."

"What? What?"

"What?" I say. I know where this is going: It is only the question of how long I want to wait to hear it, spelled out, from poor Julia. If I were her, I don't know that I'd be able to be honest.

"He is not good, Betsy."

"What does that mean?"

"Betsy—"

"You can tell me," I say. "I'm okay. I didn't even really like him that much." I smile broadly to show her how very true this is.

"I think he's hooking up with Eva," she says.

"Oh," I say. "When?" She is going to know I am lying about the not liking him part: I thought I was dancing, boxing with the truth, a feint here, a nudge there, but really I am just throwing up flares, thinking I am distracting her when all I am really doing is illuminating it. "We only started going out a little while ago," I say, intentionally vague. Maybe I can still fix this. "I don't care what he did before."

"Still," she says. "Now. The night after the Christmas party. The last day of work, before we all left."

"I thought Eva was in Goa or something."

"She was," Julia says. "I think they met up at the airport."

"Oh," I say.

"I don't think it's anything serious for her," Julia says. "You know how Eva is." What can she say to me? She's my boss, not exactly my friend, even though I like her, and she likes me. "I could be wrong," she says. "This is just what Eva says. You know that bitch is a lying cunt. I fucking hate her." She is saying this for my benefit, rallying herself against Eva, her natural antipathy invigorated by this betrayal. Now Julia sees me as her ally, or at least her charge, and there is a tiny bit of solace in that. Not enough, though, to keep me from bursting into tears so furious and fast that they spill over my cheeks into my ice cream. "Oh, dear," Julia says. "Just go talk to him. You need to talk to him right now. Clean yourself up, and go talk to him." She pulls at my face with a napkin.

"I think that might be a good idea," I say.

I return to the office alone, without Julia. I make a beeline for his desk, where he is sitting. He smiles at me, looks happy to see me. "I need to talk to you right now," I say to Ryan, parroting Julia.

It is the first time I have spoken to him in this office in my normal voice, not our secret-adventure whisper.

"Sure, okay," he says, and I am surprised by how quickly he acquiesces. Maybe I should have been like this from the beginning. Why am I going to learn all my lessons now, when they are too late to be of any practical use?

We walk out to the street. "Julia says you're dating Eva." I do not know why I say "dating" instead of "fucking." "Is that true?"

He stops short, and when I turn back to face him, he's framed by a row of Christmas trees and looks angelic. "Eva? What? I'm not dating anyone but you."

This I had not expected. This did not even occur to me. "Why would she say that? She has no reason to say that. Julia's not a liar."

"I don't know, Betsy. I don't know why either of them would say that."

I have no idea what to say. I did not expect him to contradict her. My mouth is almost completely dry. "I don't believe you," I say, but I am testing him, attempting to bait him, more than I am contradicting him.

"Betsy, you are the only girl I want to be with," he says. "You have to believe that."

I want to say: "Tell me why," and have him list the qualities of mine he finds so enchanting. Maybe if I knew how he would answer that question, I would not have approached him with such deference, such regard, and would not have awarded him such a position of power. This cannot be reduced to my own poor self-esteem. "I don't know what to say. If you want to date someone, just say it, just do it, it's okay," I say. This is instantaneously my Plan B: Be honest, let's start from here, do what you will. I still want you, if you can only want me enough to be honest with me.

"I don't."

"I don't know what to think," I say. I believe Julia. But still: Why would he lie to me now? The secret is out: If he was with Eva, then he could not want to be with me. The two were simply so completely opposed. So again: The secret is out; what possible advantage could there be in lying? First, it would be unbelievably—literally, beyond believing—stupid to think that if he were lying now, I wouldn't find out. That defies logic, and if there is one thing I trust, it is logic. And second: Surely, if it were true, he would be relieved? Guilty and pained but certainly relieved? There would be no charade to play, no excuses to invent.

"Let's go back to your place and just hang out," he says. And of course, because it is all that I ever want, I say yes.

After he leaves in the morning, I call John and Tommy and Billy, grading them on a scale from most sympathetic to least, and talking to them in that order. I am trying Ryan, laying out the case for and against, testing the explanations I am making myself believe, until I am acting as his defender, and they are judge, jury, and prosecutor, incredulous at my inability to see the crime at hand, differing only in how elaborately they express their disdain at my illogic and to what they attribute its cause: my gender, my race, my suburban upbringing, my love for lost causes or my stubborn stupidity.

The next night is Saturday, and Bridget has asked all her bridesmaids to come over for dinner. It is possibly the last place I want to be in the city of New York, surrounded by Bridget's evil handmaidens while I wait to hear from Ryan, while I wait to see if what Julia has told me will disappear into air as I hope it will. I cannot believe both of them, so I am canceling out their testimonies and reverting back to how all of this was before the troubles began, before Thanksgiving. There must be space to breathe, between what the two of them have said.

I am five minutes early when Bridget's doorman signs me in, but the apartment is already filled with the bridesmaids and assorted Callahan family members picking through a buffet dinner spread out on a table.

They scare me, Bridget's committee of vigilant nags, so I stay in the kitchen, where I am surprised to see her father sitting on a stool next to the countertop. I pile a half dozen buffalo wings onto a paper plate and sit beside him.

"All these women," Mr. Callahan says. "I have no idea what to do."

"Me neither," I say, and he laughs, which I did not expect him to do. I offer him the plate and he picks up a single wing, which he does not eat but places in front of him. He has accepted it more as a gesture of goodwill than anything else.

"And now Betsy," he says, slapping his knee, leaving a trace of orange wing sauce on his Dockers. "Did the world end last week? Bridget told me you were worried about that."

"It certainly did not, Mr. Callahan."

"It's Reverend Callahan now, but that's okay," he says. "You know, Betsy, you've been just a wonderful friend to Bridget," he says, patting my forearm. "Wonderful." This may be the most he has said to me in the past fifteen years, and the strain shows in a throbbing forehead vein. Both of us are staring into the distance, at the closed door to Bridget's room, where she is being transformed, by those devilish bridesmaids, into a creature we do not know, who will replace the Bridget we do, and I feel a sudden and complete camaraderie with this man, whose most substantial conversation with me prior to this moment concerned the location of lighter fluid for the grill during a Memorial Day picnic years ago.

"We're not losing Bridget," I finally manage. "We're gaining a doctor without a border."

Reverend Callahan nods, and I think he understands. "Just wonderful," he says again.

Later that night, when I am home watching *Saturday Night Live,* the phone rings, and I hope it is Ryan.

"Betsy?" Julia says.

"Hi, Julia," I say. This cannot be good. I lie down on Zoe's couch to enjoy the last few minutes of having someone I love in my life.

"Did you talk to him?"

"He said he didn't do it."

"I talked to Eva this morning. He did it, Betsy. I don't think she's lying. They've slept together like a half dozen times in the past couple months."

"Okay," I say.

"Are you okay? Do you want me to come over?"

"I'm okay," I say. "I'm going out with my friends later." I turn up the volume on the television.

"Are you watching *Saturday Night Live*?"

"Yeah," I say.

"Us, too," she says, and I start crying just at the way she is part of an "us." What do I have to do, to have that?

"Thanks for calling, Julia. I really appreciate it."

The thing about saying to yourself *I want to die, I want to die, I want to die* is that you don't, of course, not usually: You just want to be turned off long enough so that whatever you're feeling will die. That is the thing you want to kill, the thing that is infecting everything else. But of course, you can't, so you have to let it bleed through your body until it takes hold, like a sickness, because you carry it in you; there is no way to outrun it, to outsmart it, so all you can do is let it take over, like it wants to, shutting down every part of your head except the one you want to switch off. It is like I can feel myself sinking down into the person I was before him, like she has been waiting for me all along, knowing I would return.

I cry until I fall asleep, then wake up and cry some more.

On Monday morning I put on a black dress and black tights and black boots. Before I was going for Perry Mason, and I know I am now attempting a French widow. I buy an orange I'm not hungry for and cry on the subway, on my way to find him.

"Are you okay?" says a woman sitting across from me.

"Yeah," I say, sniffling. "I'm okay."

"Do you want my tuna fish sandwich?" she says, retrieving an aluminum foil package from her suede handbag and holding it out to me.

This just makes me cry harder, because it seems like there is a world around me full of honest love and kind gestures and even when it is being offered to me, I do not know how to accept it. "No, thank you," I say.

"You'll be all right, sweetie," she says, getting off the train at York Street. "You just need a little sandwich or something."

I find him in the stockroom. "Julia told me," I say. "Again."

His shoulders sag, and he sits on a cardboard box full of

discarded schwag—Turkish coffeemakers, CDs from obscure bands. "Okay," he says.

"You shouldn't have said you only wanted to go out with me," I say, in a voice that is small and pathetic and weak and not at all regal and defiant and proud, like a French widow's would be. "I didn't push you into that."

"I thought if I didn't," he says, "you wouldn't want to see me anymore."

"It would have been better than this," I say. "You didn't need to lie."

"I wasn't lying about you. I wasn't lying about how I felt about you." I truly, truly enjoy his use of the past tense. Because somewhere, I am still thinking: *If he still loves you, all of this can be fixed.* "It was just so fast, after all that bullshit with Stella, and there you were, and I just wanted to be with you, but I don't think I was ready . . ." He trails off. "I just wanted to be with you, but there were these other things—"

"Things?" I say. "More than Eva?"

"No, just Eva, just Eva," he says. "Do you understand that Eva could be one thing and you could be something else?"

"No," I say. "I'm a spectacularly naïve person."

"We moved so fast," he says. "We never even went to see a movie together, and then I was staying at your place four nights a week."

"I didn't make you do that," I say. "If you couldn't handle it, why not just not do it?"

"Maybe we should just talk about this later."

"Later?"

"I mean, maybe we should just think everything over and talk about it later."

"I don't know what that means," I say, which is pathetic and so true, I want to throw up at my own childishness.

"Maybe we could see a movie together," he says.

"Maybe," I say, because, horribly, I still want it.

"We should take three weeks," he says. "And then we should talk."

"Three weeks." Maybe I can just keep repeating what he says.

"I don't want to make things weird for you here," he says.

"Don't worry about that," I say. "I'm leaving."

"You don't have to quit," he says. "I'll quit."

"Are you kidding?" I say. "I'm never coming back here as long as I live."

I should leave there, but I don't, because I still believe it exists, a plausible reason for all that has happened. I am sure that if I keep talking to him, I will discover a way to bring him back to me, but all I hear is the call-and-response of *Why?* and *I'm sorry.* It takes two hours for me to recognize that this is not going to end with him dropping to his knees and begging forgiveness. How it really does end: "I really liked you," and then I run out of the building to cry on the street.

I wait for him to call, and while I wait, I sit in my bedroom and my mind replays one scene over and over:

"What are you doing?" I'd said. I had been asleep and then woke up to find him staring at me.

"Just looking," he said.

"Okay."

"I'm falling in love with you," he says.

"Okay."

"Have you ever seen *Monty Python and the Holy Grail*?"

"No."

"We'll have to make sure that you do."

"Say it again," I said.

"Which part?" he says.

"You know," I said. "That one."

He turned to face me and put him palm on my forehead, like he was taking my temperature. "I am falling in love with you."

"Tell me why."

"Because you're smart and beautiful and funny and hot. The first time I saw you, I said, that girl is something else. You were different from any girl I ever knew. And it was like you had no idea about any of it, how amazing you are."

He closed his eyes again. He had my hair in his hand. I watched him until his hand relaxed and his breathing modulated, and only then did I rest my forehead against his chest and shut my eyes.

Fade out, here. My head wants to stop here. But that is the problem, that the story did not end there, that it was so much more mundane than that sweet moment. A flash of inspiration that made it past the rewrites: the orange I brought into the stockroom as a form of emotional shield, the one I decided at some point to throw at him. I ate the orange. He threw away the peels. There are all kinds of metaphorical problems with this. But mostly it was false starts and fumbling, with someone wondering if her position will be improved by crying. Or a suicide feint. And then it ended like they all end, with two people walking in opposite directions, and only one looking back.

NINE

I expect things to stop, but they move, inexorably, onward. I call in sick to work, for the week, leaving a message on Eva's voice mail saying that I have dengue fever. Turn me in, I dare her, turn me in. See if I care. John and Billy take me out drinking, but all this achieves is a series of headaches. I come home uncomfortably buzzed, fall asleep in my clothes, wake up at one in the morning and wonder where Ryan is, if he is with Eva.

I am perfectly rational. I feel perfectly rational. I call Tommy after my beer-induced nap, because he will still be awake. "I want you to call him and tell him I've died," I say. "That I killed myself and it's his fault."

"Dude," he says. "Dude. Shut up. I am not going to do that."

"I am," I say. "You are." I give Tommy his phone number.

"I'm not writing that down," he says. "I'm not listening to this."

"If you were my friend—"

"Okay, sweetheart, as your friend, I am not going to call him and tell him you killed yourself. There's no dignity in that."

"But still."

"And he'd find out the truth. Do you want to be known as the girl who told this guy she dated she killed herself over him? Seriously, dude, I need you to get a grip."

"What do I care? I'm never going to talk to him again," I say, hoping Tommy will contradict me. He doesn't. "And he would feel really bad for a while."

"This is insane. Insane. Absolutely not."

"I don't know why you won't help me," I say, my voice cracking. "I would help you."

"Dude. Please take my word for this. You do not want to tell him you've killed yourself."

"I don't want to tell him myself," I say. "I can just call my sister and have her do it."

"You're making a mistake," he says.

I do not call my sister, who is in Denmark. I cannot wait for her to return. I do not call Bridget, who normally would have been my first choice, but—I just cannot call her, to tell her of my latest defeat, my most recent debacle. At a certain point, you just start feeling like a loser.

As Bridget pointed out, so horribly presciently, I have never been to his apartment, but I have a copy of *Texas Monthly* he lent me, which conveniently notes his address, and this is where I tell the driver of the car service car to take me.

"You're getting out here?" the driver asks, sounding dubious, pulling alongside a row of low tenement houses. The street is dark. My door stops against a garbage bag and I squeeze out. I watch the town car drive away and through a red light without slowing down. I have no plan. I am just waiting for him. I just want to see him. There is no pretending I was just walking along, which is unfortunate, but I just need to see him now, because maybe if I do, he will see his mistake. I will tell him I love him. That is ridiculous. I will tell him I hate him so he will love me.

On the corner I can see his second-story, front-side apartment, and it is there that I wait.

I am wearing a $295 Diane von Furstenberg dress I bought with my one good credit card after I saw him dancing with Eva at the office party, and ankle boots and a North Face parka, and I am still the same girl who waddled down the corridors of her middle school in red clown pants and an oversized Coca-Cola rugby shirt, the same girl who saw him dancing underneath a disco ball and knew that it was over, that whatever I had imagined was about to evaporate into nothingness.

This is the story we will someday tell: He made a mistake early in our relationship—so early, who even remembers the details, the names of those involved—he made a mistake and felt so empty and regretful that he understood his loss and came back to me. He will come with me to the wedding, and he will make fun of Georgina and her horribleness. We will be normal, happy people, like Bridget and James, but we will never be smug, because we will understand the providence of our union, as serendipitous as gravity and as inevitable as earth.

The last light goes out in the house at the address printed on the mailing label of the magazine in my hands, and either he is still out, enjoying himself, drinking with his friends, or a girl, or Eva, or he is content, content enough that he has turned out his light and gone to sleep at one thirty in the morning.

Maybe he's already brought her home, where he never took me. Maybe they are in bed right now.

I could find out. I am owed at least that. I could ring his doorbell, and he would need to answer it. He would never think that Betsy, naïve Betsy, would ring his doorbell at two in the morning.

And what do I want? Nothing. If I were someone else, maybe I would approach him with violence, with a bat. Crazier things, crazier women have happened. But all I want are answers, explanations—*words*—and my own impotence disgusts me.

I am halfway between the street corner and the entrance to his apartment when I call Tommy.

"Get the fuck off the street, dude."

"Tell me why I shouldn't."

"You want me to bottom-line it for you?"

"Yes," I say.

"Right now, you're some girl he fucked," Tommy says, and he pauses, delicately, uncharacteristically. "If you knock on his door, you're going to be some psycho he fucked."

"Oh," I say.

"Go the fuck home, dude," Tommy says. "I'll wait." And he does, wait on the phone, and as I walk three blocks up the avenue to a blinking sign for a car service, I can hear Tommy frying something, Tommy flushing the toilet. "That was just a joke," he says. "I didn't really just take a shit." I climb into the back of another town car and tell the driver to take me home. Tommy flushes the toilet again, with the mouthpiece closer to the source of the noise. "Funny, right?" he says. "You feel better yet?"

I walk through my door at three in the morning and put the cordless phone in the freezer so I will not be able to use it.

Saturday afternoon comes, and with it, Bridget's engagement party. Somehow I did not think it would come if I were not prepared for it, if I did not have Ryan by my side, but here it is, and this is a lesson to remember, how these things just do not stop, whether the narrative we'd planned accommodates them or not. In the elevator up to the restaurant on the roof, a man I am introduced to as James's best man, Bill, pats me on the arm. "So you're the maid of honor," he says. "You're like me, but a girl."

"Yep," I say. "You got it."

"Tell me this," he says. "See, you look like a normal girl. When you were growing up, was it weird having such a hot best friend?"

The elevator door opens, and I wait, for a beat, for the perfect retort to come out of my mouth, but I just stand there, waiting, mouth open, like at any moment the most cutting, Oscar Wilde–esque response will issue from that space. Bill pauses, expectantly. We almost let the doors close before I stick my arm between them.

It is as if I have cared so much, so obsessively, about what one person thinks of me, I have no more room in my head for anyone else, especially anyone like this. I will not play around anymore; I will mean what I say; I will become a person whose words are alive, and essential, and true. "Fuck you," I say, leaving him motionless behind me, and for the first time in a week I get exactly what I want.

I am seated at a table with the rest of the attendants, which means Bill and I sit across from each other. If this were a romantic comedy, and I was not a crazy bitch, maybe this would be precisely the right time to fall in love with him, but it is not, and I am, at least for the time being. On my right is Trixie, a lawyer from

Chattanooga whose husband earned a default groomsman position, and on my left is Arun. "Arun," Bridget says, pausing by our table to make introductions, "used to be my boss at the gallery, and now he's an editor at an international style magazine."

"It's true," Arun says.

"Betsy," Bridget says, "is an editor at an international women's Web site."

"It's . . . also true," I say, and I look at Arun with a mixture of embarrassment and familiarity, because I have failed where he has succeeded, and we both know it. There is nothing to do but play the pauper. "Who are you with?"

"Jetset."

"I'm with couture-dot-com."

"Be your sexy best with Couture," he says, quoting from our promotional materials. "I have a friend who worked on that campaign."

"It's a living," I say.

"So where's your boyfriend?"

"He's at band practice," I say.

"No kidding! You actually have a boyfriend?"

"What?" I say. "Do I look like someone who doesn't have a boyfriend?" Can he tell? Is it that obvious?

"Well, you know, that's the cliché, right? That you girls tell the women of America that they're useless without a boyfriend, or if they're fat, or if they don't wear eyeliner, and the big secret nobody tells them is that you're all lonely, neurotic women waiting for some asshole they gave a blow job to call them back. It's like, he's not calling you back."

"I'm not like that," I say almost inaudibly. "I have a boyfriend who loves me."

"You're all this weird mixture of frigid fashion girls with

cats and submissives who have sex in the bathrooms of Lower East Side bars."

"I love my boyfriend," I say. "And I don't have a cat."

"But you all have nice shoes," he says. "Do you have nice shoes?" He pulls up the tablecloth. "Ha! You're wearing flip-flops! I'm sorry you don't have nice shoes. Aren't your feet cold?"

"I'm okay," I say. "I wore heels here. They're in my backpack."

"It must be really hard, coming up with stories for that audience," Arun says. "It's just, like, how many times can you come up with fifteen ways to spot a cheater?"

"I'm sure there must be plenty of stereotypes about people who work at *Jetset,*" I finally say.

"What? That we're all immaculately dressed gay men and brittle, vacant women? That's also true. It's all true."

"Really," I say. I do not want to give him any more information that makes me look like an idiot and try to convey an aura of attentive, exclusive industry, refolding my napkin.

"Okay, it's not entirely true," he says. "I'm just annoyed because they didn't let me sit with my boyfriend."

"I know Bridget didn't have a lot of time to do the seating arrangements," I say.

"I'm going to stop complaining," he says. "We're going to have a lovely dinner. You're the maid of honor, right? Did you write your toast yet?"

"Toast?" I say. "There's a toast at the engagement dinner?"

"Bill's over there writing a toast," he says.

"Bill?" I say. "I hate Bill."

"Bridget told me you and her mom and Bill and James's dad were all making toasts."

"Well, that's just terrific," I say, pushing my chair away from the table. "I have to go to the bathroom."

"Do you need a pen?" Arun asks, pulling one from his coat jacket.

Twenty minutes later, Bill begins his remarks: "It was spring break, junior year, and we had just tapped the second keg of the night." I did not know people actually began toasts like this. From where I sit at the attendants' table I can see Mr. Callahan smirking at his son-in-law-to-be.

Then it is my turn. "The Callahans may have only one daughter, but I can promise you Bridget has a sister," I say, hand on my heart, sentiment thick as motor oil pouring off the toilet paper draft I have palmed in my hand. It is schmaltz, it is pure emotional manipulation, and when it is over, I have destroyed my enemy, Bill.

Arun extends his hand when I return to the table, and I shake it. "You killed him," he whispers.

Three hours later I am still sitting at the attendants' table, alone with another of the groomsmen, who appears to be as unsure about what to do next as I am.

"Do you think we can go home now?" he says.

I wonder, fleetingly, if this is how I meet my husband, this bored groomsman in a banquet hall, and I want to hit myself for thinking it.

"Have you seen Bridget?" I say.

"I think she and James went home already."

"No shit," I say.

"No shit," he says.

In the taxi home I cry so hard, the cabbie offers me his cell phone. "Is there someone I can call for you? Someone who can take care of you?"

I shake my head, and then he opens the window, letting in the January air, letting out this uncontrollable sadness that neither one of us knows how to handle.

I have no intention of reporting to work on Monday morning, after my dengue fever has, I suppose, cleared itself up, but there is nothing else for me to do, and anyway—he is there. What more do I need to know? I take such a theatrically deep breath getting off the elevator that Sybilla, who appears beside me, asks if I am taking the new lunchtime yoga class.

I watch Eva organize her things at her desk, arranging invitations to past fashion shows on her office wall. She is too insubstantial to be hated. (*Where is Ryan?* my other head is saying, because we do not see him. We see Eva, but not him.) Part of her recognizes the fact that she is valued chiefly for her looks and her connections, and that part of her wonders why it is those and not other qualities of hers that are so highly valued. It is nicer feeling sorry for her than it is to hate her, because hating her, I am discovering, puts me at a disadvantage. *Where is Ryan?*

I sit and stare at the ceiling until Nancy's assistant, Carrie, who is usually allowed to leave her desk only for food and errands, taps me on the shoulder and leads me into Nancy's office.

I've never been in Nancy's office before, and it is underwhelming, a sliver of a window looking out onto a parking lot. This? This is what I've been coming here for?

"I'm very sorry, Betsy," Nancy says as a greeting, taking off her glasses in what appears to be more stage direction than an organic motion. I think she is trying to look concerned and caring, and she is failing.

"Thank you," I say.

"Did Eva tell you?

"Not really," I say. "Julia did."

"How did Julia know?"

"From talking to Eva, I guess."

"But why would they be talking about cutting your feature?"

"What?"

Nancy does not stumble, even though I clearly have no idea what she's talking about. Nancy's genius is that she has absolutely no tolerance for curiosity, intellectual or otherwise. "We have to cut your Topeka story," she says.

"Oh," I say. "Oh."

"It really just plays too Midwest for us. But you did a lot of work on it, and in Julia's absence, I wanted to talk to you about it directly."

"We did a lot of work on that story," I say. "I interviewed like two dozen girls from Kansas. It's a real issue, and coming from us, those kids would listen." The last part is totally made-up bullshit, but of all my options, appealing to Nancy's vanity seems the one most likely to bring success.

"Still," she says. "Too Midwest."

We sit quietly for a moment.

"Ginger candy?" she says, passing me a dish of wrapped sweets.

"I quit," I say.

I look for Ryan on my way out, taking more time than I need to put on my hat and mittens, but even after this charade has reached its most ridiculous limit, he does not appear. Something is wrong with me, when I am more concerned about that than about the fact that I just quit my job.

I pack as slowly as I can, unpinning pictures of Jack Cole from my bulletin board, rolling up my posters and fixing them with hair elastics. Everyone sees me, but only Casey comes up to me, when I have finally gathered everything in my arms and begin my lurch forward toward the door.

He takes a carrier bag full of pilfered beauty samples and a stack of books under his arm. "I know what Ryan did," he says as I wait for the elevator. The door opens into an empty carriage, and I step into it.

"He's a dick," he says, passing me my things. He runs his hand through his hair, so that it points even more toward the ceiling than usual. "And he's not even smart."

"It doesn't matter," I say, and the doors close before I need to say anything else.

I cannot keep from dialing his number at the office, but for the first few days I restrict myself to calling at four in the morning, when I am sure he will not be there to answer the phone. Every day now my calls migrate closer to working hours, until I am surprised when he does not pick up and say, "This is Ryan," in that slow Texas roll.

I am about to call at noon, and have already dialed the 212 area code, but instead finish with Billy's work number instead.

"The dude was an asshole," Billy says. "Don't you be an asshole, too."

"You don't understand," I say.

"I understand that he slept with your boss."

"You're missing the point," I say unsteadily, because I can

hear how absurd I sound, how ridiculous, how deluded. "He was everything that I wanted. Nothing like this has ever happened to me before."

"And it never will again," Billy says. "The number of boss-fucking dudes out there is small."

"I mean, I'd never been so happy with someone before," I say, struggling with sniffles that threaten to become sobs.

"Jesus Christ," Billy says. "You're screwed."

I return the phone to the freezer.

In the mailbox I find an envelope from Eva, with her Dolce & Gabbana shawl inside.

There is a note. *I figured you should have something nice from your time here,* she writes. There is a PS: *He's a dumb shit.*

Mostly I watch TV. I become the crazy friend. I can talk to my friends about Ryan and nothing else; in six years of friendship I have banked acts of goodwill and kindnesses, too slight to count for much by themselves, but, in the aggregate, they are stores from which I am now withdrawing. I am moody and mean and they know that every conversation they begin will somehow wind its way back to Ryan, and how much I miss him, or how much I have cried. "Dude, just two seconds ago, we were talking about *The X Files,* and you weren't crying," Tommy says, exasperated, after a cheer-up mission at one of our neighborhood bars has ended with me dissolving into tears, having reenacted, for the hundredth time, my last conversation with Ryan, this time focusing on the irony of the orange. They know that scene backwards and forwards, like one from a movie they would like to forget.

The fact that they still begin those conversations, ever hopeful that the subject will change, makes me more devoted to them than ever before. I want to tell them that they are my anchor, my lighthouse, my mooring, or any of a number of less nautical metaphors, but it is one of the saving graces of my life that they already know it.

Only once do I threaten to break our three-week agreement, and that is with an e-mail I type, describing, at length, my current position, my feelings for him, my feelings for Eva, and, the centerpiece of the missive, the story of my only scar: I tell him the unglamorous truth, that it was the result of a misunderstanding between me and a slide, when I was seven, and young enough to be intimidated by playground equipment. I am telling him this because it is the only thing he ever asked me that I failed to answer fully, and once this is clear, I delete the message before I can close my eyes and send it (hoping for his immediate rendition, of course): It is certainly pathetic, this attempt at courtship by words, though which is more pathetic—the ongoing attempt at courtship, or the fact that I do so with words—is difficult to judge. Tommy was right: Why do I strain with this endless, circuitous self-expression, when all I really ever needed to do was answer my door wearing nothing but my underwear? Why have I always believed, mistakenly, I am now sure, that these things exist so determinedly in the mind, to the exclusion of the body? What books was I reading? What lies did I believe?

I am learning to call things by their names and to identify them fully: I am living with whatever this is with Ryan, for Ryan—but also . . . something else. It is the something else of no longer going to couture.com. It is becoming the silver lining, the second-place prize, and while I would never have suggested that trade, love the one you're with, and I love waking up at noon, and once

I register that Ryan is not with me, also registering that I do not have to go to Couture. There is room here, of course, for an evolving perspective, and it evolves particularly noticeably every night, as I settle down for another bowl of couscous and hamburger. My biggest mistake, maybe, was mistaking a global apocalypse for my own tiny event. The upshot is that piss-poor planning for the former is still more than adequate for the latter, so I have as much food as I need, and for the first week, my checking account stays static at three hundred dollars.

The two car services to Ryan's house and back cost seventy-three dollars. I turn out my pockets, collect the change from the couch and coat pockets, and count seventeen dollars. My new health insurance will be $410 a month, but someone said something about a ninety-day grace period, and I am just going to have to hope that is true. I need a job. I can fax and FedEx, and I can also remember everything Ryan ever said to me, including the fact that he once "had the best strawberry shake of [his] life" at a restaurant called You're Fresh, which he said was "near the bridge," in Brooklyn.

You're Fresh has its own Web site, with a hiring section advertising the need for a server.

Apparently You're Fresh is an organic restaurant. The walls are lined with thousands of pieces of plastic fruit. It is like walking into Carmen Miranda's headdress.

A man in a baseball cap sits alone at a corner table.

"Are you looking for a waitress?" I say. "You had a sign on your Web site?"

"Have you waitressed before?"

"Yeah," I say, extracting my waitressing résumé from my backpack.

"I didn't think people actually had these," he says, folding the paper into ever-smaller halves. "What's your name?"

"Betsy Nilssen," I say, and he writes it down on the back of my résumé, spelling my last name like a Japanese carmaker.

He extends his hand. "Frank," he says, but the "Frank" that rhymes with "honk," even though I know his type, down to the silver buckles on his suede loafers, and he grew up within fifty miles of Trenton. "Friendly. You, not me." He writes FRIENDLY in large block letters beneath my name. "Show me your wrists."

"Sure," I say, extending my hands toward him, palms down, but midway through the word, he's pushed up the sleeves of my shirt, leaving my forearms bare.

"No needle drugs," he says.

"Okay," I say. This is a part of the interview we never had in Margate.

"Anything else, you do it in the bathroom," he says. "I don't need that shit in my kitchen."

I start training in the morning.

I had not guessed that "training" would mean running gigantic stacks of food from the kitchen to the tables. For free. There is too much new information, a static of names and ingredients and table numbers. In the lull between the morning rush and lunch, Frank sticks a menu in my hand and sends me off to the back of the restaurant to memorize it. I have not eaten most of these vegetables. I have not heard of most of these vegetables.

"I usually eat frozen dinners and rehydrated couscous and hamburger," I say to Frank after he corrects my pronunciation of "jicama," offering my best approximation of a warm suburban grin.

"That's disgusting," he says, a look of both horror and reproach on his face.

I have played this role before, the role of the incompetent waitress, and my sincere, hand-wringing apologies usually averaged out to 22.1 percent tips, especially on Monday Night Football nights. But that was then, at a golf club in Margate, where the local dads, in their old fraternity T-shirts and Dockers, were too blissfully buzzed to worry about an overcooked hamburger or an absent dish of jalapeño poppers. This is not then. "This isn't soy," says one woman, frowning into her milk shake. "This is skim. I wanted soy."

"Well?" says one of the two waitresses—Sasha? Susan?—half a decade younger than me. Light bounces off her pink glitter eyeshadow as she raises her eyebrows at me, while I stand transfixed in front of the doors to the kitchen. "Excuse me," the other waitress says, banging a plate against my elbow.

I've never seen this milk shake before, so I shrug my shoulders and walk backwards into the kitchen. I remember this feeling from sixth grade, when I was the new girl at Margate Middle School, and Tonia Serrod, the class president, passed back the book reports and instead of handing me my glitter-paint picture of Halley's Comet, threw it to the floor and laughed as I bent over to pick it up.

"Are you okay?" the blond cook asks as I pause before reentering the dining room, a stack of plates piled from my hand to my elbow. "Is that soup running down your arm?"

"It burns," I say.

He dabs his apron against the bowl, sopping up the excess vegetarian gumbo. "Much better," he says.

I dash out of the kitchen, deposit the plates, and rush back, pretending to look for knives.

"Are you surviving out there?" the cook says.

"It's awesome."

"Sarah only works on Mondays and Wednesdays," he says.

"I appreciate that."

"She's like that with everybody."

"You have an accent," I say. Spenser for hire, here. "Where are you from?"

"Dublin."

"Are you a chef?"

"A sous-chef."

"I'm Betsy."

"Ian," he says.

"You probably make food for yourself all the time."

"I do."

"What did you have for breakfast?"

"Banana nut waffles with syrup," he says. My mouth is watering. Here is what turns me on: waffles. "What did you have?"

"A Krispy Kreme doughnut and a Diet Coke," I say. "And a Snickers." The last part is a lie.

"You should eat better," he says. "You know, I made the waffles here. We all eat together in the morning sometimes. You could come by for that, if you wanted."

Could it be this easy? I think, trying to figure out what the plot of this story might be, whether he is the guest star sent in to catch the emotional Hail Mary, or a walk-on, an extra, an elusive distraction.

Apparently the soy/skim milk shake debacle does little to interfere with my prospects for continued employment. When I come in for my first double shift, I discover I have been scheduled for additional training shifts, six lunches, and another double on Sunday. Bridget calls while we clean up after dinner, and I walk outside, away from the clanking kitchen sounds.

"It's not a good time," I say. "I'm going to be in my office until like midnight or something."

"Jesus," she says. "You've totally disappeared. I just need to know if you're bringing this boyfriend you're always talking about."

"You need to know now? It's not for another month or something."

"Are you insane? Everyone else RSVP'd months ago. You're only getting away with this because it's you."

"Oh," I say.

"So is he in? Or out?"

"He's in," I say. "In. Nilssen plus one."

"Very good," Bridget says.

"Very good."

"Is something wrong with you?"

"No, no, no," I say. "I just have a lot of work to do. I have a very important job."

"I thought you hated your job."

"Bridge, I have a meeting in like two minutes."

"You have a meeting at ten forty-three P.M.?"

"It's about the season's best nail shapes."

"You'll have to let me know how that turns out," Bridget says sourly.

It is my ninth shift at You're Fresh, and I am still officially "training," which means I still have yet to take home a dollar. Sarah is taking home all my money, and I hate Sarah. But it is Thursday, so she is teaching her morning yoga class, which means it is not so bad, just Frank and Marni, his perpetually stoned waitress-girlfriend, Ian, and the rest of the kitchen staff. Midway through my shift, I discover I have been scheduled for five more "training" days.

"This is why there are unions," I say to Ian. "This is terrible."

"Let me make it up to you," he says. "Want me to buy you dinner tonight?"

At least I have learned to tamp down the incredulity, which had undoubtedly been my default emotional setting with Ryan. "That would be just marvelous," I say.

There is not even an opportunity to plan, or be nervous, or contemplate whether I would take his last name or dash ours together. It is an altogether better position to be in. Bridget always said that the secret to a successful relationship was to care less than the other person. Bridget also said not to fall in love prior to the first date. I would never have been able to achieve either of these two if I'd wanted to, but now that I have been given little choice in the matter, I feel like I am coming around to her perspective.

Ian and I walk up to a Mexican restaurant on Bedford Avenue, where he steers us to a table in a corner, in the back. I am hoping this is because it is private and not because he has a girlfriend who may at some point walk by.

"Can I get some apple juice?" he asks the waitress, who, I hope he does not notice, is much prompter and more professional than I have ever been.

And: apple juice. Priceless.

He is excellent. He has dogs. He grew up in a town—a village!—called Kilcullen and moved to Dublin only after his parents separated. He wants to own two restaurants—one in New York City and one in Ireland, where all the ingredients will be raised in the backyard and his dogs will watch over sheep. When he speaks quickly, he pronounces the word "think" without the *h*. He is exactly what I need: a viable option to Ryan, five feet and eleven inches of perspective. Ryan. For the last two hours, I have been thinking about him only in the sense of not thinking about him.

After dinner is over, we both kind of pause on the street, in front of the L train entrance, walking around in small circles, neither one of us making a definitive move in any direction.

"I live in Gramercy," he says. "Do you think you'd want to come over and walk my dog?"

I begin to laugh, thinking he is using this as a euphemism, or at least a joke. "I would just love to," I say. He is not. "Where's your other dog?"

"Other dog?"

"You said you had 'dogs,' plural."

"Oh," he says. "One's my ex-girlfriend's."

"You count your ex-girlfriend's dog as your own? That seems weird." I am not walking around in small circles anymore. I am still, one foot on the railing of the subway stairs, one foot below it, on the top step.

"Well—weird?"

"She's your ex. She's your ex, and you count her dog as your own. That's kind of weird, right?"

"They used to both be ours."

"Oh," I say. "That's nice."

"It was," he says.

"They used to be both of yours when . . ." I take a step down the stairs, so now I am looking up at him, chin cocked, eyes open and wide.

"When we were engaged," he says.

"That's funny," I say. "You didn't mention you were engaged."

"Yeah."

"And now you're broken up."

"Yeah," he says.

"Yeah," I say.

"Well—"

"Yes?" I am sharp. I am getting better at this. I take another step down the stairs, and he begins to follow me.

"Technically, we're on a break."

"Until . . ."

"We have chosen a date."

"To break up?"

"To get married."

"Oh, you're kidding," I say, shaking my head, almost laughing. "What are you doing here then?"

"We can see other people," he says. "Until then."

"Oh," I say, turning around, my back to him. "I have to go. Seriously."

He rushes down a few steps, takes my hand in his. "Come on, Betsy," he says. "I really like you. Why don't you just come back to my place and we'll just hang out."

I pull our hands, entwined, to my face, so that I am rubbing my cheek with the back of his hand.

"That's it," he says.

His wrist is in front of my mouth. I pull his hand further up, toward my ear, and bite into his flesh, hard and sharp. Explain that, motherfucker.

"Go home to your girlfriend," I say. There are only ten feet between me and the turnstiles, and I make it through one in time to look back and see him still staring at the impression of my teeth in his arm.

I am surprised to see that it is not even midnight by the time I get home. As soon as I walk through the door of our building I know that whatever I had hoped for with Ian was a ruse, a distraction that I prayed would keep me from doing exactly what I am about to do. It is three weeks to the day after Ryan and I last talked. I have given him what he asked for, and I am following our rules. I am not being demanding. My heart is beating so hard as I dial his number that I put my hand to my chest, both to steady it and to prove to myself that I can actually feel it pounding beneath my skin. I want to remember this, this betrayal. I do not want him to make my heart beat like this.

He picks up after the third ring. He has caller ID. He knew it was me, and he picked up. He has figured things out. I knew this would work.

"It's Betsy," I say.

"Betsy," he says, and there is a long quiet, not filled, as I had hoped, with an apology, however halting.

"You said three weeks," I say, even though it is obvious that I should not have to remind him.

"Right," he says, like he had forgotten. Could he have forgotten all that, that quickly?

"Would you want to get a drink or something? Just talk?" There I am again, with the talking. What is so great about talking? That's what's supposed to seduce him?

There is a pause and I hear voices in the background. "This week is really bad for me," he says.

"Huh," I say.

The voices stop.

"I thought you wanted to talk again," I say, trying to make this sound like a fact, like I am only doing what he had requested.

"No, I totally do," he says, "but I have this show in a couple weeks, and we have to finish the electrical work in the gallery, and my friends are coming in from L.A. . . ."

"I get it," I say.

Silence again. I had not expected it to be this hard. The last time I saw him there was so much to say, too much to say, and I thought we would just pick up where we had left off. But why would he? Want to pick up there? Unless he loved me?

All I can think is how fast this is going, how fast this is disappearing, how whatever length of rope I had imagined was exactly that, an imagination, and I recognize that these last three weeks have been nothing but a lie, but one I needed to believe, and I do not regret telling it to myself. "How's Eva?" I say. I don't think it matters much, what I say now.

"She won't talk to me anymore," he says with regret in his voice, and that is just so right, that is just so perfect. There is a lesson to be learned here.

I hear the voices again. I know them. He is watching *South Park,* the episode with the chicken fucker.

"I like that one," I say.

"Me, too," he says.

I can hear Cartman complaining about hippies.

"I should probably go," he says.

"Me, too," I say, and that's it.

I have done ten loads of laundry, I have learned to bake muffins, I have watched hours and hours of Court TV, but I have not slept the night through for the last twenty-one days. I do not know how you can sleep, not knowing if the person you love, the person you think about endlessly, the person you want, so literally, more than anything else you have ever experienced—not knowing if that lost person will find a way to return to you, or not. Now I do, and now I can sleep.

I pack in the morning, and then I wait for Zoe to come home. "Hello!" she says, apparently delighted to see me sitting on her sofa watching the *Today* show. "How are you?" She pushes a piece of my hair out of my eyes. "I hope you had a nice night," she says, stroking my arm.

Even though this encounter is fueled more by drugs than by her feelings for me, it makes me sad, and lonely, and mortal, to think that Zoe and I might have been friends, if I had only worked a little harder at it, if I had made an effort. If I had not spent all my time obsessed with Ryan, if I had taken a wider worldview, one not limited to the expanse of his shoulders. Maybe I am just emptily eulogizing her to myself, honoring something that never existed, but I don't think so, and it makes me want to leave as quick as I can. To cut my losses. "I have to go," I say, pointing to a garbage bag full of clothes on the floor. "I can't stay here anymore."

"I knew it," she says. "I hear you crying all the time."

"It's been," I say, "a difficult time."

"Don't go yet," she says. "And don't worry about the rent. I'll give you your security now. What was it?"

Part of me wants to say "seven hundred and fifty dollars," but that is a lie. "Nothing," I say. "You didn't ask me for one."

"But I have to give you something. Your mail!" she yells, running into her bedroom, and returning with a stack of envelopes, some of which bear postmarks from March.

"Thanks," I say. There are several months of American Express bills. One includes a platinum Optima card with a ten-thousand-dollar limit. "I don't know what is going on," I say.

"And take this," she says, digging into her clutch for something, and then closing my fingers into a fist around it.

I look: It's a plastic baggie full of blue pills, red pills, and some straws.

"I don't know what to say," I say.

"Just be well," she says. She smiles, displacing silver glitter from the creases of her eyes to the tops of her cheeks, and hugs me, genuinely, across my shoulders. I wish again that I had found a way to be her friend.

"I'll miss you," we say simultaneously, and although I cannot speak for her, I think we are both surprised to discover that we mean it.

TEN

There is only one place to go for regrouping, particularly when you have neither a job nor, any longer, an apartment, and that is home.

"Do you realize," Bridget says over the phone, "that you have only three weeks to prepare for my wedding?"

Another three weeks. I need a friendlier unit of time. "More than you know," I say.

"Did you buy your tickets yet? Do you have a passport? It's going to cost like three thousand dollars for you and the boyfriend."

"It's cool. It's covered," I say, trying to sound breezy and confident and effortlessly international, like an assassin.

"You know," she says, "you have to go to the wedding. And it's in another country. So to go to it, you need to buy plane tickets."

"I think people who are getting married should just add up the travel and the present and the new outfit and send invoices instead of invitations."

"That's almost as funny," Bridget says, "as your joke about the wedding invitations being like bills in your mailbox."

"You know my routine," I say. "I didn't think you'd remember."

The girl sitting across the aisle from me is pressed against her window, taking a photo of the Statue of Liberty's back.

"Where are you?" Bridget says suspiciously, because she knows I am doing something she would not approve of.

"I'm going home for a bit," I say.

"Why? What's going on? Why are you going home on a Monday afternoon?"

"Research," I say.

She doesn't even bother to accuse me of lying. "Are you sick? Are your parents home?"

"No, and no," I say.

"Are you sure?"

"I am."

"And you're going to buy your tickets? Tonight?"

"Okay," I say. There is a pause, as if she is waiting for me to explain myself. "Did you ever think about how unfair it is that we get the Statue of Liberty's back? Don't we need liberty just as much as everyone else?"

"Not as much as the immigrants, in the boats," she says, "coming into the harbor."

"That was then," I say happily, because I have successfully changed the topic. "You think they could at least turn her to face the airport."

"That," Bridget says, "would be the best prank of all time. Do you think we could do that?"

"Do you have access to an underwater demolition team?"

"Not yet," Bridget says. "But I'll work on it."

I have nothing to do at my parents' house but watch *Forensic Files* and *Oprah*. My friends leave messages I do not return, and I sit in our living room, the television muted, staring at the screen and waiting for something to happen.

On Wednesday, I drive over to the only travel agent in town, the official transportation coordinator for the Callahan–Templeton nuptials, and somehow I am not surprised to see my favorite teacher from high school sitting behind a desk.

"Mr. K.!" I say.

"Betsy! What are you doing here?"

"What are you doing here? Aren't you teaching anymore?"

"It's intersession," he says. "It's my wife's family's business. I'm just helping out for the day. What are you down here for? Working on a big exposé of underage gambling rings?"

Mr. K. was the advisor on the high school newspaper when I was the editor-in-chief, my first and last position of editorial authority. I am glad to see him: He does not know the person I have become, sad and lonely, and because of that, I do not have to be her. As that thought occurs to me, it stops me for a second, and I pinch myself so that I will remember it. "Do you remember my friend Bridget Callahan? She's getting married. You guys are handling all the travel stuff."

He points me to a chair. "Some island, right? You guys sure are doing it big."

I think about trotting out my invitation/invoice joke again, and decide against it. "Her boyfriend's a doctor something or other," I say.

"I hope he's paying for your ticket," he says, and I laugh. I loved Mr. K. He opens a folder and pulls out a list of names. "You're buying two tickets? Married?" he says, glancing at my left hand.

"Boyfriend," I say.

"That'll be $1,365.50 each. Or . . . let's see, $2,713.30."

I want to throw up. I am buying a plane ticket for a phantom. "Here you go," I say, pulling out my new credit card.

"You kids today," he says. "What's his name?"

I don't know why I hadn't expected to be asked this, but I hadn't. "Casey Murphy," I say. I fill out some paperwork, writing in Tommy's cell phone number for Casey's.

"Did you keep up the writing?" he says as I pull on my jacket.

"I'm an editor at a women's Web site in the city," I say. "That's how I met my boyfriend. I just came home for the weekend."

"It's Wednesday," he says, but casually, carelessly, like he is accustomed to a former student dropping three thousand dollars on plane tickets for her and her ghost and then telling even more lies about her nonexistent career. "Why don't you come into class and talk about your job? The kids would love to hear about it, I bet."

"Sure," I say, not wanting to disappoint Mr. K. "I would be delighted."

Immediately after I leave Mr. K. with my tickets, my cell phone rings, and an unfamiliar 212 number shows on the caller ID display. I am not going to pick it up until it occurs to me that perhaps it is a new number for Couture, and Ryan has changed his mind. I am not above thinking this. "Hello?" I say, trying to sound calm, cool, aloof—things I have never actually been.

"Betsy?"

It is not Ryan. But it is someone from Couture, and although I am not displeased to hear Julia's voice, my stomach twists, just knowing that these people exist, that Julia's life goes on, which means that Ryan's life goes on without me in a way that my life has not gone on without him. "Hi, Julia," I say. "What's up?"

I do not tell Julia where I am: that is the miracle of cell phones. I do not say that I am waiting in New Jersey to figure out a way to stop wanting Ryan back, and that I spend all my time watching Court TV.

Julia has called to offer me a job. In New York City. "I can't pay you much," she says, "and you wouldn't be on the books until the first of March. But until then you could freelance a few pieces and make some money."

"Like what?" I say. "Not, like, food quizzes, right?"

"Seriously," Julia says. "I will never edit another food quiz in my life. You'd like it—art and music and movies."

"That sounds good," I say.

"And the first assignment—that would be my present to you, especially after those bitches killed your Topeka story," she says. "Since you wouldn't be getting any health insurance."

"What could be better than health insurance?"

"You like that actor, right, Jack Cole?"

Julia says this so confidently that I am sure she thinks I would prefer Jack Cole to health insurance, which is nearly, but not completely, correct. "Sure," I say.

"We're doing a feature on him," she says. "If you want to do it, it's yours."

"Seriously?"

"The junket's next Wednesday, and you'd have forty-five minutes with him. We could give you five hundred dollars for a thousand words. Could you do it, do you think?"

Five hundred dollars is half what Couture would pay for a food quiz. "The piece or the job?"

"Both," she says.

I am sure there are all sorts of questions I should be asking. "How much does it pay?"

Julia names a figure approximately 65 percent of my salary at Couture.

"Can I . . . ," I say. It occurs to me that one way of dealing with past mistakes is to stop adding to them. "Can I take the piece and think about the job?"

"That's what I assumed you'd say," Julia says, but I do not know whether this assumption is based on her trust in my sturdy, thorough, deliberative mind, or on her belief in my inability to recognize a lifeline when I see it.

It occurs to me that I could replace Ryan with Jack Cole, and no matter how much I want to wring this thought from my head, it stays there, like a sickness, like an infection.

After a week of haphazard trips to the mall and the Borders and the QuikChek, Monday afternoon marks my first official appointment since I returned home: my scheduled presentation to Mr. K.'s journalism class.

"Betsy," he says, greeting me in the lobby of my old high school, a pass on a lanyard hanging around his neck.

"Hey, Mr. K.," I say. "What's up with the metal detectors?"

"All the schools down here have them now," he says. "Knives and things. And what are you now, twenty-four? You can call me Richard."

I have no intention of calling him Richard. "I don't think kids brought knives to school when I was here," I say.

"Oh, sure they did," Mr. K. says. "We just didn't know about them."

He leads me down familiar halls to his classroom, the same one where I once heard a presentation by a sports reporter for the local community college paper, and there they are, two dozen interchangeable faces.

"Hello," I say.

Nothing.

I give them the two-minute version of my career, which is ninety seconds longer than it deserves.

Nothing.

"I'm sure someone has a question for Betsy," Mr. K. says.

"How do you get a job?" one of the boys says.

"Knowing the right people," I say confidently. "Networking."

"And how do you get to know the right people?" he asks.

"Parties," I say, equally confidently.

"So how do you get to go to parties?"

"Your friends will get invited, and then they'll invite you," I say. Honestly, I give up. "Just make sure you go to college where there are lots and lots of rich kids. They don't have to work for their money, and they always know people who can give you jobs, at least in something stupid like fashion."

"But what about politics or something?" says a small girl with a huge head of curly hair. "Or, like, being a war correspondent?"

"That I wouldn't know about," I say. "I'm sure they have their own parties."

Silence.

Now I have a question for them. "Would you guys rather stay in Margate or interview movie stars?"

"Movie stars," a few of them say, which, in this case, is sufficient for a consensus.

"I'm going to meet Jack Cole this week," I say.

The usual silence, but then: "No way," one of them says.

"Way," I say.

"They really perked up when you told them about interviewing that actor," Mr. K. says, walking me back to the parking lot as his students work on their class Web site.

"I would, I guess, if I were sixteen," I say. Or twenty-four. "Tough room."

"Tough room," he says.

What do I do now? I want to say, but of course I don't: I hand him my own lanyard, with my guess pass attached, and I walk back to my mother's car. He is not Mr. K. anymore, but Richard. I am an adult now, and on my own.

I am still thinking about this at ShopRite, and I search the produce aisle for adult purchases. Star fruit. Mangoes. Complicated, unfamiliar vegetables, like kale. These all go into my basket. I am wondering exactly how I will prepare them when I backpedal, seeing my last opportunity to pick up a Kit Kat, and in the process hit the woman behind me with my basket. "Ow," she says.

I look up, fluttery. "Sorry, sorry, sorry," I say. But I know this woman. "Ms. O'Connors," I say. "Sorry—sorry about that. I just wanted some chocolate."

"It's okay," she says, and we both place our purchases on the conveyor belt, Kit Kat included. She looks pretty and delicate and thin. "Betsy Nilssen, right? I saw you at Thanksgiving."

"Yeah, that's right," I say. "I love T.G.I. Friday's."

"You were with Bridget Callahan, right?"

"I'm just home for a few weeks before Bridget's wedding," I say.

"Weddings," she says. "Let me tell you, Betsy. They're not all they're cracked up to be."

The man ahead of me signs his credit card receipt, and I watch my purchases go up the belt, but I try to hang back, wanting to hear what she is going to say. "Really? You don't think so?"

The cashier rings up the fruit and vegetables I am never going to eat. "I was thinking about getting married, you know," she says. No shit. "But then I decided not to. It was like I was in a fairy tale, and you know what? Fairy tales aren't real."

I don't know if she is offering this as a warning or a lesson or a lie. "Okay," I say.

"I mean, wouldn't you rather be free?"

"I hadn't thought of it that way," I say, paying for my groceries. "I guess I shouldn't tell Bridget that, should I?"

"Of course you should," she says. "You should tell her as many times as possible."

"Will do," I say, grabbing my bags. She is coming apart, the way I was with Ryan, but in a different way. I know this verbal spew, this inability to keep anything to yourself, this innocence of barriers. But as much as she seems to be disintegrating, she also seems to be reassembling herself in an entirely new form. Watching someone change is an unsettling thing, especially when you see them at a distance, a distance that allows for a sweeping vantage: They make you wonder how they did it, who told them it was okay to do so, who you could become if you only had the guts.

Wednesday arrives more quickly than I expect it to, and with that I am on a bus back to New York, in the same shoes and expensive denim I wore to the Couture Christmas party. I feel like I am dressed in another woman's clothes, and the distance between us is a curious, unexpected thing.

The junket is being held at the St. Regis Hotel in Midtown, and I walk there from Penn Station. I am greeted in the lobby by Anne, my favorite contact at the PR firm handling his movie. "Jack's just going to be five minutes," she says. "He's finishing up with the guy before you. Isn't he dreamy? So dreamy. We played backgammon for forty minutes waiting for the guy from *Newsweek*."

"I'm sure he is," I say tightly, partly because I am trying to project a veil of professional, critical distance and partly because I am extremely jealous that she got to play backgammon with my movie boyfriend.

"You know he doesn't like to be interviewed very much, right? He's only doing these because he really loves the movie."

"Okay," I say.

"Are you still at Couture?" she says. "We had someone from Couture in this morning. I mean, I know you're not writing this for them, but are you still on staff there?"

"They were planning a piece on this when I left," I say. "Who's the writer?"

"Eva . . . Hausenfeffer?"

I like someone not knowing her name. I like knowing that her power is finite. "Eva Pfenning," I say. "She was my boss there."

"She's so pretty," Anne says, and I want to throw up.

"I followed my other editor there, Julia Newberry, to *Glossy*."

"Glossy," she says. "That is such an amazing magazine."

"You think?" I say. I could have said *Soldier of Fortune* and she would have found something to compliment: She is a professional well-wisher. She is my age, in a pale yellow skirt and white blouse and silver bangles around her wrist. I recognize the blouse, from Ralph Lauren's new spring collection. She looks like an adult, a successful one. For the second time in two minutes I am envious of her.

She tilts her head toward the ceiling, and I follow her gaze, looking for whatever chandelier anomaly is about to be the subject of our chitchat. But then I realize she is pressing an earpiece to her head. "He's ready for you," she says.

Jack Cole is taller than I expected: When he answers the door, I have to look up at him. He is taller than Ryan, even, and I feel my neck relax when he sits down, eye-level, on his bed. "Do you want something to drink?" he says, pointing to the minibar. "Jack Daniel's? I have like thirty little bottles of those airplane whiskeys."

What am I doing shaking my head? How insecure do I need to be, to assume that this is a rhetorical question? *Just hold on one fucking minute here,* I hear myself say. *If you're so fucking annoyed with yourself, stop being yourself. Jesus Christ.* "Actually, I changed my mind," I say. "Let's have it."

"Shakes her head, takes the drink," he says. "It's a good beginning." I expect glasses to materialize, but they don't; he just hands me one of his little bottles, unopened, and clinks it. "Here's to the power of the press," he says.

"Oh my God," I say. "You've been doing this all afternoon."

"Makes the interviews go faster," he says. "If you were on this end of the bullshit, you'd understand." He closes his eyes. "It's cool, though. Everybody's just doing their job." He lies back against the pillows and picks up a remote control. "This is my favorite song in the whole world," he says, turning up the volume. It is a clanging, industrial noise. "Tom Waits," he says.

"I like Tom Waits," I say. "I'm from New Jersey."

He makes no sign of understanding the connection, but he turns the volume back down. "Do you want to hear the song from the beginning?"

"Do you want to talk about the movie?" I say. I can feel the whiskey beginning to take effect, that wispy thing that only barely precedes the headache I am about to have. But for the moment, it is nice. I put my bag on the floor and hit the RECORD button on my tape recorder.

"Do you?"

"I don't know," I say. "Of course. That's why I'm here. But up to you, I suppose."

"How about I ask myself the questions? 'What drew you to the script? What was it like working with this director? How do you prepare to play this character?' "

There is little use pretending that I hadn't intended asking him these. "I would also like to know if you would ever like to own a castle."

"Like in *Dragon Keeper,*" he says, nodding his head. "I hated that fucking movie. That's off the record. They were nice guys, but stupid."

"Why don't you tell me your favorite story from childhood?" A plan is taking shape in my head. He can be my proxy. He has to answer all my questions, and he must at least pretend to answer them fully. "Something involving a pet."

"I once gave a cat mouth-to-mouth resuscitation," he says. "Our cat fell into a pool, and I dove in and pulled him out."

"Did he live?"

"Course he did," he says. "I wouldn't brag about it otherwise."

"Okay," I say. "I'm going to ask you a bunch more questions, and I want you to lie to every single one." This is my experiment, and it is to destroy the power of words—or not to destroy them, but a lesson in mistrusting them. I ask him all the things I didn't ask Ryan, because the truth would have terrified me; I ask him whom he loves, if he could ever be faithful, if he finds me attractive. He tells me about the prostitute he visits in Los Angeles, a one-armed gimp trained in the Kama Sutra; he tells me about the groupies he serviced the summer he spent as an Aerosmith roadie. He tells me about working in a carnival, and how he shared his razors with the bearded lady. "You should write kids' stories," I say, meaning it, switching off the tape recorder. I have all I need. Better these conscious lies than the others.

"What?" he says. "We're done?"

"Is there anything else you want to tell the readers of *Glossy*?"

"You don't like my stories?"

"No," I say. "They're really good. But this is my last assignment ever. I don't think I need to worry about it so much, you know?"

"It's not a bad job, what you do," he says. "It's a great job. There are some great people who do your job."

"I know," I say. "I'm just not one of them."

"My grandfather was a coal miner in Pennsylvania," he says. "I think that's the first true thing I said. Except about *Dragon Keeper.* This is all off the record. It sounds like a lie I made up, to sound more blue-collar. That's work. What we do isn't work."

"I know," I say. "But there's a big world out there."

"Fair enough," he says. "You have something already lined up? What are you going to do now?"

"Paint," I say, lying. "Waitress," I say, lying. "I'm not sure," I say.

We sit quietly for a moment, until I remember that I am in charge of this social occasion. "I have ten minutes left," I say, "but I'm going to give you some quiet time to yourself. That would be nice, right?" There is, remarkably, no part of me hoping he rejects my offer.

"It would be," he says.

"Well, okay, then," I say. I gather my things and open the door to the hallway.

"Hold on," he says, sitting up on his knees, fumbling with the remote control. Suddenly the room is filled with Tom Waits singing "Jersey Girl." "Think of it as your exit music," he says.

"If there is one thing I have always wanted," I say, "it is a processional."

I take one measured step, and then I am standing in the entryway. I turn around, and smile back at him, and then I close the door behind me.

The next morning, I call my sister on my way to Baltimore, and tell her I am coming down for a haircut.

"Do as you will," I say, when I am seated in her chair.

"Are you sure? Is it Christmas? Is it my birthday?"

"I'm going to close my eyes," I say, "and when I open them, I want to be a different person."

"You got it, dude," she says. I keep my eyes closed, but I can feel the hair snipped from the bottom: inches of it, falling to the floor. I do not understand the biology of hair, exactly, but I do know there is something in hair that is like a tree trunk's interior circles, the way they record seasons of drought and flood. If there is anything of Ryan in my hair, I want it gone, and my sister, unknowingly, obliges.

I open my eyes to bangs. It is not too short. She did her job well. "Audrey Hepburn-y," my sister says. "But if you don't blow out the bangs every morning, I'll kill you."

Three days later, I put Casey's ticket to Bali in an envelope with a note that reads: "This is yours. It was free. I am not in love with you. Please have a nice time if you would like to go to this private island in the South Pacific." I e-mail my story to Julia: "Lies Jack Told Me." It is twelve hundred words of total bullshit, but I do not care, because I feel like that particular well is completely dry. "I'm sorry," I write at the bottom, as a postscript. "I was drunk." However disorienting it is to fail at something, to do poorly at something, it is equally liberating: For so long I have wanted to succeed at this, but now, it is difficult to muster the energy to guess what it is that someone else wants. I feel as though I have used all of that up, and now there is only one path ahead of me, one foot in front of the other, and wherever they lead, it is not to where I expected.

My story finished, my career, such as it ever was, finished, I pack my bag and call a car service that will drive me all the way to LaGuardia for the flight that will take me to Tokyo, and then to Singapore, and then somewhere else. I have packed only three T-shirts and a sweater and the rehearsal dinner dress and my Vera Wang confection and three pairs of jeans. If nothing else, I have learned how to pack economically.

It is a gray, unhappy day, a day for leaving somewhere, not arriving, and I am glad to be going. At the Holland Tunnel approach, the driver, Gus, turns to me and removes his sunglasses. "You know, we don't get a lot of pickups for LaGuardia, mostly Philly and A.C. You think you could give me some guidance here?"

"Actually," I say, "I know a special shortcut."

We cross Canal Street and the Manhattan Bridge. I do not even know what I am looking for, at this late date, at this late hour. I direct Gus to within a few blocks of Ryan's apartment, which I only know from the one night I spent outside it, waiting for him to come home and recognize that I was his one, true thing.

And then I see him, for the first time in a month and a half, coming out the subway stop. The hood of his parka is unzipped, and I see him clearly, though he cannot see me behind the dark glass of this borrowed limousine. We are both at a red light, waiting to cross, and I take him in, tucking his hair behind an ear, readjusting a mitten. I did not expect to see him, but I had hoped he would have changed, would have been in some way unrecognizable, but he is still the same person that I wanted. I want to finish that thought, to think, "the same person that I wanted and the same person I still want," present tense, but somehow this is no longer true. The person I want belongs to a time and a place that I can no longer access, and that is the person who will keep haunting me, who is a ghost to me. The person standing ten feet away from me is no one I know, no one I love, and no one I want.

"Are we done with the field trip?" Gus says.

It occurs to me that as inaccessible as my old Ryan is to me, in the present, the Betsy I am now, at this moment—sad and empty and unmoored—is rooted to this moment as well. I will not be her forever. Whatever happens, I am going to be someone else—someone not unrelated, but not identical, either. How will I view myself, this Betsy, in a month, three months, a year? Maybe I will look back on myself, at this moment, and say: *Man, she was pathetic.* Or: *Boy, do I feel sorry for her.* More charitably: *If only she knew that from here on in, it's nothing but good times and birthday cakes.* Unhappily: *If only she knew that was as good as it would get.* I shake my head to rid myself of the last thought. This is simultaneously the most depressing and the most reassuring thought I have had in ages: It never ends, as long as we live. Our future self will likely look back at our present self, and weep.

However: We must focus on the good times and birthday cakes.

"We ready to go?" Gus asks again.

"I think yes," I say.

"Personally, I've enjoyed it," he says. "A change of pace is good for the heart."

The light changes to green, and we are gone.

Eleven

Bridget and her brother Owen, one of the triplets, meet me at the airport. I am part of the advance reconnaissance team. I am on this team because I am unemployed and have nowhere else to be, but thinking of myself as some sort of bridal delta force operative is pleasantly, and sufficiently, distracting from the business at hand. From the lack of business at hand. Everyone else will arrive over the next days. Even the groom, busy saving the lives of those unfortunate enough to require his services, will not be here until a couple days before the wedding. Until then, it is just Bridget and her family and me, and it is easy to pretend that this is a summer vacation with the Callahans like all the ones that came before it, except on a private island built with the profits of evil.

"How was your flight?" Owen asks, behind the wheel of his rented Jeep.

"I kept dreaming that the world was over, and everyone was dead except for us, and I kept talking about how no one understood that for the rest of time, no one would ever be able to make Diet Coke again."

"You're retarded," Bridget says, kicking the back of my seat. "Surely there would be more important things to worry about, like fried chicken."

"What's so hard about chicken?" I say, turning around.

"There are still plenty of chickens around. That's nothing compared to Diet Coke."

"Banana splits," she says.

I turn around to face her, so she can see me roll my eyes. "We could still make banana splits," I say. "The power was still on, so there was electricity to keep the ice cream cold."

"But who's going to keep making the electricity?'

"I don't know," I say. "The sun. I'm sure we'd find solar energy somewhere. Or, if we really had to, we could make ice cream in one of those buckets with the turn-y things."

"The crank?"

"Yes," I say. "The crank. Like in Girl Scouts. And then we'd just eat it before it melted."

"But where's the ice coming from?"

"From the *sky,*" I say, pedantically. "There would still be winter and things. And then solar power. So there would be absolutely no problem keeping the ice cream cold."

"Yes," Bridget says, contemplatively, staring out the window at the ocean. She wraps her arms around the headrest and looks directly at me, nose two inches away from mine. "But who will make the bananas?"

"You two are freaks," Owen says.

Owen drives up a dirt road to a hut on top of a hill, where Mrs. Callahan, Jake, and Ben are playing gin rummy. I wish, once more, that I had a brother, if only to provide me with a teammate at events like these. And to beat up people at my command. Once, when we were younger, Bridget and I had decided that we could have simply married each other's brothers if only my mother had done us the service of producing one for Bridget, and we badgered her about it ("Why can't *I* have a brother? *Why* can't I have a brother? Why can't I have a *brother*?") until she said that maybe there had been a son: Maybe his name was Christopher, and maybe he had black hair and green eyes and a heart-shaped scar on his wrist. "And maybe I loved him very, very much," my mother said, and then stomped off toward the garage. Bridget and I were sure that we had goaded my mother into sharing some horrible, twisted family secret, something involving a baby, forgotten on a bus, maybe, or left on a convent step. I am fairly sure now that she went into the laundry room, poured herself a half glass of wine and had a nice long laugh about it. I always thought it was quite selfish of Bridget, to demand a trade instead of simply providing a gift, for me, in the form of one of her brothers.

"How was your flight?" Ben asks me.

Ben would always have been my choice in the brother-swap, except for the fact that he is kind to his mother and to Bridget and not to another female in this world, including the lacrosse team manager he fucked in front of a video camera before literally broadcasting the results to most of our high school. The fact that I am intellectually over him, or that he is a video pornographer, has nothing to do with the fact that whenever I am around him I get a tiny bit sick to my stomach.

I do not need to explain to Ben about the Diet Coke and the banana splits. "Turbulent," I say.

"That's too bad, sweetheart," Mrs. Callahan says, licking her thumb and rubbing it on my chin, presumably removing a spot of toothpaste or jam I had yet to notice. I remember once reading about a porn star—something about how she would perform blow jobs the way others would shake hands: as an element of making introductions. Somehow it made me think of Mrs. Callahan, however incongruous a comparison that was. There is no stopping her from laying her hands on some part of your body, arranging an errant curl or, in my case, removing food from my face.

"Oh, I love turbulence." I say this because it is true, but also because it distracts Mrs. Callahan from studying my body for other flaws. This is not the first time I have felt so dissected, and found so inadequate, by her, and I have always wondered if her exacting eye did her daughter good, or bad: Bridget will not leave her apartment without mascara and eyeliner and the right sort of shoes. Did I win? Because I will go to the supermarket in running shorts and a sweatshirt with holes in the seams?

"You do not," Bridget says. "Nobody does."

"Well, I love roller coasters, right? And turbulence is like that. The only reason people get scared is because they think they're going to die. But the thing is, if the plane's going to crash, it's going to crash. It's probably not, and even if it is, it's not like you can do anything about it. So you might as well enjoy it."

"And this from the person who thought the world was about to end like six weeks ago," Bridget says.

I do not want to discuss this with Jake and Owen and Ben, so I am glad when Ben has another nothing question to ask me. I am enjoying the nothingness, dinner-party nature of his questions. "What are you doing now?"

"Nothing," I say. "I quit my stupid job."

"What are you talking about? Is that what that was about, going off to Margate?" She turns to her brother. "Right after the wedding's over, she's going to go back to New York and get a real job, like a real adult."

"Maybe I don't want a real job," I say to Bridget. "Maybe real jobs are for suckers."

"Amen to that," Jake says.

"You're an investment banker," I say to Jake.

"Still sucks," he says, and returns to arranging the playing cards into a houselike structure.

Mrs. Callahan is uninterested in the bickering. "I'm so happy you're here, my sweet Betsy," she says. "Doesn't Bridget look beautiful?"

"I guess so," I say as Mrs. Callahan pulls a face, the same face she pulls whenever I respond to this question in this way, which I do whenever she asks it, which is frequently. "I mean, sort of."

"Average, I'd say," Jake says.

"Yeah, just okay," Ben says, pulling her ponytail.

Bridget, after blowing down Jake's house of cards: "Will you all just shut up?"

This is what I do not want to lose: my place at the Callahan family table. I know that those places are hardly fixed: I had never imagined the Callahan family table without Mr. Callahan at its head until I saw it, after he left, Mrs. Callahan still sitting in her regular seat, to the side. I had walked in with Ben, and he had seen the table, and his mother, and the empty seat at the head of the table. He'd sat there, when neither of his brothers, nor Bridget, for that matter, had thought to do so. This was the height of my infatuation with Ben. I am not sure Ryan ever did anything more to convince me to love him—if love, anyway, was what it was, rather than a sort of love-based obsession. My first thought is: *Ryan never made me do anything to dislike him, like Ben and that videotape,* but then, I think: *fucking your boss*. I was in love with him after that.

"Bridget does look beautiful," her mother sniffles, and this time none of us have the inclination to disagree with her.

Owen stays behind with his brothers and mother, so Bridget and I take the Jeep back to the Callahan family resort compound, a collection of thatched huts hovering above a lagoon.

Bougainvillea sprouts over the balconies. "Who's paying for this?"

"My father owes us for the rest of his life," Bridget says, and she leads me to the hut farthest from the fountain in the center of the complex. "This," she says, "is the bridesmaids' suite."

"And when are they getting here?"

"Not until Thursday," she says. "It's Sunday. You have four days until they get here."

"I can't wait," I say. "Then we can start sharing important life lessons, like whether or not you can get HIV from a blow job."

"They wouldn't care about that," Bridget says, but I am not sure if she means they would not care because they already know the answer, or because they're not giving out random blow jobs. "They will arrive and do exactly as I say, which is how any bride should be treated. Not that I get that from you."

"You'll be lucky if you get a wedding present from me," I say, laughing, although this is probably true.

Bridget sits on the hammock, kicking the ground so it sways back and forth. "Did you remember the Frank Sinatra CD?"

"Of course," I say. Fuck. "What do you take me for?"

"Unemployed and irresponsible," she says.

"You know, Bridget, you really are a hater."

"Are you going to get something else?"

"I have an offer from this magazine called *Glossy*," I say.

"Well, you're going to take it, right?"

"I think they're going to retract it." I explain about the American Express card. "I don't think I have to worry about things for a little while."

"You mean, as long as you can pay for things with an American Express card," she says.

"Exactly."

"So what the fuck are you going to do when they only take Visa?"

"Oh," I say. "I just won't stay at that hotel."

"You're insane."

"I want to see things," I say. "I want to see the world."

"Is that an occupation?"

"Explorer," I say. "You know, Bridget, just because you're ready to tie yourself down for the rest of your life doesn't mean the rest of us are."

I did not intend for that to sound like an insult: I meant it as an excuse, a way of saying, *I have nothing, and you have everything, so let me at least enjoy my nothing.* I did not think for a second that it sounded like bragging, or a challenge, but judging by the way Bridget hops off the hammock and marches back to her hut, I probably should have.

Bridget returns later to tell me to unpack, which I do not. Instead, I shove my backpack beneath the teak frame of my bed and fall asleep with a 1997 copy of *Scientific American,* which I found in the bedside table, covering my face. When I wake, it is 11:30 A.M. in New York City and 12:30 A.M. here.

"Good," says Bridget, who has materialized behind the mosquito-net door out of nowhere. "You're awake."

"How did you know I was awake? I've been asleep for nine hours."

"Magic," she says.

I remain on my bed.

"You turned the light on. Duh," she says. "I'm bored. Let's go out."

"Go out where?" I say, stepping on to the porch, looking

from dark hut to dark hut, from the poolside cabana to the empty sauna. "Where are we going?"

"Just to the bar," she says.

"I don't want to go to the bar," I say. "I want to sleep some more."

"Honestly," she says. "Are you a thousand years old?"

She turns to go down the steps and the dynamic of our relationship being what it inevitably, indelibly is, I follow.

"Oh my God," is the first thing I say to Bridget as we walk into the nightclub down the street from the hotel's entrance. "Oh my God," I say. We walk in beneath a sign reading NO FIREARMS, through a set of metal detectors, into a heaving mass of people who seem to be jumping up and down in unison to the music of MC Hammer. "You've got to, you've got to be kidding me." The lighting changes every few seconds from purple to lime to orange and then goes brilliantly bright, so that you have a few milliseconds to make out the features of the person you are about to sleep with. "This is the worst place in the world. I didn't think they had these places on private islands." I feel ridiculous in the Surf-a-Go-Go T-shirt I picked up in the airport, the wardrobe of choice among women seeming to be string-bikini tops and denim miniskirts.

"Did you notice that bridge we crossed? Now we're on another island. And they have this everywhere."

We keep walking, squirming our way between sweaty backs, past the bar, to a mercifully quieter space. Pools of water are illuminated from above by strands of Christmas lights hanging from the ceiling, and Bridget takes a table next to one of them.

"Why's it so much quieter in here?" I say, sitting beside her. "It's so much nicer."

"There's no dancing."

"And there's *eating*?" I say, discovering a pair of plastic menus on the table. Suddenly I don't mind this trip so much. "How much is twenty-six thousand rupiah?"

"About three dollars," she says.

"Three dollars for Australian beer-backed ribs? And we just get to sit here? I changed my mind, Bridget, this was a really good idea."

"Don't say anything about anything," Bridget says, and I have no idea what she means but assume it has something to do with how wonderfully inexpensive the ribs are. I am holding my hand up, trying to catch the attention of a waiter when I see two decidedly American-looking men walking toward us.

"They're not waiters," I say. "Who the hell are they?"

"Jace," one says. "Chris," the other says.

"Where are they from?" I am still talking to Bridget.

"Austin," they reply in unison. *Could they know Ryan?* I think, nauseated at the idea.

"They go to school," Bridget says. Unlike a minute ago, when she was absolutely impassive, she is now grinning a very small grin behind her hand, which she holds in front of her mouth.

"UT," they reply in unison.

Jace holds up the pinkie and forefinger of his right hand. "Horns up," he says.

"Indeed," I say, and sadly put down my menu.

Jace is a history major and Chris is an economics major and I want to strangle Bridget with the puka beads encircling his neck. Two hours into our evening together, they leave, at last, to inquire about the availability of the "magic mushrooms" advertised in the men's room. "How," I say to Bridget, "did you find the only two University of Texas seniors in this country?"

"What are you talking about?" Bridget says. "That's, like, the biggest university system in America. I'm sure that there are more than just these two."

"You're getting married at the end of the week," I say. I see a note on the bottom of the menu: In the time Chris and Jace have been here, the kitchen has stopped serving dinner, and I explode. "What the fuck are you doing here? This place is for people like me, desperate, lonely single people. Like me." It feels completely disingenuous, saying that, which is a triumph I will observe later. "You're an idiot. Why the fuck are you getting married?"

We sit there silently, my question hanging in the air, unanswered, like a thundercloud, until Chris and Jace return.

"Who's ready for some magic mushrooms?" Chris says, holding a paper bag high in the air.

"I'm just pretending," Bridget says as we walk back to the huts from the club. "There's nothing wrong with that. I'm sure James will have strippers at his bachelor party."

"Have you made out with them?"

"Of course not," she says. "I'm engaged."

"I think what you did was go to that bar the last two nights just hoping someone would talk to you, and you knew they would, because they always do, because either you're a terrible person and you're just bored, or you're hoping that something is going to shake you loose from this wedding."

She doesn't say anything, just walks on, kicking the sand, head down.

I have no idea what to say to her. How could I possibly know about any of this? Is this jitters? Is this something else? How would I ever know the difference between the two? For the first time, I really, truly want to be the perfect maid of honor, even as the definition of what that is is changing as we speak. "Do you want me to hire a private plane so you can escape?"

"You don't have enough money for a private plane."

"I," I say reproachfully, "have an American Express platinum card. And," I say, starting to yell again, "beggars and choosing."

"I want to go back there tomorrow," she says. "I just want to have fun."

"No way," I say. "No fucking way. Or I will kill you."

"You can do that tomorrow, too," she says.

I stay up until six in the morning reading about the new science of algae-powered batteries. I feel out of season, timeless, rootless: not in the good way, not in the sense that I am immortal, but aimless, like a planet whose sun has dimmed, and the gravitational force that once held me in orbit has abandoned me to drift through space.

I awake at 7 P.M. The Callahans—with Mr. Callahan, who has been given a sort of brief pardon, his Denver wife nowhere in sight—have visited a temple and the beach and are eating a dinner of fish and some sort of tropical fruit salsa on the gazebo between the huts and the ocean. "It's a shame you missed it, Betsy," Mr. Callahan is saying. "Did you know that the year here has only two hundred ten days in it?"

"I wonder how that works," I say, keeping an eye on Bridget, who, in a white sundress and no makeup, looks like one of the models we would use at Couture when trying to convey an appearance of sun-kissed sauciness or some other semiappropriate alliteration.

She meets my glare and shrugs. “Dad, did you tell her about what they do here on New Year’s?”

“Now this is really unbelievable,” Mr. Callahan begins. “Every New Year’s, all the traditional people turn off any electrical appliance . . .”

It goes on like this for several days: The Callahans tour various environmental, cultural, and religious places of interest, I sleep until sunset, and then I read my copy of *Scientific American* until five or six in the morning. Tracey arrives, with her headset and her checklists. “You girls are so lucky, you have no idea,” Mrs. Callahan says at one point, after refinalizing the dinner order with Tracey, who rides up our driveway on a scooter, clipboard under her arm. “Tracey’s taking care of everything.”

“Too bad that cost you two hundred and fifty grand,” Owen says, and I gasp so loudly, everyone turns to look at me.

“Oh, Betsy,” Mrs. Callahan says. “Don’t worry. You’ll have your turn.”

The problem is that every night this routine is broken by Bridget, knocking on the door of my hut. Tonight I see her walk up the steps, and I know from the sheen of her shimmery Pucci top that tonight is different. There it is, my legacy from Couture: Fashion has become a tool for prognostication, for psychological diagnosis. “Oh my God,” I say. This is all I ever say now. “What do you think we’re doing tonight?”

“You know everyone gets here tomorrow,” she says. She lies on my bed, the one beneath the ceiling fan. “It’s my last night of freedom.”

“I thought that was the bachelorette party,” I say dissolutely.

“That means this is the last night we have to each other.”

"By 'each other,' you mean . . ."

"Chris and Jace called."

"Ooh," I say. "Big surprise there." I sit on the bed opposite Bridget's, not putting on my sandals, not brushing my hair. "Why can't we just stay here and play cards?"

Of course we can't do that, so I follow Bridget down the path to the club, five paces behind her, scowling at no one. This, really, is just too much: Bridget is supposed to be the good one. Bridget has always been the good one, the honest one, the one whose every civilized breakup ended in hugs and genuine offers of friendship. She seemed neither less nor more in love with James than she had with anyone else. They just appeared to be the perfect match: matching looks, matching interests in third world nations, matching SAT scores: "They're identical!" she'd said, happily. Now that I think about it, maybe the happiest she sounded, this tiny measure of coincidence. There had never been an occasion to doubt her.

Is this, then, the price of being good?

Does it all blow up in your face?

Is there a reason I hadn't considered this earlier?

As I follow her, I feel something horrible happening, and it is that I can feel myself becoming less of her friend, more an observer. This is what I want from her, for making me believe in her fairy tales, if that's what they are: I want to know if they're true, or not. A tiny part of my head hates itself for stealing this from her, when I am sure that she needs me most—but I want more to know how this ends, and if all the crap I have bought into over the last six months is nothing but smoke and mirrors, a deft sleight-of-hand by a magician rapidly running out of tricks to perform.

Chris greets us at the door with a bottle of Cuervo in one hand and a joint in the other. He grabs Bridget's hand and pulls her down on the sofa next to him. "We've been waiting for you girls all night."

"Hello," I say to Jace, who must be delighted that he has landed Grumpy McGrump and not the prom queen.

"We're playing the game, right?" Chris says to Jace.

"What game?" I say, scowling again.

"The Question Game!"

"I love that game!" Bridget says.

I do not love that game, but I know how to play it.

"C'mon, Beth," Jace says. "Don't be a downer."

I hate Jace. "Okay, whatever," I say. My clinical interest, my evidence-gathering, seems not to be dependent, at all, on my attitude.

Chris divides the Cuervo between four plastic cups. "I'll go first," he says. "Am I too sexy for you?" he asks Bridget.

"Who's the cutest guy here?" Bridget says to me.

"I hate this game," I say.

"Drink! Drink!" Jace yells, pinching my upper arm between two fingers. "Dude, you suck at this game."

I raise the cup to my lips but keep them closed. It is my turn to restart the game.

"Just go," Bridget says, and I am not displeased when I hear the annoyance in her voice.

"What's the atomic weight of mercury?" I say to Bridget.

She frowns at me and turns to Jace. "Is your friend always so cute?'

"Dude, how hot is she?" he says to Chris.

Chris turns to Bridget. "Are you a naughty girl?"

"You're so adorable!" she squeals.

"That is not a question," I say, pounding my cup so hard against the floor that Cuervo splashes onto the cream carpet. "Party foul," Jace says, wiping it up with his sleeve in a surprisingly kind, gentle manner I imagine he uses with whatever Austin-based girlfriend he's hoping to cheat on.

"I am going to watch CNN," I say, sitting on the sofa, entirely unsure of where to take my snit. There's no room to hide in this hotel room except for the bathroom, and I'm not going in there, because I will not know how to go back into the room. And whatever interest I had in Bridget's misbehavings is disintegrating. In any case, I've had my answer since we walked through the door, and Bridget morphed, immediately, into this girl I hate, the kind of drunk nothing girl we have made fun of together. That is what I am protecting, more than anything else, more than her relationship with James: It is my vision of her I am defending when I stomp my foot and stand up. If this is selfish, I couldn't care less, because in this instance, James's interests and mine happen to be identical, and that is getting Bridget out of this room as quickly as possible.

"Bridget, we're leaving," I say, yanking her to her feet by her wrist.

"You can do what you want after all those other girls are here," I say as we walk, once more, down the dirt path from the hotel to the huts, "but until they get here, and the responsibility for you is divided between us, you are not going to do anything fucked up. Period." Bridget is not responding to any of my speech-making, and I don't care, because I at least need to know that I have said all these things: They are my acquittal, my preemptive I-told-you-so. "If you want to be a drone, if you want to be a little bee, then you can go ahead and keep doing this and be crazy"—and

I am not even sure now what I am madder at her for, making me believe in these things or refusing to relinquish them—"but—you do not have my blessing." *Oh, Jesus Christ, could I not do better than that?* "What are you doing with those stupid kids?"

She stops walking, spins around on her heels. "Don't you understand what it's like to feel like you'll never feel that way again, all excited about someone new, ever in your life? Doesn't that seem like a horrible thing to you?"

"To me, it does," I say slowly, because I do not trust myself to speak any faster. "But to you, it shouldn't."

"Don't you think this is normal?"

"Do you?"

Her shoulders slump, and she looks up at the sky. I wonder for a second if she is trying to stop herself from crying, but I think it is frustration more than sadness I hear in her voice. "How are you supposed to know?"

"I have no idea," I say. "Why aren't you asking any of your friends who are married?"

"Because they're all unhappy," she says. "But then, they're always unhappy, so I could never figure out what it was."

"Don't you think," I say, "that none of this is working, that there might be something else you can do? Some other way? Why do you want to be like Georgina?"

"It's not fair," she says. "That I have to be the first one."

Oh my God. I have been here the last six months, and no one has ever suggested that Bridget's dream wedding was anything like a burden. More like the yardstick every other accomplishment was measured against, and found superior. "You can do anything you want," I say. "You can get on a plane tomorrow and go back home. That happens every day."

"I'm going to get married," she says. "What do you think?"

"You don't have to do anything," I say. "It is a huge world and you can do anything you want in it."

"I am going to get married," she says. "You're going to go back to New York and get a normal job and a new apartment and be with your boyfriend."

"We broke up," I say. Why have I kept this from her as long as I have? What was the point of it? "He slept with my boss."

"That's horrible," she says.

"You told me so," I say, for both of us. There seems to be nothing to discuss: She has been in my head, with this, the entire time, and at this point, there is nothing she could add I haven't heard her say, in my head, already. For once, the fact that he is dwarfed by Bridget's wedding is a relief.

"Okay," she says, recovering. "You'll go back to New York and get a nice new boyfriend, and a normal job, and a new apartment—"

"Now you're trying to do it to me, just like that bitch Georgina did it to you," I say. "You're trying to make me want something you don't even want, just so you won't be the only one who fucked up."

"That is a terrible thing to say," Bridget says.

"Well, you be the judge," I say, "and tell me if you think it's true or not."

We both stand there, looking up at the stars.

"I think we should go home," Bridget says. "It's almost four. And people start getting here tomorrow."

"You're the bride," I say.

"Don't say it like that," she says.

"Like how?"

"Like a jail sentence."

"I don't think I did," I say.

"What are we going to do?" she says.

" 'We'? What is this 'we'?" I do not stop myself from saying. I am still mad at her for making me believe in something I am not sure she ever believed in herself.

"What am I going to do?"

"I don't know," I say, and I don't.

Twelve

I wake up the next morning with that feeling: the feeling that something horrible has happened, but it is impossible to say exactly what, and so I just stare at my face in the mirror, keeping it at the edges at first, because what I do know is that as soon as I do remember, it will require action of some kind, and at this moment, all I want to do is remain still, and unencumbered. But then I remember: It is Bridget, and the bridesmaids, and the way that all of this is happening, even just this minute, as I keep staring at my own reliable face, but it is too late. I know there is a calamity on the horizon. Alarms are sounding, and they cannot be ignored, so I watch myself shrug my shoulders in the mirror—the smallest of shrugs, as if to say: *I will do what I can, and beyond that, I cannot be held responsible*—and then leave behind my hut—empty, tragically, for the last time—to find Bridget.

Instead, I find my parents on my hammock, swaying slightly, awkwardly, as their feet push against the wood-plank floor in two steady but noticeably different rhythms.

"Rise and shine," my father says. "Look who's up with the early worm."

"What?" I say to my father. "That doesn't make any sense. What are you doing here?" I say to my mother, "Where did you come from?"

"Don't you like a surprise?" she says, putting her hands on either side of my face, pulling my head to her breast, so that I bow increasingly forward, at my waist, as her end of the hammock swings backwards. "Aren't you glad to see us?"

"Did you plan this? Was this the plan all along? To come to Bridget's wedding?"

"Well," she says, releasing my face, so that I am able to stand upright. "We weren't going to miss the wedding. Bridget's practically part of the family." She stands up, and over me, and runs her fingers through my hair. She is not admiring it. She is evaluating it. "What did you do to your hair?"

"Whatever, Mom," I say, pulling away. "Blame Rebecca." Two minutes: This is all it takes to forget the orphaned longing of the last five months. Maybe it is simply another way of celebrating their return, taking them for granted again, and so quickly. "How did you get the invitation on the boat?"

"She e-mailed us," my mother says. "We asked her to keep it a surprise."

"Do you have any more surprises?"

"We're selling the house and moving onto the boat," my father says.

"You're making that up," I say, although I am glad there is news like this to discuss, because it means we can concentrate on this and not on the orphaned-longing issue. "What about Boomer?"

"He's here," my mother says. "He's at the bar."

"The dog," I say, "is at the bar?"

"Not by himself," my mother says. I immediately think of our dog on a bar stool, licking a beer out of a glass. My mother shakes her head, and as she does so, I watch oversized gold hoops, hanging from her earlobes, swing back and forth. She is also wearing a Dries Van Noten sarong. And she looks weird. Younger. It is not just the tan, or the sarong. My mother looks happy. "With your sister."

I find Bridget having an animated conversation with that wretch Georgina, and another one of the bridesmaids, Martina the tax attorney, behind Bridget's hut. Bridget is pinning laundry to a line hung between two palm trees, which seems like an absurdly proletariat touch for this resort.

"Pear cut," Georgina is saying, holding Bridget's ring to the sky. "I've seen this ring a hundred times and I still can't get over how much I like the pear cut."

"But I like yours, too," Martina says, holding Georgina's hand aloft, so that it looks like the three of them are involved in some sort of backyard prayer session. I cannot figure out, in any case, why they have decided to do this, holding the rings to the sky, since it means that they are staring directly into the sun. It is like they are superheroes waiting for their powers to activate. "I told Mark I wouldn't accept anything less than two carats and I didn't care what shape it came in. How many carats is yours, Bridget? One point five?"

"My parents are here," I say to Bridget before she can respond. "And I'm not entirely positive, but I think my sister is, too. And Boomer!"

"I know," she says, dropping her hand to her side, breaking the chain. "Everyone's here. Georgina and Martina are here."

I don't look at them. Ugh: them. "What am I supposed to do with my family? Did you hear the part about Boomer being here?"

"I saw him. You should really teach him to heel or sit or stay or any of those basic commands. He slobbered all over my

T-shirt. Just think," she says, touching Georgina's arm. "It could have been the dress."

She is doing this for my benefit, but Martina speaks before I can. "Is that your dog?" she says. "He was practically assaulting Bridget."

"He is a very special guest of the wedding," Bridget says, making it sound like perhaps Martina is not. I knew Bridget would not betray Boomer. "He just needs to have his jaw wired shut."

"Have you seen my sister?" I say.

"By the bar, I think," Bridget says. "With the dog."

"Show me your ring again," Martina says, making it very easy for me to leave.

"Holy shit, dude," my sister says. "You look like crap. Do you know what time it is?"

It is not just my sister sitting beneath a cluster of palm trees in front of the pool, nor just my sister and Boomer, but Rebecca, Stevie, Boomer, and Stevie's guitar, which is being employed in an impromptu reworking of "Hotel California." *"Welcome to the Hotel Private Island,"* Stevie sings. *"Such a lively flight, such a starry night."*

"My boyfriend," Rebecca says. "He's a genius."

"Welcome to my girlfriend Rebecca," Stevie sings back. *"Such a lovely mass, such a pain in my ass."* He waggles the pin pierced through his lower lip at her.

"I know," Rebecca says, "you can do better than that."

Stevie picks up the guitar to try once more, but I stomp my foot, which is, horribly, becoming a habit. An effective habit, however, as they stop moving. "What are you all doing here?"

"It's a reunion," Rebecca says. "Didn't you hear? Mom and

Daddy set the whole thing up. They paid for all of our tickets. Did they tell you that they're selling our house? They're going completely around the bend. But I thought they'd be all poor and homeless by now. I thought somebody was going to put a pound of opium into Mommy's Channel Thirteen tote bag, and we were going to have to break her out of a women's prison in Bangkok."

I look at our dog, who is passed out on a lounge chair, tongue flapping slightly. "But how did you get Boomer here?"

"Apparently Daddy's about to do business with the immigration secretary's son-in-law or something," she says. "Boomer got through customs before we did."

I put my head against Boomer's chest and listen to his heartbeat. "I can't tell you how happy I am that he's here."

"I told Bridget he should carry the ring down the aisle in a bandanna, but she didn't like the idea," Rebecca says.

"Now that would be a good wedding. You could have a good wedding here," Stevie says thoughtfully, deliberately. "But you would have to have certain things."

"Like Boomer as a ring bearer," Rebecca says.

"And a mango-eating contest."

"And people who hide the presents in the rambutan trees," Rebecca says. "Bridget's dad told us about them when we got here. They're kind of like coconut trees."

"He's a real expert," I say. "Are you coming to the bachelorette party tomorrow night?"

"No fucking way," she says. "Are you kidding? A bunch of girls being girls?"

"I didn't think so," I say.

"Let's take Boomer down to the beach and make him chase sticks."

Not once did I ever consider that at this moment, in this place, I would even consider this thought, but I am piercingly happy my family is here.

The bridesmaids' hut has been overrun with bridesmaids. While Rebecca and Stevie spread sleeping bags over the deck of our parents' boat and built a pit in the sand for a campfire, I am stuck in the thick of them, sitting on the floor beside my bed, below their line of sight, reading my magazine. It is truly a sorority, a sisterhood: They are sharing both the material and nonmaterial, cheerful appraisals of too-tight dresses I am sure are motivated by the appraiser's interest in seeing the appraised humiliated in public. Also: hair dryers, ionic and travel-sized; pins, bobby and safety. Someone, someone who has been determinedly nursing a level of drunkenness achieved, and maintained, since about ten minutes after boarding her plane in Los Angeles, attempts to hike her breasts up with a roll of masking tape found in the desk, and fails. I am safe in my bubble of *Scientific American* until Georgina trips over my outstretched leg and pretends she has not. "Do you want some concealer?" she says, bending over and pointing a beige stick at me.

I am sure this is an insult, as much as it is a cover for her disregard of my personal space, but it is so obvious that I do not know how to address it except directly. "It's okay," I say. "I have nothing to conceal." Because I do, I smile like I know exactly what she is insinuating, and because the best she can manage is an attack on my under-eye circles, I do not care.

"But what about those?" she says, touching my skin just above my left cheekbone.

Apparently she has lost all her patience for psychological subterfuge. It was really not that long ago that I envied Georgina, with her streaked blond hair and green eyes, that lawyer boyfriend and the Saab convertible and the summer house on Moulton Road in Amagansett. And her lack of under-eye circles. "It's all just one big cover-up," I say. I am not sure if she realizes the many things other than concealer to which this description can be applied. "And besides, didn't you see the spring looks? Everything's totally bedhead and 'jet-lagged Euro trash,' they're calling it."

Georgina puts the top back on her concealer. "I didn't know that," she says. She stands there, blinking. She licks her index finger, smudges her eyeliner a tiny, almost undetectable bit, and walks away from me.

Fashion as weapon. It has so many more uses than I ever would have imagined. I have done my rehearsals, and now I am playing my part.

"I said, 'Are you ready to party?' *Whooo!*" This is Bridget's friend Caitlin, standing on top of a picnic table, screaming into a crowd of unfamiliar people, pointing her index fingers at the stars above us, hopping up and down so violently to the music that her breasts, barely sheathed in a cranberry tank top, look like they are flapping against her chin. She is not an elegant drunk.

I have told Caitlin twice that I could not hear her, mostly because I am hoping she will say something different. I raise my arms, the local equivalent of Long Island iced teas in each hand. I am halfway through both, shifting between left and right, hoping to look busy so that one of the nicer girls, like Caitlin, does not think to pull me up alongside her on the picnic table in some misguided mission of sympathy. *"Whooo!"* I yell back at her. This is all she really wants from me, anyway: company, permission, the security of not being the only girl from the party to dance drunkenly on the picnic table.

"Whooo!" Caitlin says again. She reaches for my hand, and I think she is going to take my drink away from me, possibly not a terrible outcome, so I lean toward her, allowing her to grab my wrist. She pulls on it hard enough, and long enough, that I step on the bench and then the table. She bounces her hips left and right, with a rhythm that is more aerobic than sensual, bumping me until I begin to mimic her movements. We are, I am sure, following some sort of fitness video routine. *"Aren't you having the best time of your entire life?"* she yells. *"I'm so glad my kids aren't here!"*

"Absolutely!" I say. I do not know what to do on the table, where Martina and Georgina have joined us; three girls whose names I cannot remember are bouncing and holding hands on another table, across from us. None of the other girls, still on the dance floor, are talking, just hopping and silently holding their drinks to their lips, studying the crowd and occasionally screaming into it, except for Georgina, who, as far as I can tell, has just poured a club soda down her shirt and is now shimmying for a crowd of young men who are deliriously applauding this impromptu peep show.

"I can't believe that bitch did that," Caitlin screams. "What are you drinking?"

"It's kind of like a Long Island iced tea," I say. "Three clear liquors and Sprite."

I am about to follow this with, "But I don't know what the liquors are," when she says, "Do you mind?" and before I can reply she lifts it to her chin and tilts the glass toward her chest, so it cascades down her white shirt. *"Whooo!"* she shrieks. Her black bra becomes visible beneath her white T-shirt, and the pack of boys makes its way from Georgina's end of the picnic table to ours. *"Whooo!"* The boys applaud. One throws his polo shirt at her, and she picks it up and slides it between her legs, riding it like a wooden pony, before roping it around her head like a lasso and flinging it toward the back of the club. The shirt's owner looks peeved and turns away from the stage to look for it. I know this because while Caitlin is doing her routine, I am still on the picnic table with her, still bouncing from one foot to the other, roughly in time with the music. ("Tub-thumping.") Caitlin is in the midst of relieving herself of the burdens of her T-shirt, having seen Georgina wriggle out of her tube top, and she is running her fingers beneath her bra straps when I touch her on the arm to get her attention.

"Oh my God," she says. "Isn't this the most fun ever?"

"Totally," I say, cupping my hands around my mouth and leaning against Caitlin's ear. "Have you seen Bridget?"

"She's over there," Caitlin says, pointing to the other end of the club. "She's doing the twelve things.

The twelve things—the "dirty dozen"—was a plan dreamed up by one of the subgroups of girls when it became clear that I, crap maid of honor that I apparently am, had neglected to organize bachelorette party entertainment beyond conferring with Bridget as to where she wanted to go. "No penis cake? Nothing?" one of them, an Abby, had said as we entered the bar—not the Chris and Jace club, but another looser, younger spot. "You always want to have a penis cake, they're so funny."

"I got us three bottles of champagne," I said, hoisting the grocery bags in my hands to a level where she could appreciate them for what they were, which was two hundred dollars worth of alcoholic beverages. "That's enough for the ten of us, isn't it?"

"I'm sure it is," Abby had said, smiling, and I thought it was, but as soon as we sat down and uncorked the champagne, while I waited for everyone to settle down so I could give my rhyming toast, Georgina had announced the dirty dozen: twelve dares written down by the ten of us (Georgina got to go three times) and stuffed into a clutch. Someone stirred them with a fork, and Bridget reached in to select "Kiss every bartender on duty." And there she was, a sylph in a gold tank top, rubbing a man's shoulders as he tosses a martini shaker up and down, while I stand on top of this picnic table and wait for the music to stop.

I find two doors at the end of a dark, uneven subterranean passage, with two melons on one and a banana on the other. I close my eyes and push my way through the one with the cantaloupes, and although I have chosen correctly, in that there are stalls and not urinals in this bathroom, I have made the mistake of not listening for the sound of two people having sex on the sink. "Georgina?" I cannot stop myself from saying, because it is, indeed, Georgina, with her engagement ring on her finger and her magenta thong around her ankles and her back pressed against a mirror and some man in a Take Me Drunk I'm Home T-shirt between her knees.

All I want, in the world, is to vomit all over them. I do not. I reverse, backwards, through the door, into the hallway. So here is more proof that Georgina is a big, fat fake. I do not mind her having sex in the bathroom. I mind her rubbing her fancy boyfriend and her big, loving, respectful relationship in my face and then having sex in the bathroom. I stand still for a moment and then enter the banana door. I lock the door behind me, and I have two urinals and two stalls to myself. This bathroom is like a pit stop on the path to hell. I want to get as far away from these people as I possibly can. I want to go home so badly: I want to go home and be with Ryan, in a way that I feel is as much in my stomach as in my head. I have not thought about him this way for at least a day or so, and I hoped I wouldn't again, but I am recovering from something I cannot control. When it stops, it stops of its own volition.

Our first day of sixth grade was postponed due to a hurricane that hit Cape May the night before; the morning after, Bridget and I had gone to the beach, with the rest of the town, to see the waves, higher than we could ever remember seeing them before, and, we were sure, higher than they could ever be again. We felt as though something had changed, forever, that the ocean was profoundly altered. The next day, classes started. I walked to Bridget's house on the corner of Ocean Drive and Mollusk Way and we stood on her parents' deck and looked at the waves, which were no longer extraordinary. Bridget showed me the clear lip gloss her mother had agreed to let her wear on the first day of school. If anything changed permanently that day, it was not the ocean.

The lesson, then, was not what I expected: not every squall is as lasting as it may seem. It passes. I am not thinking of the ocean anymore. This is how it is going to be, and this is what I must remember: These storms, these moments of weakness and desolation, are not destined to endlessly intensify. They can blow themselves out, too, one weaker than the next.

I go back to the dance floor. Everyone is where I left them. Caitlin is now, officially, dancing in her bra. The desperation and the adrenaline are gone, but I feel emptied out, raw, wildly alone: the way you feel alone in the deep woods, when there is no visual evidence that anyone else exists. But then I look at my watch and do the math: It is only two thirty in the afternoon at home, and I go outside to a pay phone in the parking lot, sit down on a little bench, and charge a call to Brooklyn on my American Express card. "Dude, you are not going to fucking believe this shit," I say when Tommy answers the phone. A fraction of my unhappiness is optional, it seems, and easily mitigated, and to think of it as anything else is both an indulgence and a lie.

Before I disconnect the call, I place another one, to my own voice mail. There are three messages.

Zoe has found, along with an old bag of potato chips I had for some reason stowed in the bathroom cabinet, a pair of diamond earrings she thinks might be mine. "And your closet is ready for you whenever you want to come back."

Then: "Betsy, I loved your piece so much." Julia. "And I can't wait for you to come home and work for me at *Glossy*! Call me the minute you're back."

That is completely unexpected.

And then: "Hey, Betsy." Pause. "It's Casey." Pause. "Thanks for the tickets." Scuffling. Mumbled: "I didn't think you were in love with me." Ha! Pause. Louder: "I quit Couture, that place sucks." Pause. "That's really cool that you got that free ticket for me." Pause. "So I'm going to come." *!!!* "I had to come a day later, but that's cool." Pause. "If you want to hang out, here's the number of the hostel where I'm staying." He gives the number. Pause. "Actually, it says it's the number for the store across the street." Pause. "Okay, well, hope I caught you before you take off."

Casey?

There is nothing I can do about this now: It is too late, too early, to call the store across the street from the hostel. What am I going to say to him? Could hanging out with Casey even be any fun? He's just like a grumbling, moody mouse, with that fucked-up hair going at all different angles. I tap my flip-flop against my heel, trying to figure out what all of this means.

What I do know is that the Ryan malaise is utterly gone, and I feel foolish for having felt so desolate.

This is the most amazing series of voice mails I have ever heard in my life, and I kiss the phone before replacing it to its cradle.

Now I really, really want to get out of here and see what is going to happen next, but there is nowhere to go: I am sitting on a velvet lounge, watching the sky above me progress from purple to lilac. It is six o'clock in the morning. Caitlin's shirt is missing, and she is across from me in her black bra and jeans, shivering. Georgina is sleeping on one of the picnic tables.

I haven't seen Bridget for ages, so when she strides up to this ragged collection of bridal party members, I am surprised to see her so casually sober, unlike the rest of us drunkards. "I've done them all!" she says, and the girls who are awake brighten and applaud.

It takes me a moment to realize that she is talking about her dirty dozen. She is saying that within the last six hours she has squeezed a girl's left breast, made a bouncer show her his underwear, and convinced ten men to buy her a tequila shot. "No, you didn't," I say.

"I didn't do yours," she says. "It was outside the scope of the game."

Even the girls who were not awake for the original announcement are coming around, and they all look at us to see where we will take them, what drama we can provide them. "It wasn't," I say.

"It was," she says. "So I asked Abby to write me another one."

"That's cheating," I say.

"You get yours back," she says, pulling a slip of paper out of her pocket, crumpling it into a ball, and tossing it to me. "Now we're going home."

With a wave of her hand, Bridget's attendants rise and stagger behind her, toward the club exit and the waiting minivans outside. I sit there a moment, with the paper in my hand, before smoothing it out. "#1: Ditch these bitches," it says. Not very politic, that. "#2: Don't be such a goddamn pussy," it says, because I was tipsy when I wrote it and had come to the position that the only way to deal with this is tough love, and also because I could not believe we were talking about things like stuffing her bra with bar napkins when there were serious, unresolved issues, like why, exactly, this wedding was still taking place. I stare at the material proof of my impotence, the hopeful loops of the *p* in "pussy," the space I had made for exclamation points before deciding against them. And then I roll the paper back into a ball and hold it over a candle until it begins to burn.

I do not comprehend how drunk I am until I am halfway between the lounge and the door and I walk directly into a stripper pole.

The ride back to the huts is silent, except for Abby's snoring and the driver, speaking a strange language into a cell phone. I feel like I am on a ride at Disney World, a matrimonial Pirates of the Caribbean where we are ferried from one venue to the next, and no one is even considering getting off before the big finish. They all want to see what will happen, and I wonder if Bridget knows that she is their entertainment, their star, their proxy, the living symbol of the wisdom of their own decisions to have traveled the same path she is traveling. Their concern ends there, after she joins their club, which they have sold to her like a time-share, all sunshine and bouquets of lavender on the kitchen table.

I have wondered how Ryan has changed me, and here is his transformation: naïveté corroded into something cynical and suspicious, a reverse-alchemy as ordinary as iron submitting to rust. But there is something harder there, too, revealed at the bottom: Forces of nature eroded the valley. It is up to me to focus on what was swept away in the current, or the view from the ridge.

When we get back to the huts, one of the bridesmaids whose name I cannot remember is sleeping in my bed and although I want so much to just roll her onto the floor, I turn around and commandeer the hammock on the porch, facing the sun as it rises over the ocean.

I wake up only because someone, who turns out to be my sister, is poking me in the head with a stick. "Quit it, ass!" I say, grabbing the stick. "What's your problem?"

"I need you to do something for me," she says.

"What? God. What time is it?"

"It's two in the afternoon, *ass,*" she says. "We let you sleep as long as was reasonable."

"Who made you the god of reasonable?" I say. "What do you want?"

"We need you to hold these," she says, offering me a bunch of birds-of-paradise.

"Where did you get these? Did you steal these from a nature preserve?"

"You can pick them anywhere," she says. "Maybe if you weren't so drunk, you'd have seen them." She points to a clump of them growing six feet away. "There, for example."

"What am I supposed to do with them?"

"Come with me," she says. "Everybody's waiting."

"Where's Bridget?" I say. "Is she part of this?"

"We're undecided about Bridget," Rebecca says. "Do you think she should come?"

"It's her wedding," I say.

"Not today," Rebecca says.

"Are you serious?"

"Just come on, will you?" Rebecca says. "But I guess we should get Bridget. Nobody else. Meet us at the boat."

My sister leaves me standing there with a bouquet of birds-of-paradise in my hand. And then I go to find Bridget.

"Dude," I say to Bridget, whom I find painting her toenails on the back entrance to her hut. "You've got to come with me. My sister is up to something insane."

"I can't go anywhere," she says. "I'm busy. And James is going to be here in an hour or something."

"Bridge, seriously. She is planning something crazy."

"Like crazy how? And what are you doing with those flowers?"

What I end up doing is simply yanking Bridget to her feet and pulling her down the path to the marina where my parents' boat is moored, or parked, or however that is described. When we get there, we see that my sister has changed into a plastic nurse's uniform, commonly purchased at stripper stores, and Stevie is wearing a blue suede suit jacket, a white shirt, a tie, and a kilt. An unfamiliar man is quizzing my father on his research. "It means the end of skin cancer!" he is saying, nodding enthusiastically, while my father smiles benevolently, pleased to be recognized.

"Finally," my sister says, when she sees us climb aboard.

"How much did that dress cost?" I ask.

"Forty-five dollars and ninety-nine cents," she says, "which is about thirty-nine dollars and ninety-nine cents more than I thought it would be. But isn't it hysterical?"

Bridget and I are introduced to Pastor MacInness, who moved here twenty-five years ago as part of a Scottish Rolling Stones tribute band.

"What is going on here?" says Bridget.

"They're getting married," I say.

"Right now?" Bridget says. "Who's doing things? Who's making food?"

"We got KFC," Rebecca says. "Can you believe they have KFC here? And Stevie wanted to have a mango-eating contest, but he was the only entrant. We're going to make him the big winner so he'll finally shut up about it."

"You shut up," Stevie says.

"You shut up," Rebecca says.

"So," I say, eager to be helpful, to make clear my enthusiasm for the right sort of wedding. "How does this start?"

"Places, everyone!" Rebecca says, but no one moves. She rolls her eyes, and then points to my parents, who have seated themselves on two reclined beach chairs. "Mom and Daddy, stay where you are. Stevie, stay where you are. Betsy and Bridget, you may sit next to Mom and Daddy."

We do, spreading out a towel beneath us. "Shouldn't we be standing or something?" I whisper to Bridget, who just shakes her head, not so much replying to my question as expressing her bafflement.

My sister is paying no attention to us. She has an all-business, CEO thing going on that I am sure has yet to make itself known at the hair salon where she works. "Pastor MacInness, you may begin."

I am expecting him to open with some sort of Psalm or something, but apparently this is his cue for the processional, which is sung by Black Train Jack, Stevie's favorite band, and played on a large boom box. Because Stevie and Rebecca are standing almost directly in front of him, however, there is nowhere really for them to process, so they just stand there, waiting for the music to end. "I love this song," I hear Stevie whisper to Rebecca.

Eventually, it ends, and Pastor MacInnes begins his ceremony. "We're gathered today in the splendor of God's pasture to unite, in this realm and all that is to come, the eternal souls of Rebecca and Steven," he says. I expect him to finish with "yadda, yadda," but he does not. "I understand that you've written your vows?"

"Yeah," Stevie says.

"Rebecca?" Pastor MacInnes says.

"I promise," Rebecca says, glancing at her wrist, which is covered in black ink, "to do whatever I want, whenever I want, and I expect you to love me all the time, no matter what. I'll kill you if you ever betray me, and you can kill me if I ever betray you. I promise to always believe in you and your band and never make you get a job you hate." She pauses. "Plus, I want my own dog, and a pickup truck." She curtsies. "That's it."

Bridget and I look at each other, and as happy as I was to have my sister here to shield me from Bridget's insanity, I am equally happy to have Bridget here to witness this spectacular spectacle.

It is Stevie's turn. "I will kill for you, I will die for you, I will walk to hell and back for you, and anyone who fucks with you is going to have to get through me first."

Now Bridget and I are both tearing up and wiping our eyes. Together we stand and clap, while the pastor restarts the CD, even though Stevie and Rebecca are standing still. "Oh, right!" he says. "The rings!"

My father leans back in his chair and pulls them out of his pocket, holding them out on his palm to the two of them. "We tried to make the dog do it," he says, explaining this to the pastor, pointing at Boomer, who has been bedecked with a garland of daisies he is trying desperately, and fruitlessly, to lick off his neck. "But that only works in movies. He kept trying to eat them."

Rebecca and Stevie put the rings on each other's fingers, and that is it. Rebecca runs behind my parents' chair and returns with a bucket of fried chicken, which has been mysteriously hidden there. My mom passes out paper plates and little Styrofoam dishes of baked beans and mashed potatoes. "I'm so glad you girls could make it," she says. "Rebecca was getting antsy when you weren't here straightaway."

" 'Straightaway'?" I say. "When did you start saying that?"

"We met people from all over the world on our trip, from Ireland and London and Albuquerque," my mother says. "And I'm sure we all cross-pollinated each other a little bit."

I want everyone around me to stop changing: I think it so hard, I almost stomp my foot again, and then I think about how embarrassing it will be if I throw a tantrum ten minutes after my sister gets married, which is all that keeps me from doing it. "It was a great wedding," Bridget says, a plate of biscuits and chicken thighs in her hands, and I nod my head in agreement, with increasing enthusiasm. I am not the cynic, I am not the wedding-hater. I loved this wedding. This wedding was not about fairy tales; this wedding was about love and family. Specifically, it is

Bridget's wedding that has me so ill at ease, and though I am still nodding, I feel a little bit of the terror, of the significance of that idea. And as Bridget takes in the scene, Rebecca and Stevie and my dad throwing scraps of carefully deboned chicken meat toward Boomer, she starts staring at her feet.

"That was how a wedding should be," she says.

My mom looks at her, all momlike. "Now, Bridget," she says, in that way of hers, the one that says: *Are you being your most authentic self?* Or at least it has since she started watching *Oprah*. The look existed before that, even if the wording had previously been more diffuse.

Bridget knows what is coming, because this is what my mother said to her every afternoon she came over during our junior year in high school, after her father had left his job to become an evangelist. "Now, Bridget," she would say. "Would you like some milk and cookies?" she would ask, even when we didn't have any cookies in the pantry, my mother knowing and not caring that she was speaking an easily decipherable code.

"I should go," Bridget says. "James will be here soon." She turns to the newlyweds. "What are you guys going to do now?"

"Well," Rebecca says, "Boomer couldn't carry the rings, and we didn't have the mango-eating contest, but there was one element of Stevie's perfect wedding we managed to put together."

"Hold on," I say. "You hid the presents in the coconut trees?"

"Not coconut," my mother says. "Rambutan. They're like coconuts."

"Well, congratulations," Bridget says. "And see you all tomorrow."

"Good luck, Bridget," my mother says. "I'm sure you'll be beautiful. Everyone knows you'll be such a beautiful bride."

My mother is a quick study, and my mother means to injure. My mother was the one who had always looked past Bridget's beauty, and who had gained her trust for it. It sounds like well-meaning blather, but the three of us see it for what it is: an admonition, and a slight, and a call to something better.

We are both silent for the first ten minutes of the hike back to the huts. I do not know what Bridget is thinking, but I am racking my brain for a metaphor that does not involve *The X Files*. I fail. "Bridget," I say. "This could be just like the episode where Mulder and Scully are trapped in the hallucinogenic bog. All they had to do to get out was realize they had to get out."

"Don't you know this is all your fault? All that time I thought I had what I wanted, and then there you were, and you were all, like, obsessed with him, and I could see it and remember and I never felt that way with James, which I thought was good, but then I got all jealous—"

"You," I say, "you were jealous of *me*?"

"Well, who wouldn't be? You're walking around in this daze because your boyfriend's so great. . . ."

"He cheated on me! With my boss!"

"I know," she says. "But what if I'm missing out? I don't know what it's supposed to be. I don't know if it's supposed to be like you have it, or like I have it."

"Maybe," I say, "maybe there's a happy medium, and neither of us have found it yet."

"That would be really fucked up," she says, "considering the fact that I'm going to get married in like twenty-four hours."

"Well then, you just can't," I say. "You can't if you're not sure."

"But maybe nobody's sure."

"Sure-ish, then," I say. "Rebecca was freaked out, but she was sure."

"Okay," she says. "Forget it. Forget I said anything. It's too late. Everyone's here because of me." She holds her hands to the sky, palms up. "Everyone bought us these presents."

"The only good answer is that it's because you love him."

"Of course I love him," she says. "This isn't about that."

"Then—?"

"What if I don't know if I love him enough?"

"Then you can't go through with it," I say. "You can't. I mean, I don't think you can. I don't know." There is also this side of me that is terrified of successfully talking her out of it: It could be like one of those stories where a man saves another man's life, and is then responsible for him, forever. What if she really never does find anyone else? What if she is unhappy, and I am to blame? In the midst of this, I feel, for maybe the first time, sorry for her: If I am this confused, she must be the same, only exponentially more so. "Maybe everybody feels like this before they get married."

"How am I supposed to know?" Bridget says.

"What does your mom say?"

"My mom thinks this is the only good decision I've ever made in my entire life," she says.

"Bridge," I say. "You have to be brave. Don't be a pussy. You can't be a pussy."

"No," she says. "We have a plan. We're going back to New York, and everyone will be married, and we'll get a married-person share in the Hamptons and you'll get your Saab convertible and an apartment on Central Park West, and everything will be perfect."

"Is that really what you want? Is that what you really want with this person?"

Bridget stops walking. "You know that feeling, when you love that person more than anything else in the world? How did you feel when you were dating the asshole?"

"Like every day I could not believe this person was going out with me."

"See?" she says. "Shouldn't I be feeling like that?"

"Bridget," I say, pedantically, "you would feel that way if you were dating an asshole. I felt that way because, you know, evidently, there was good reason to believe that this person should not be going out with me. And the thing about it was that I was right. I am going to believe that there is something between apathy and obsession."

"Do you think so?"

"I guess so," I say. "I don't know what else to think."

"You know," she says, "this would be a lot easier if you knew something about anything, like Georgina."

"Oh, yeah, Georgina?" I say. "Georgina who got fucked in the women's bathroom? This is all bullshit, Bridget, and if you want to go on believing it, that's cool, but don't come calling me when you realize that they're all full of crap."

She is quiet, staring down at her flip-flops.

"Okay, you can call me," I say. She hasn't moved. "Do you realize that all you do anymore is stare at the ground?"

"Georgina had sex in the women's bathroom? With who?"

"I don't know," I say. "Some guy. He was wearing a Take Me Drunk I'm Home T-shirt."

"I don't want to be like her," she says. "I don't want to be with a guy like that." I am unsure as to whether she means that she wants to stay with James, and thus avoid reentering the dating pool, or if it means she wants to leave James, because she doesn't want to be with someone she does not love. I am about to ask her to clarify when she starts walking ahead of me back to the huts. And I know, too, that she is on the edge, of something, and as sure as I am of the decision she should make, I am too much of a pussy to say so again: Now that it seems like she might take my advice, I am sufficiently aware of my own shortcomings to recognize that I want her to take it in a way that will prevent her from holding me accountable if it all goes to shit.

The rehearsal dinner starts at eight. I have moved out of the bridesmaids' hut, onto the patch of my parents' boat now vacated by Rebecca and Stevie, who are spending their wedding night in a hotel room paid for by my parents. "Shrimp on the barbie?" my father keeps saying, peering over the top of his George Foreman Grill.

"It's a rehearsal dinner," I say. "They're going to give us food for free."

"In that case," my father says, "keep your paws off mine." He pokes my arm with one of the shrimp skewers.

"Maybe we could just have a variety show and travel the world," I say. "And you could do the poking skewer thing in front of international audiences."

"Isn't that what we're doing now?" he says, looking at my mother. She puts down a copy of *The Economist* and claps until he turns back to me. "We're living the dream, Bets, and don't you forget it."

I do not feel like I am living the dream as I climb up the steps to this hacienda-on-the-sea, the Grand Mariner Lodge Ballroom, by myself. It is a cultural and professional Noah's ark: There is the pair of tax attorneys (Martina and her fiancé); there is the pair of hedge fund managers. Actually, that is the hedge fund manager—the best man, Bill—and his actress girlfriend, who tells us that she once had a chorus part in *Oklahoma!* and wore braids every day, working or not, for the three-month run. "I'm Method," she explains. The more I study them, going slowly up the steps to the ballroom, the more I see that my initial impression was wrong, tainted by Martina and a man I learn is her boss. I see how imbalanced these couples actually are: there is a man who makes the money, and a successfully attractive woman: the venture capitalist and the artist's assistant, the corporate lawyer and the catalog model.

The first person I both (a) recognize and (b) fail to hide from is Arun, Bridget's old boss. "I remember you! I liked you! Where's your boyfriend?"

"Oh, he's looking for the men's room or something," Arun says. "We're not joined at the hip or anything."

I wonder if this is how people in relationships talk about each other when they are considering breaking it off. "Oh," I say. "Are you still at *Jetset*?"

"Oh, no fucking way," he says. "We quit our jobs and moved to Spain. Andy's grandfather has a house in the hills. He's setting up photo shoots and I'm working on a book."

My dismay at my inaccurate relationship reading is far outmatched by my delight in his response. "That's unbelievable!" I say. "I thought you were such a magazine guy. I thought you thought I was so stupid for working at a Web site."

"Are you kidding?" he says. "That was all self-loathing. All I talked about every day was ten-thousand-dollar seating units. I wanted to shoot myself in the head."

"No shit," I say.

"No shit," he says. "I'm sorry if I made you feel bad."

"I was going through kind of a weird time," I say. "But it's getting better now. I actually got an offer to go to *Glossy.*"

"Oh, really?" he says. "Are you thinking about it?"

"Yeah," I say. But on the other hand . . . "But I also am beginning to feel like I just got out of jail. Like that episode of *The X Files* where Mulder and Scully are caught in that hallucinogenic bog."

"I saw that one," he says. "That was a great episode."

"I was all set to take this new job," I say. "But now I sort of feel like . . . looking around a little. Exploring. I always wanted to see new things, and I haven't seen anything new for ages."

He waves to Andy, who has appeared across the ballroom. "You should be brave," he says. He looks over my head, to the crowd, and I imagine that he is judging all of them, everyone here except me. "And don't be a robot."

After my miraculous series of voice mail messages last night, I decided I would go back to New York. What else could they mean? I would live at Zoe's and work for Julia, and my life would pick up more or less where it left off. There would be nights out with my friends, and free drinks at promotional events, and there would be another guy to become obsessed with—if not Casey, someone else. I would be an integral part of Bridget's new life: I would be the Unmarried Friend, and I would serve that crucial role, the living proof of her virtuous decision. Bridget and I would meet for brunch on the Upper East Side, and I would complain about the trip in from Brooklyn, and when we divided the bill, she would pay slightly more than half, as a sign of her position more than of her relative wealth. I would complain about the men in New York: "The only problem with them," I would say, "is that for every one who will marry you, two will push you in front of the A train." I would not get a cat, even if I would want one. I would invent, and play out, this role: Crazy Betsy and Her Hilarious Adventures. Watch her as she dates losers and assholes! Laugh as she spills juice down her shirt! Cry as she celebrates another birthday alone!

But maybe it does not have to be like that. This is what I am thinking while I eat my air-freighted Maine lobster and accompaniments, wedged between Georgina's boyfriend, Todd, and Craig, a cousin of Bridget's I have not met before, a hospital accountant who appears to be so nervous around these movers and shakers that he keeps saying things like, "Our bottom line has a bit of a curve to it," painful, punning, nonsensical things. They're assholes, I think. You don't need to be like them. You don't have to compete with them.

Craig says something about how the capital gains tax "hit me in the gut," and that's when Todd leans back and says, "I paid more in taxes than you made last year."

Craig blanches and focuses on cracking a lobster claw. I am so happy I know something Todd does not. I hope Georgina's partner has crabs.

I turn away from Craig and Todd, and at the other end of the table two girls are talking about how many shoes they are going to buy with their bonuses. They are doing the math, dividing an amount not too far from my would-be salary at *Glossy* by the price of one pair of shoes. The price they are using for one pair of shoes is five hundred dollars.

I do not have to stay here. I don't have a boyfriend. I don't have a job. I don't have anything. I can do whatever the fuck I want.

I debate waiting for the chocolate coconut cake to arrive,

but it does not show up fast enough, so I leave my napkin on my chair and go to the bathroom with my copy of *Scientific American* in my tote bag, and that's where I spend the rest of the dinner.

When I emerge, there is only the coffee-and-chitchat period preventing me from returning to my parents' boat. Abby, who, it turns out, is a social worker, is discussing the fellowship her husband won, which will take them to an Alaska glacier for two years to study something about oil. "I hate to leave my job and my friends," she says. "But it's what's best for him."

"That sounds terrible," I say. I don't care what these people think of me anymore. "Can't you just visit him on weekends or something?"

"You know how men can be when they're left alone." She says this like she is making a joke, but her expression is blank and somber. "And I'd be so lonely without him."

"Sometimes I really don't think this whole marriage thing is all it's cracked up to be," I say. "All this doing what the other person wants to do because they'll freak out if you don't."

"Amen to that," Todd says. He holds up his hand for me to slap, which I do, and we both shoot pointed glances at his girlfriend.

At that, I walk out again, to find a pay phone, and I call Casey, or at least the store across the street from where he is staying. A lovely woman with an English accent answers the phone, and she says that Casey is surfing, but that she will give him a message. I detail where the post-wedding reception will be, and when I hang up the phone, that is that: There is no small death, no sense that everything has ended, that I have lost all control. He will come, or he won't. What a wonderful feeling, one I have never known before: either I was indifferent or obsessed. Casey is hot but a bit of a grump, and again: that crazy hair, sticking out in all directions. Again: He will come or he won't. There is nothing else to say. I wait for it, and still: nothing. I had never known it could be as easy as that. If I can figure out how to maintain this, I will have learned something valuable.

Next, I call my bank.

I don't see Bridget until after dinner is over, as everyone mills around, shaking hands and saying complimentary things about each other's outfits. "Why are you grinning like that?" she asks me.

"All is becoming clear," I say. "I have had a series of revelations, and things are different now."

"What the hell does that mean?"

"It means," I say, "that I'm not going back to New York. I have six thousand two hundred dollars in credit, and thirteen hundred dollars in cash. I'm sure I could see a lot of stuff on that. I am going to be an explorer."

"Who needs explorers? Everything's already explored. What about that new job?"

"I hate that new job," I say. "Fuck that new job."

"What about that boyfriend you want back?"

"There are others," I say haltingly, forcing myself to mean it. I have not missed Ryan for the last time, but there are only so many times I will miss him, and I am one closer to reaching zero than I was before she asked.

"That's just as much of a cliché as anything else," Bridget says. "Backpacking. It's just as expected, it's just as regular as everybody else in Manhattan doing their own thing."

"Maybe," I say, "the problem is not living out the cliché, but living out a cliché you think is stupid. And I think that other stuff is stupid."

"I think you're going to regret it," she says. "You're going to want that job back."

I wonder if Bridget is doing to me what yesterday I had done to her: failing me because the alternative was so messy, would require too much of her. "You don't mean that," I say, "and don't try to pretend like you do, because I know you too well."

"Stop sounding so confident!" she says. "Enough is going wrong without you flipping out."

"You should get out of this while you can," I say. I hold my breath after I say it, like: *I tried to keep it in, but it escaped.*

"You're telling me this now? You couldn't have told me a month ago?"

"I didn't know it a month ago," I say. "I didn't think you could criticize weddings. I thought you knew better than I did. I'm so stupid about that stuff. I didn't think you could be wrong."

"But now you do? What if I look back on this in a year, and I realize that I screwed up? That I'm actually as happy as I would ever be?"

"First of all, I don't think that's the case," I say. "And second, we need to focus on the good times and birthday cake."

"What does that mean?"

"It just means that you are not choosing between this wedding and nothing. It's like, this wedding, or a thousand different other things, or other people."

"I know that," she says.

"Then why are you going through with this?"

"Because I want to," she says. "And it would break his heart."

"I don't believe the first one," I say. "And the second one isn't good enough."

"I love that you've figured this all out now, the night before the wedding." It is the most inadequate sarcasm I have heard from her.

"I did the best I could," I say meekly, because I should have done better, and we stand there silently until James takes her arm and leads her out of the room.

I walk by myself back to my parents' boat, alongside the beach, skipping a little when no one is watching me, because I have realized that there are benefits to not relying on another person, another person whose name begins with an *R,* to provide me with my happiness, or my Saab convertible, and also because before I left the reception I drank four glasses of champagne.

When I wake in the morning, I stand and fall. And stand and fall. It is Bridget's wedding day and I am lying flat on my back, watching the clouds spin counterclockwise above me. I close my eyes, and then it starts to feel like I am the one spinning, so I open them, and everything stops. This is not an auspicious beginning to the day. I pull my sister's sleeping bag over my head and stay there until I hear my parents shuffling around their cabin, and then I begin to lurch my way toward the huts.

We are due at Bridget's hut at eleven, and I am the last to arrive, a few minutes late; all of them are sitting around in their dresses, except Georgina, who seems to be enjoying walking around in her underwear. Caitlin and Bridget's mom are buttoning up the back of her dress. "It's just nerves," I hear Mrs. Callahan say, but Bridget's eyes look red and raw.

"Oh, give me a break," I say to the three of them, speaking to their reflections in the dressing mirror because I cannot bear to look any of them in the face. Mrs. Callahan hesitates enough for me to know that she is hurt, or at least surprised: *My sweet Betsy,* she always calls me, and now it must seem as if her little poodle has gone all feral on her. I think of Mrs. Callahan as family; I barely distinguish her from the aunts who share my genetic code, but it is always here, when there is discord, that that relationship reveals its weaknesses. We have always been joined by our mutual goodwill for Bridget, and now that we are not, there is no shared blood to silently comfort us, to deny our disagreements. I know she loves Bridget more than I ever could, but I also believe that she is basing Bridget's decisions on her own failures. My only advantage is that I have relatively more failures in front of me than behind.

"Doesn't Bridget look beautiful?" she says, to Caitlin, I suppose. It is our old call-and-response: *Doesn't Bridget look beautiful?* And then my reply: *Sure she does,* rolling my eyes if Bridget can see them. I am about to roll my eyes, but as spitefully and meanly as they could possibly be rolled, when I stop, and I see Mrs. Callahan holding Bridget's hand. She is as terrified as I was to be on the wrong side of a bad decision, I think, and she long ago decided her position. She is gambling she is right because if she is, she will lose no ground, and if she retrenches now, she certainly will, even if that loss will pale in comparison to the one she is risking. And then there is the simple fact of James, and the simple fact of Bridget's father: Why would Mrs. Callahan prize anything above security, stability, calm? "I've never seen her look so radiant," Mrs. Callahan says.

"Radiant's one word," I say, but I say it so that the other word might, in fact, be "ecstatic." I do not know how much I can fault a mother for wanting her daughter to have a better marriage than her own.

"This is what I've dreamed of since she was a little girl," Mrs. Callahan says, and I believe her.

From here it moves so quickly: Tracey returns, darling Tracey in a Chanel suit, and leads the bridal party to the bridal party holding area, a thatched-roof cabana. I have read about how ceremony is used in different cultures to force people into accepting extraordinary circumstances, and Bridget looks—she simply looks like she is literally in another place, and we have been left here to orchestrate her physical movements. But Tracey is in charge of her fate now, and Tracey is going to make sure that all the trains run on time.

"I need the bridesmaids outside and the mother of the bride ready to be escorted down the aisle to the front row," she says, both to us and into a headpiece microphone positioned to the right of her mouth, like McDonald's crew chiefs wear. It is nice thinking about Tracey working at a drive-through window, unable to keep up with the seasoned employees around her. Maybe later they could rub french fry grease into her pores. "You two have five minutes for final adjustments. Your dad will be here in a second."

I was not expecting to spend any time with Bridget alone.

"What?" she says to me.

" 'What'?" I say. "If you don't want to do this, just leave! There's a window. Just go! There are plenty of movies where that happens."

"Name one," she says.

"The Graduate," I say.

"Name another."

"Er . . . Hold on. Hold on."

"You can't name two?"

"You can't get married because I can't name two movies. It

happens every day. That's why it's a cliché, being left at the altar. You can do it, too. He'll get over it."

"I can't," she says.

"Why not?" I say. "Do you want me to raise my hand when they ask if there's a reason why you shouldn't be married? Is that how I'd be a good maid of honor?"

"Oh my God," she says. "No. Don't do that."

"So what do you want me to do?"

"Don't do anything," she says.

For a moment, both of our mouths are full of words, and then, almost simultaneously, they spill out:

"You don't love him," I say.

"I don't know how not to do this," she says.

The door opens, and Tracey is there, holding her hand over her headset's microphone. Three women passing by all clasp their chests and smile. "Beautiful," one of them says.

"I need you out here now," Tracey says.

"Can you think of another choice?" Bridget says to me.

I stand there, my mouth open.

Tracey points at me, and to a spot on the asphalt path leading up to the aisle. Bill is there, waiting for me. Bridget's dad comes in and offers her his arm, and she takes it.

This is what I remember after that point: James looking nervously, theatrically, at his groomsman's watch, Bridget and her father, the wedding march, her father offering a little practiced bow that looked ridiculous to anyone who had known him for longer than six months, which was pretty much everyone on the right-hand side of the aisle. And then—really, what could I expect after a half bottle of champagne and the four Long Island iced teas the night before?

First, unexpectedly, Bridget's dress went black.

Then, I realized that this problem extended beyond Bridget's dress, and that all the whites in my field of vision had turned black, and all the blacks had turned white, and that I was looking at something that resembled a photo negative.

And then I hit the floor.

Here is the part that proves my memory lies—and there is such a relief in knowing that, in knowing that if it can lie about this, it has lied about Ryan, made him increasingly desirable as he becomes decreasingly attainable.

It is also the part that makes me a little less afraid of dying, because what I remember next is a gentle swoon to the floor: a swoon, the back of my palm to my forehead. Perhaps I would be revived by a doctor.

And I was, by a doctor without a border. "You hit the floor like a brick," Bridget says, even as I am propped up against the lectern. "We thought you were dead."

"I didn't swoon?" I ask as James unwraps a straw and sinks it into a can of Sprite someone has contributed to the save-Betsy fund. He offers me the can, and I drink from it. "Oh my God," I say. "Is the wedding still going on?"

"We're taking a break," Bridget says. "You were out for like fifteen minutes. Your mom and dad went over to get the resort doctor, but James just thinks you're a big lush who can't handle her liquor."

"I'm sure you'll be fine," James says, patting my head, which is, of course, level with his hand, since I am sitting on the floor and he is still standing. Sitting on the floor while Bridget's entire guest list stares at the retard who destroyed Bridget's wedding.

"Oh my God," I say. "I did it. You knew I would do it. I killed your wedding."

"It's okay," she says. "Really."

She says this just sharply enough for James to look over at her, but he literally bites his lip and softens his gaze and I know why she loves him, as much as she does, and it is because of his patience and his devotion and because he is everything her father is not, reliable and true. She needs him so much more than she loves him, and now that her needs are taken care of, she will find someone else to love, and I don't think it will end well for either one of them.

"I feel like Cassandra," I say. "I feel like I am uncovering great truths, and not all of them are good."

"And you didn't swoon, by the way," Bridget says. "We thought you were having seizures."

"I would have liked to swoon," I say. "But I'll have to live with my great truths."

James leaves to find some wet paper towels for my forehead, and Bridget and I sit together, behind the lectern, with our backs to the crowd. "I just gave you a reprieve," I say.

"You did that on purpose?" she says. "I thought about it for a second, but then there was all the seizing and there was no way you were acting."

"No, no," I say. "We must view this as a gift from God. I'm giving you a reprieve."

"We all have to clear out now," Bridget says. "We can have the church back in the morning. They're holding up the wedding after us until you can walk out. And believe me, they're pretty much ready to throw you over somebody's shoulder if we don't make it out of here soon."

"Maybe," I say, "the best wedding present I could have gotten you was another twenty-four hours to make the right decision."

"This would be a lot more persuasive," Bridget says, "if I didn't already know that it meant you didn't bother to buy a present."

"That's not it," I say, and I know she knows it's not.

The wedding party is diverted to the pool area. Everyone is frowning at me, the wedding-destroyer, but I know, even if they do not, that I have done my job, that I have been a good maid of honor. Except with the bachelorette party. I should have thought of a better bachelorette party.

The entire wedding party is here: There are Georgina and Todd, at the swim-up bar, sharing a margarita. Maybe they are discussing the satisfactions of their open relationship, and Georgina is not a hypocrite but something more complicated, something as sophisticated and complex and vaguely European as she hoped that gilet would make her. I think, however, they are talking about firing their housekeeper. There are Abby and Caitlin practicing cheerleading routines in the water: Those two, especially, they are not so bad—a little sad, maybe, but trying, I think, and trying is something I can support. Mrs. Callahan is laughing, sitting at a table with her three sons, swatting one on the shoulder, and I can see she is testing her supports, and seeing that they hold: Her husband left her, but she has these sons, and they are, each one of them, in the truest sense of the words, fine specimens, for regarding them as such somehow excuses their misdeeds, their predilection for strippers, their shared, guiding philosophies, best boiled down to the word "unperturbed." I have been looking down on them so long, it seems only right that I should now see that they are only occupying a position on a spectrum, a position as extreme as my own.

I do not know how my family was allowed past the security guards into the resort and its pool, but they are all here: my parents on lounge chairs, under matching wide-brimmed straw hats. Stevie is doing cannonballs off the diving board while my sister, sitting on the rim of the pool, applauds and scores the splashes on a scale from one to ten. I see Casey, sitting beside her: Later on, I will have to find out how he realized who she was, but for now, I am content to let them be. Part of my head is going: *Casey! What the fucking fuck!* But it is happy, and unconcerned, and I let it puzzle over that: It is a puzzle, nothing more, and one easily solved. Maybe this is what Bridget meant all along, that it is better be truly aloof: to not care, to not care about not caring. I am closer to it now than ever before, and I think, about this, she has been right all along.

Bridget floats by herself. I want her to be happy more than anyone I know, partly because, unlike my sister, unlike my parents, I think it is possible that she might not be, that she may fail herself. You shouldn't, I think. You should not do this. You can be so much better than this. I will die if she is the girl with the monogrammed towels and the Valium addiction.

I do not need her to know what to do next, and that is a first. In two days, we will leave the huts, and she will go back to New York and practice being a wife, and I will get on a plane: I will go to New Zealand and find those fjords everyone has been talking about. And then after New Zealand, somewhere else I have never been, and somewhere else after that. I can hear myself telling Ryan about this, my plans, but I let it go on, like background noise. Like white noise, like static, like buzzing, like nothing.

I am leaving her, as much as she is leaving me: What an

awful, thrilling feeling, being left behind. Bridget sits up on her float and sees James; she glides toward him and then walks up the steps, out of the pool. He is a good man, and maybe she will realize that he deserves her love. I will be there, in her world, either way, wherever I've been, whoever I am. I do not need to move to a glacier, I do not have to remake myself in the mold of the artist's muse, or the rose-tender's girlfriend. That is not how this story ends. I could be anything. I am so excited to begin.

"Be brave," I whisper, across the pool. "Be true." Before the words are out of my mouth, she has already drifted a few steps back, toward her husband, her hand outstretched, waving goodbye.

I wave back.